Shearwater
Point

By

Denise Beddows

Denise Beddows

MISBOURNE PRESS

First edition

Published in 2022 by Misbourne Press

Copyright @ Denise Beddows

ISBN: 9798787762570

A CIP catalogue record for this book is available from the British Library.
Cover design is by **Will Aldersley at:**
www.willaldersleyphotography.com

What readers have to say about Shearwater Point:

"Possibly the next John Le Carré, (she) has produced yet another winner. Gripping, enthralling and bang up to date." – Robert Howe, author of 'Men of Letters'.

"Secrets, assassins and betrayals, with a lost boy who finds himself at the centre of a deadly storm, Shearwater Point is a fast-paced thriller set on the beautiful Northern Ireland coast by an author who clearly loves the place." – Paul Waters, author of 'Blackwatertown'.

"With sinister themes including identity theft, historic institutional abuse, an assassination plot hatched by a murderous neo-Nazi group, and a detective with a heart-breaking cross to bear, the intense beauty of the story's location conceals the dark cruelty of its past, and yet, there are spotlights of humour to lighten the darkness." – Murder Monthly Blog.

"Beddows has concocted a fascinating mix of old influences and new challenges in her modern Ulster Noir. Gripping, and with a terrific sense of place, a worthy addition to this burgeoning genre." – J.A. Marley, author of 'Standstill'

Chapter 1

They arrived at night, exhausted after their flight of seven thousand miles from Argentina and Brazil. Tossed around by winds and battered by squalls, under cover of darkness they descended, making their approach into the prevailing wind. Landing with pinpoint accuracy, they sought out their spring quarters. Lighthouse Island was home to them, but only for the spring and summer. Each pair of Manx shearwaters would locate the same redundant rabbit burrow they had occupied the previous year and, once settled, would begin the annual breeding process.

Secure and warm underground and safe from predators, the determined seasonal migrants had timed their arrival to coincide with the richest bounty of the northern seas. Lured by the abundance of sprats and sand eels, and guided by the magnetic map of the earth and the star compass of the heavens, these gypsies of the skies had returned, as they did every spring, to the depopulated solitude of the Copeland Islands. As they continued to arrive in squadrons, they filled the silent skies with their eerie cries, the same cries which, across the ages, had fed superstition and given rise to local legend about the keening of the *bean sidhe* and the tortured souls of drowned fishermen.

Safe here in these islands off the coast of County Down, the shearwaters would remain through the spring and summer, renewing old acquaintances with their nesting neighbours and scything through the deep, dark waters for fish to feed their hatchlings. The arrival of these regular migrants was always warmly welcomed by the local people who would turn out in hardy droves to watch them. This idyllic spot would be the birds' home until the shortening days would herald the end of summer and signal the time to return, this time with their young, half way across the world again to the south Atlantic. Sadly, not all migrants enjoyed as warm a welcome in Northern Ireland as did the Manx shearwaters.

Bilan made her way to the Bryson Intercultural Centre, accompanied by her two small children. Aminah, five years old now, had quickly taken on the role of a second mother to her two-year old brother, Omar. There had been a third child, a baby boy, whom Bilan had named Aaden. He had been born on the road and, tragically, he had died on the road. Bilan had been pregnant with Aaden when she had fled Somalia. Her husband had never seen his youngest child, and now he never would. She had received no word from him or from their fellow villagers who had been taken by Al-Shabaab. Assuming he was dead, she had taken their savings and their children and had set off on a three-month journey to Europe. Along the way, she had been robbed and both verbally and physically abused, but she had made her way at last to a place where she hoped she might feel safe. It was a place where people were tolerant and kind – at least, most were.

Here, in Belfast, she believed she and her little family might have some kind of future. She was learning to speak English and, soon, Aminah would be starting school. The money they received as an asylum seeker's allowance was very little, and their accommodation was very poor, but it felt safe. At least, it had felt safe until last night. Last night, the house which she and three other refugee families occupied had been burnt out. Of the few, paltry possessions she had lost in the fire, it was her paperwork which caused her the greatest anxiety. She must now apply once again for her refugee papers. She hoped her details would be on file at the centre and that obtaining a new application registration card would be a straightforward matter.

When the shouts had awoken her in the night, for a moment, Bilan had thought herself back in her village near Juba. She had feared the militiamen had returned for her and her children. Leaping out of bed, she had rushed to the bedroom window. Down in the street, she had seen the man wearing the woollen hat and face mask. She had sensed the cruelty and hate just from the resolute and challenging way he stood, watching the building burn. She had seen the flames erupting from the broken window of the ground floor room and licking the front of the building, curling up as far as her windowsill. Quickly, she had awoken the children, grabbed an armful of their clothes and made her way down the smoke-filled stairway, to escape out via the back yard. She and the Afghan families, whom the fire had also made homeless, had spent the night in a local church. There they had been shown kindness.

As she now headed past Belfast's City Hall, its white dome bathed in April sunlight, she heard a sudden commotion across the street to her right. It sounded like a dozen umbrellas being shaken and furled after a rainstorm. She glanced across and saw it was just a flock of starlings taking off from the grounds, disturbed by the screeching of the brakes on a bus as it halted at the traffic lights. She paused for a moment to shift her sleeping son to her other weary arm, and she and Aminah watched in wonder as the birds took to the skies. How magical and effortless was their ascent; how unlike her own flight from Somalia. Would she ever be free like the starlings, she wondered? Could this place ever really be home?

Chapter 2

The weather was mild and breezy that morning, as the three men in the black BMW headed out of Belfast. The open-top tourist buses were full and there were queues for the city's many visitor attractions. The traffic began to ease as the men gradually left the city behind.

'Hughie, why are we taking the B170?' the rear seat passenger asked. 'This way takes longer, doesn't it?'

'A wee bit, but there's fewer security cameras this way,' the crop-haired driver replied.

The back seat passenger nodded. The young man in the front passenger seat turned to look over his shoulder.

'Are you sure you're okay sitting in the back, there, Mister D? Would you not be more comfortable up front?'

'No, I'm fine here, Alistair.'

Ten minutes further along the road, Alistair's burning curiosity got the better of him. He turned to face the man in the back seat.

'May I ask you a personal question, Mister D?'

'You can ask, son. Can't guarantee I'll answer.'

'I was wondering about the sunglasses – why you always wear them.'

'To keep the sun out of my eyes, naturally.'

'Yes, but you wore them at Mackey's funeral, the day it rained heavens hard.'

'Aye, that was a bleak day, right enough. Just the weather for a burial.'

'So, if you don't mind me asking, why the dark glasses?'

The older man sighed. He removed his sunglasses and looked straight at Alistair.'

'Now d'ye see?'

Alistair stared hard. He could see nothing unusual to begin with. Then he noticed. Each of their passenger's eyes was a different colour.

'Oh, how did that happen?' Alistair asked.

'Heterochromia is what they call it. Superstitious Ulster folks would say I was touched by a fairy at birth. Native Americans call it 'ghost eyes'. They'd say I have one eye looking into heaven and the other looking at the earth.'

'That must be awful rare, so it must.'

'Quite rare, yes. Me and Michael Flatley have it. Of course, one of us is a great dancer. The other's an American.'

Laughing at his own joke, the back seat passenger replaced his dark glasses.

Further down the road, it was the driver, Hughie's turn to ask a question.

'You'll not be getting out of the car when we get there, sure you won't?'

'I certainly will,' the older man replied. 'I don't want to miss the action.'

'I thought mebbe you wouldn't want to be seen, though.'

'I want *him* to see me. And I want to see him. I want to see the look on his face when he realises. I want him to know who it was done it.'

The three continued their journey in silence. Their route took them across country, past lush, green fields, dry stone-walled farms and small, neat villages, until, some forty-five minutes later, they arrived at the pretty harbour town of Donaghadee.

Turning onto the coast road, Hughie cruised slowly along until they reached their destination. The large, Georgian house with the big windows had a sloping front lawn, edged with lavender bushes. The driveway swept down towards the road. There were no trees or tall shrubs to impede the sea view.

'That's us, Mister D,' Hughie said, switching off the engine.

'Look at that, boys,' the older man said, pointing at the house. 'That's what sending your fellow Ulstermen to prison gets you.'

Alistair stepped out of the vehicle and held open the rear door for their passenger who alighted. Hughie glanced up and down the road. There was no traffic. All was as quiet as might be expected mid-morning on a weekday. The three men walked up the driveway towards the house. Hughie climbed the three stone steps and rang the doorbell then stepped down again, slipping his hand inside his jacket.

Moments later, they saw, through the frosted glass of the front door, a figure coming slowly down the hallway. A man in his seventies opened the door, he smiled expectantly at the two younger men whom he did not recognise. Nobody spoke. Then he glanced at the middle-aged man who stood slightly behind them removing his sunglasses. Recognition immediately wiped the smile from the householder's face.

'You?'

It was the last word he would ever speak. Hughie produced the Glock from inside his jacket and pumped three rapid shots into the old man's chest. Mortally wounded, the man staggered backwards for a second then toppled forward, falling head first down the stone steps. His assassins calmly walked down the drive and back to their car.

The sound of the shots immediately brought the man's wife to the hallway. Puzzled at first to see no-one beyond the open door, slowly she walked down the hall. As she reached the front door, she spotted her dying husband, lying motionless at the bottom of the steps.

'Oh, no!'

Horrified, she bounded down the steps, fell to her knees beside him and cradled his head in her hands.

Inclining her face down towards his, she kissed him and whispered to him as she felt his life ebbing away.

'Oh, no! Georgie, my Georgie. I love you, my darling. I'll always love you.'

Chapter 3

Feeling surprisingly fresh following his three-thousand-mile flight from Boston, the American entered the lobby of the Belfast hotel. With his laptop case slung over his shoulder and wheeling his suitcase behind him, he approached the reception desk.

'Good morning. Welcome to the Europa,' the cheery young woman on reception beamed.

'Good morning. I have a reservation. Dominic Caffrey.'

The receptionist checked her computer.

'Ah, yes, Mr Caffrey. And how long will you be staying with us?'

'Well, two weeks initially. I may stay a little longer if the research works out okay.'

'Have you stayed with us before?' she asked.

'No. This is my first visit to the Europa. First visit to Europe, in fact.'

'Well, you may have heard that the Europa is famous for being the world's most bombed hotel. But all that's in the past, of course. You'll be perfectly safe with us now. You're in room three-oh-one. That's up on the third floor. The lift is over there. Will I get someone to help you with your bags.'

'No, thanks. I'll manage,' he smiled.

'Well, all the information you'll need for your stay is in your room,' she added as she handed him his key card. 'Let me know if you need anything else. I hope you have a pleasant stay in our city.'

'Thank you. Oh, say, there is one thing you might be able to help me with.'

'Yes?'

'Like I said, I'm here to do some research – family history research. Where would I go to get copies of birth certificates and find out about baptisms and suchlike?'

'Ah, you'll be wanting GRONI and PRONI.'

'Excuse me?'

'GRONI is the General Records Office of Northern Ireland. They hold all the birth, death and marriage registers. They can issue you with certificates. Lots of other public documents, such as church records, they're held at PRONI the Public Records Office.'

'So, where will I find this GRONI? That sounds like a good place to start.'

The receptionist tore a printed tourist map from a pad of such maps and, with her pen, circled the hotel and the General Records Office.

'Here you are. This is us, here, and GRONI is over here at Stranmillis. It's less than half an hour's walk from here. They're open till four o'clock.'

Caffrey took the map.

'Thank you very much, miss. You've been very helpful.'

He took the lift to the third floor and let himself into the room. It wasn't huge like some of the hotel rooms he had stayed in back in the States, but it was beautifully appointed and it felt very serene, especially for a place that had withstood numerous attempts to destroy it.

He had managed to sleep quite well in business class from Boston and he was keen to get started on his quest, so he decided to freshen up quickly and try to find the amusingly named GRONI. Giving his face and hands a very quick wash, and dabbing on some of his expensive cologne, he removed a document wallet from the side pocket of his laptop case, then locked the laptop case inside his suitcase. Armed with all the documentation he needed, including the receptionist's map, he set off for Stranmillis.

The stroll across the city was quite a pleasant one and the records office was not too busy when he got there. After

9

a short wait, it was his turn to be seen by the rather dour looking records clerk. He produced the letter from the American adoption agency and handed it to the clerk.

'Hi, I'd like a birth certificate for Killian Devereux, please. The birth was registered here in Belfast in nineteen-seventy-six.'

The clerk looked at the letter for a moment, then looked at Caffrey. Caffrey noticed his mouth tighten slightly. Caffrey wondered why. Was it a religious thing? He didn't know whether Devereux was a Catholic name or a Protestant one. He understood the Catholics and Protestants over here had stopped killing one another. At least, so far as he knew, they had. Of course, Devereux didn't seem to be a regular Irish name. Caffrey thought it was most likely French originally. Maybe the guy didn't like the French. Or maybe it was Americans he didn't like. Perhaps he was sick of Americans coming here in search of their roots, and maybe he was tired of going through the registers and making out certificates all day long. But, heck, that was what he was paid to do. Caffrey imagined it was ancestor seekers like himself who kept the guy in a job.

'Killian Devereux, you say? The list of fees is displayed in this leaflet. Is it just the one copy you're wanting?'

'Yes, please,' Caffrey replied, and the clerk pointed him towards the row of mostly vacant seats then disappeared into the back office.

Eventually, the clerk returned with a freshly printed certificate and Caffrey handed over the required fee. He decided he'd wait until he was back in his hotel room to have a good scrutiny of his birth certificate. He was excited to learn all about his birth parents and the circumstances of his adoption, and yet he was also quite nervous about it. After all, he might not like what he would find. He tucked the certificate into his document wallet and headed for the door.

He decided to explore the city a little first and then find somewhere to have a snack lunch. He walked down to the River Lagan and then headed up to Donegal Place to have a look at the impressive City Hall. He wanted to get a feel for the province his ancestors would have known. He explored the Titanic Memorial in the neatly kept grounds of the City Hall, then he followed the signs for the Titanic Quarter.

He knew the city had an industrial heritage but he hadn't expected it to look so twenty-first century. The Titanic Experience Museum dominated the area, its jagged roof corners, shaped like the prows of the great ocean liners, pointed skywards, as if challenging the heavens. He gazed down into the depths of the graving dock, the actual dry dock where Titanic herself had been fitted out. He wondered whether any of his ancestors had contributed to her construction. He hoped they had. That would certainly be something to write home about.

It was late afternoon when he arrived back at his hotel. He made himself a coffee using the kettle in his room, and settled down, at last, to examine the certificate. He didn't unfold it immediately. As he held it in his hands, he felt a strange sort of trepidation. This would be an important moment in his life and he didn't want to rush things. To be on the cusp of discovering his own early history seemed odd, scary even. For forty-six years, he had been Dominic Caffrey – Dom to his friends and to those he had supposed to be his family. In all those years, the couple he had called Mom and Dad, the Caffreys, had been, to the best of his belief, his biological parents. It had been a shock to discover they were not.

The truth had only emerged a few months earlier, when he had needed to obtain his first passport for a trip to a law symposium in Canada. He recalled how the Caffreys had obfuscated and made various excuses, ranging from being unable to locate it to having accidentally destroyed it during

11

a house move. It wasn't until he had demanded precise details of when and where his birth had been registered, so that he could apply for a duplicate certificate, that the Caffreys had come clean and admitted he'd been adopted.

His surprise at the discovery that he was not their natural son was compounded by their admission that he had, in fact, been born overseas. His birth was not registered in his home city of Boston after all, but in Belfast, they told him. That was Belfast in Northern Ireland, they had added, not Belfast, Maine. Announcing his intention to come to Ireland and seek out his real family had caused the Caffreys a great deal of offence. How could he not consider *them* his real family, they had asked. Hadn't they raised him and nurtured him? Hadn't they educated him? Hadn't they helped fund both his law studies and his business venture? Weren't they responsible for his comfortable status in life, for his success? How could they not be his real family? He had tried to explain his motives to them, but that hadn't healed the hurt.

Putting off the act of revelation for a moment more, he asked himself why he was here and what he hoped to gain. Why, at the age of forty-six, had he crossed the Atlantic to find his birth parents? Why, as his adoptive mom and dad had continually asked him, would he even *want* to learn about the people who had given him away?

Well, he could think of a lot of reasons. He wanted to know more about his ethnicity and his heritage. He told himself there were also good, practical reasons for finding out, such as whether he might have inherited any particular medical conditions. When he'd been asked about family illnesses at his doctor's practice and by his insurers, he had listed a couple of things he knew the Caffrey's had suffered from, such as his dad's arthritis and his mom's cataracts. Now, however, he knew that information was irrelevant.

He guessed some adoptees decided to trace their biological parents because they had experienced a void in their lives, perhaps following the death of an adoptive parent. Others probably found that, when they became parents themselves, they were so overwhelmed with feelings of love and protectiveness for their infant that they began to wonder why they had been rejected in their own infancy. He felt they were probably looking for some kind of reassurance that poverty or difficult personal circumstances had been the reason for their rejection. If he were honest with himself, however, Caffrey thought his main motivation was intense curiosity.

Since learning that he had been adopted, Caffrey had started looking more critically at his mom and dad. He couldn't think why it was only now that he'd noticed how little he resembled them physically. He now recalled every disagreement he had ever had with his mom; every argument with his dad, and now he put that down to the fact that he wasn't like them in temperament either. He was curious to see what his birth parents looked like and whether he looked just like them. Also, he'd been raised as an only child. For all he knew, however, he might not be an only child after all. He might have a full or half brother or sister somewhere. He knew *what* he was; he was a successful attorney-at-law, a university educated Bostonian, but he felt that finding his birth family would tell him *who* he was.

Well, the moment of disclosure had arrived at last. He would put it off no longer. He put on his reading glasses, and, with slightly trembling hands, held the certificate beneath the reading lamp on the room's small desk. There, before him, was his true identity. He was Killian Devereux. That much he had learned after weeks of pestering the US end of the adoption chain. He was born on 26 April 1976. That, too, he already knew. But here, before him, was the name of his biological mother, Alice Devereux. Alice. He liked that name. It was feminine and a little old-fashioned. It sounded like the rustle of a silk taffeta gown. Alice.

His eager eyes moved along the lines of his early life to see if there would be a father's name. Yes, indeed there was. John Devereux was a farmer. So, this suggested his parents had been married. He'd not actually expected there to be a father's name. He imagined most mothers forced to give up their babies would be single mothers. So, if his parents *had* been married, why would they have given him up for adoption? Perhaps poverty had been the driver.

John, a simple name, but a strong one, he thought. John and Alice Devereux. Their faces began to take shape in his imagination. They would have dark brown hair just like his, and pale blue eyes. They would not be too tall, for he was not exactly tall. The Irish, he knew, were not a tall race, and nor were the French, if that was where his earliest ancestral origins lay.

The birth informant was shown as having been his mother, and here, too, was her place of residence. To his surprise, this was given as Ballyglass in County Wexford. Caffrey had a vague idea Wexford was a county further down south, somewhere down in the Irish Republic, yet the place of his birth was given as County Down, specifically a place called Shearwater Point. From his laptop case, he took out his tourist map of Ireland and spread it out on the bed. He saw that the city of Belfast straddled both County Antrim and County Down, but, look as he might, he couldn't see anywhere in Down which was named Shearwater Point. He did note, however, that from County Down in the north east right down to County Wexford in Ireland's south east corner was a fair old distance.

Next, he plugged in his laptop. Perusing the room's literature, he found the code to enable him to log onto the hotel's internet. Googling 'Shearwater Point' soon identified this as a small headland on the Down coast, a spot beloved of birdwatchers, apparently. So then, this would be his next port of call. He determined he would go there in the morning. The tension and apprehension of discovery having subsided now, he felt he had a lot of thinking to do. He decided he would head down to the first floor to the piano bar to have a drink before dinner. First, however, he would change his shirt.

He gazed at his reflection in the bathroom mirror as he changed.

'So, Killian Devereux, son of John and Alice. Turns out you're a Wexford boy. Whaddaya thinka that?'

Chapter 4

It was around two o'clock in the morning when the white transit van cruised slowly along Belfast's Ormeau Road. Slowing down as it came to the row of terraced shops and cafés, it gradually came to a halt outside the smart façade of the Star of Bengal restaurant. The fairy lights which normally illuminated the two potted bay trees standing sentry at each side of the entrance were turned off, but the street lights cast a light reflection on the highly-polished silver lettering above the restaurant's large front window.

One of the van's passengers quickly alighted and approached the restaurant. His face obscured by a woollen hat and scarf, he held a glass bottle with a twisted rag protruding from the top. Glancing furtively up and down the road, he took a lighter from his pocket and lit the rag. Almost immediately, the petrol-soaked cloth ignited and the man took aim and threw the bottle at the large picture window. On hearing the glass shatter, he bounded back into the van which took off at top speed.

The flames had taken a firm hold of the restaurant's interior by the time fifty-five-year-old chef Shamsuddin appeared at the window of the upstairs apartment, alerted by the sound of breaking glass. He glanced down into the street but could see nothing amiss. Shrugging, he closed the curtains and went back to his bed.

Six hours later, distraught restaurateur Joytul Miah and his wife Aliyah stood and stared at the burnt out remains of the Star of Bengal. The recently applied midnight blue paintwork was blackened and blistered, and the classy silver lettering above the big picture window was melted away. The window was now missing its plate glass, and the neatly trimmed bay trees were shrivelled and dead. Gazing into the blackened interior, the couple saw all that remained of the business they had built up together, from humble beginnings back in the nineteen-seventies: the skeletal chair frames and overturned tables, the scorched walls now devoid of plaster, and, everywhere, shards of glass, some inside the property, some exploded out onto the pavement. Upstairs also, the staff flat had been gutted by the fire. Mercifully, the charred mortal remains of Shamsuddin, their Sylheti employee, had been removed to the police mortuary earlier that morning, before the Miahs had been informed of the fire.

Detective Sergeant Dan McKittrick stood alongside the couple. He shook his head. He hated this sort of crime. It reminded him of the fire-bombings and shootings of his Belfast childhood. As a kid, back in the early 'eighties, he would play on the bomb sites and in the ruins of people's homes and businesses. With the occupants frightened away, chased out of town, all that would remain was the rubble and the smell of burnt paper and wood – the same smell which assailed his senses right now.

Back then, he and his mates never gave a thought to the misery of those who had lived in the buildings which then lay in ruins. It had never occurred to them that people might even have died there. The kids would often twist their ankles on half-buried bricks as they played, but they would still have fun, pretending to shoot at each other around partly demolished corners. Not for them were television inspired games of cowboys and Indians. Belfast boys played games of soldiers and balaclava-wearing gunmen.

There would be a post mortem, McKittrick informed them, although there was little doubt as to the cause of their chef's death.

'Mr Miah,' the detective said gently, 'I'm sorry to be asking questions at a time like this, but the firemen suspect this was arson. There's evidence of petrol in there, you see.

Would you have any idea who would have wanted to do this? Any business rivals, mebbe?'

Joytul Miah shook his head. Aliyah squeezed his arm. 'Racists,' she said.

'*Ota bolo na!*' her husband silenced her sharply.

'Have you had any racist threats?' the DS asked.

'No,' Miah shook his head.

Tight-lipped, Aliyah glanced at her husband and, reluctantly, shook her head, too.

A car suddenly drew up and a well-dressed Asian man in his early thirties stepped out. He approached the Miahs and slipped an arm through Aliyah's. His expression was one of great concern. McKittrick could not understand the earnest conversation which quickly ensued, since they spoke in Bengali.

'Excuse me,' the detective butted in. 'I'm DS McKittrick. Who are you?'

'Apologies,' the young man said. 'I'm Aminullah Miah, their son. I just heard. What happened, do you know? Was anybody hurt?'

'It seems likely it was an arson attack, Mr Miah. And I'm sorry to say that the occupant of the staff apartment, Mr Shamsuddin, perished in the fire. Do you have any idea who might have done this?'

Joytul Miah immediately began berating his son. Though the detective spoke not a word of their language, he was in no doubt that the older man was warning his son not to say anything. McKittrick had experienced this reaction before. Folks in Belfast's immigrant community didn't like the spotlight turned on them. They never welcomed a fuss, no matter how badly they were treated. They didn't like to make waves or draw attention to themselves. As much as they might resent the way they were treated, they would suffer in silence, fearing that resentment breeds resentment. The DS waved over one of

18

the uniformed officers who was standing guard outside on the pavement.

'Constable, would you drive Mr and Mrs Miah home. And offer to make them a cup of tea when you get there. They've had a terrible shock.'

The constable led the couple to a waiting police car. McKittrick turned to their son.

'Mr Miah, if you know anything about this, please tell me. We need to catch whoever did this before they can get rid of any evidence, and before they kill someone else.'

The young man bit his lip pensively as he gazed in at what was left of his parents' livelihood. His face now seemed familiar to the detective sergeant.

'Don't I know you from somewhere, Mr Miah?' the DS asked. 'I'm sure I recognise you. We've met before, haven't we?'

'Yes. we met three years ago when you investigated my elder brother's disappearance. Remember Mohinullah Miah? There were witnesses who thought they'd seen him being forced into a car. He was never found and no-one was ever charged in connection with his disappearance.'

'Oh, of course. I do remember. I thought your parents seemed familiar, too. Your brother was married, wasn't he, and he had a young boy? And now this. Do you think the incidents might be linked?'

'I'm sure they are. I was a law student back then. Now, I work for Northern Ireland's Human Rights Commission. I'm sure you know as well as I do that racism is on the increase. In the period since my brother's abduction, racist attacks in Northern Ireland have more than doubled' Not just attacks on our community, but also on the Jewish community. And that's not all. There have been numerous attacks on gay men and on transgendered individuals.'

'You think that's what this, then, a racially motivated attack?'

'Yes, I do. My parents are probably too scared to tell you, but they've been getting death threats. You know the kind of thing, 'get out or else'. But they've lived here most of their lives now. Oh, there's always been a degree of racism aimed at them and the other Indian and Bangladeshi-owned businesses, but it's definitely on the increase. And, as you can see, it's getting more and more deadly. Something needs to be done, Sergeant. And soon.'

Chapter 5

The taxi summoned by the Europa's receptionist pulled up outside the hotel and Caffrey got in. The driver turned to him for instruction.

'Did the receptionist mention I'd like to go out of town?' Caffrey asked.

'Yes, somewhere on the Down coast she said.'

'It's a small place called Shearwater Point. I don't suppose you'll know it, but I think I can pinpoint it on the map.'

'No bother. I know it well. It's not far from Donaghadee. I used to go birdwatching there as a boy. Is that what you're going there for? For the seabirds?'

'No, I'm actually hoping to visit the place I was born.'

'Well, you chose a beautiful spot to be born, right enough. I'm Joe Doyle, by the way,' the driver said as he pulled out onto Great Victoria Street.

'Dom Caffrey. I can't tell you how much I'm looking forward to this, Joe. It feels like I'm coming home.'

'I hope you like it when you get there. Wasn't it Doctor Johnson who said 'it's better to travel in hope than to arrive'?' Doyle asked.

'Well, I believe it was Robert Louis Stevenson, but I'm sure going to enjoy the journey anyway,' Caffrey said as he settled back in the seat.

Soon they were heading out on the A2 and Doyle pointed out various sights along the way.

'This here's Holywood, home to no film studios whatsoever. Up ahead is Cultra. That's well worth a visit for the Ulster Folk and Transport Museum. You can see how Ulster folks lived two hundred years ago, and how folks down in the Republic still live today,' he joked.

Eventually, they reached Donaghadee, where Doyle turned onto the coast road and headed north. A short drive beyond the pretty harbour town, Doyle pulled up in a layby.

'Well, this is Shearwater Point. Do you wanna have a wee dander round?'

As Caffrey got out of the taxi and stretched his legs, he was immediately struck by the stunning beauty of the place. The sunlight-dappled emerald waters stretched out ahead of him as far as he could see, and gentle waves turned to foam on the jagged rocks below him. Above, all manner of seabirds circled in the blue skies, some dipping down and skimming the waters of the Irish Sea in pursuit of the abundant fish, others soaring skywards and hovering on warm air currents. Doyle joined him to enjoy the view.

'I had no idea it would be so beautiful,' the American marvelled. 'And what's that out there?' he queried, pointing to a landmass not far from the shore.

'That's the Copeland Islands,' Doyle informed him. 'There's a National Trust bird observatory there. I used to go there as a boy. You've certainly come at the right time of year, for the Manx shearwaters are here to breed, right now. They nest in the deserted rabbit burrows on the island.'

'It's truly stunning. I didn't expect this, Joe.'

'You know, the oldest known wild bird in the world was recorded as breeding on Copeland. It was ringed when it was about five years old. That was in nineteen fifty-three, the year of the Queen's coronation. It was last recorded here in two thousand and three, when it would have been fifty-five years old. For all we know, it may be here again this year.'

'Wow! Really?'

Caffrey looked around him. As uplifting as the sight of the birds was, he wasn't here to see the wildlife.

'There don't seem to be many houses here, though.'

'There aren't. Some wee fishermen's cottages and a coupla nice holiday homes owned by well-do-do city folks, that's all. Do you have an address or a house name?'

'Yes. It seems to be a house with a French name – 'La mare doo bon pastooer'. I have it written down here.'

Caffrey fumbled in his inside pocket for the birth certificate.

'Ah, I know it,' Joe nodded. *'La Mère du Bon Pasteur.* That's French for Mother of the Good Shepherd. It was a maternity home run by an order of nuns of the same name. It's a bit further up ahead. Hop in and I'll take you there.'

They drove a little further up beyond the point and Joe turned off the coast road, headed up a sharp incline and, passing through some broken iron gates, pulled up in front of a large old building. Chipped, whitewashed pebble-dash and sun-bleached woodwork gave it the distinct look of an abandoned institution, which, as Joe explained, was exactly what it was. A few of the window shutters were hanging off and most of the ground-floor windows were boarded up. Weeds sprouted up between the cracks in the paved driveway, whilst overgrown hedges and untended trees surrounded the grounds. Caffrey turned back to look again at the view. It was just as beautiful from here.

'It closed down back in the 'nineties,' Joe informed him.

'As you say, Joe, a beautiful place to have been born. Would it have been expensive, to have a confinement here, I mean?'

'No. The nuns who ran it didn't charge any fees.'

Caffrey took a photo of the former maternity home using his camera phone. He also took many more shots of the views out to sea.

Back at the hotel in Belfast again, Caffrey settled up with Doyle. He wasn't used to sterling but he gave him what he hoped would be a generous tip. Doyle's raised eyebrows confirmed it was.

'Thank you, Mr Caffrey. Here's my card. If you want me to take you on any more trips, don't hesitate to give me a call.'

'Thanks, Joe. Yes, I'd like to take another run out to Shearwater point, maybe in a coupla days' time. In the meantime, though, I'm thinking of taking a train down to County Wexford.'

'Okay, Mr Caffrey. When you want me, just give me a call the night before and I'll make sure I'm free.'

'Thank you, Joe. Oh, and it's Dom, by the way. Please call me Dom.'

Chapter 6

Carole Murray caught a taxi from Belfast City Airport to her aunt's house on the coast road at Donaghadee. Paying off the driver, she put her suitcase down on the drive and turned back to look at the view. How she had loved that view as a child. So little had changed. So many happy memories suddenly came flooding back. She recalled the long summer days when Uncle George would take her and her aunt out for the day on his boat. Aunt Ellen would make the most wonderful picnics, with buttered soda farls, Dundee cake and lemonade. Of course, back in those days, the Special Branch officer had to come, too.

Several times – it must be nearly forty years ago, now, she recalled – they had sailed as far as the Scottish coast. So many of her school holidays had been spent here with her father's younger brother and his wife. It had been idyllic and the summers had been so long back then. Oh yes, she had been deliriously happy here.

She now felt guilty that it had been eighteen months or so since she had last visited. On that last visit, she'd brought her fiancé to meet her only living relatives here in the beautiful province. She'd imagined they would have given up hope of their niece ever marrying, and they'd certainly been surprised to hear she had become engaged soon after she'd turned fifty. On that last visit, Ellen had introduced her and Dave to Steensons, the Belfast jewellers, where they had chosen their wedding rings. For his part, Uncle George had introduced Dave to the delights of fishing for trout and plaice out on the sandbanks. Dave had declared this the most beautiful place he had ever been.

Carole rang the bell and saw her aunt come to the window first to check who the caller might be before opening the door.

'Aunt, Ellen,' she said as she hugged her aunt tightly. 'I'm so sorry. It's devastating.'

'I know, love. Come you in.'

Carole found it pleasing once again to hear her aunt's local accent, though she thought Ellen looked much older than when she had last seen her. Perhaps it was the shock of sudden bereavement which had tightened the skin over her cheekbones and drawn dark circles around the pale grey eyes. Ellen's hair, too, was greyer than Carole remembered.

'Sit down, dear, and we'll have a cup of tea. How's … er …?'

'Dave? He's grand. He couldn't get time off this week to come with me unfortunately. Here, you sit down, though, and I'll get the tea.'

In the kitchen, Carole was surprised to find the fridge empty, save for a bottle of curdled milk. She found a packet of coffee whitener in the cupboard, so she made them each a coffee instead. Heading back down the hallway, she spotted her uncle George's waxed jacket and waterproof hat hanging on the hallstand. Putting down one of the coffee mugs, she stroked the sleeve of the jacket fondly. Alongside stood his fishing tackle and wellingtons. The sight of them brought a lump to her throat.

Back in the lounge, she handed her aunt a coffee and sat down beside her on the sofa. All around the elegant lounge there were framed family photographs. The only child in the photos was Carole herself, a swim-suited tomboy pictured on the beach, clutching a child-sized keepnet and brightly-coloured bucket. George and Ellen Murray had never been blessed with children themselves. Their niece Carole had been their surrogate daughter and had been the sole beneficiary of their love and generosity.

26

'I'm so glad you're here, our Carole,' her aunt said. 'There's so much to do and I really don't know where to begin.'

'Don't worry. I'm here to help you make the funeral arrangements and to do anything else that needs doing.'

Her aunt nodded gratefully, then her eyes seemed to slip into faraway mode.

'We'll pop down the shops in a bit, if you like,' Carole suggested. 'I'll pick up some food for dinner. I think we could use some fresh milk and other provisions.'

It broke Carole's heart to see her aunt looking so thin and fragile. Her childhood memories of Ellen were of a strong woman who raised chickens and grew potatoes in the back garden and baked wonderful lavender and lemon shortbread. As for Uncle George, he'd been an intelligent and kindly man with a strong social conscience and a keen sense of humour. It was hard to believe he was gone. There were questions Carole was desperate to ask her aunt. Perhaps it would be best to ask them now, and get them out of the way.

'Aunt Ellen, have the police told you anything about their investigation? Have they arrested anyone?'

'They've told me nothing, dear. Not a thing. The ones who came to the house surmised it would be something to do with his judicial role. They said he'd put away a lot of villains over the years. They said it'll take them a long time to look at all the possible suspects.'

'I imagine you didn't see his killer yourself?'

'No, dear. I just heard a car pulling away. I didn't go down to the road to look. I wanted to be with your uncle in his last moments.'

Carole grasped her aunt's hand and they sat in silence for a while.

'That was a grand cup of tea, Carole,' her aunt said at length, as she drained her cup.

'It was coffee,' Carole corrected her.

'Of course. I meant to say coffee.'

'You've no milk, auntie.'

'Well, we'll get some at the shops. I've other messages to get. I could get some of McCracken's sausages for George's supper. He loves their sausages.'

Ellen caught her niece's surprised look, and she remembered why Carole was here.

'Oh,' she said and she shook her head at her foolish memory lapse.

Carole glanced across at the nineteen sixties' wedding photograph on the mantlepiece. A fresh-faced Aunt Ellen, in a white satin, full-skirted dress with Bardot-style portrait neckline, her hair backcombed into a once fashionable beehive, clung onto the arm of her youthful, dark-haired George. As a teenager, Carole had always thought they resembled Katherine Hepburn and Cary Grant – a golden couple, inseparable, invincible. The couple fixed in time within the silver frame seemed to be gazing beyond the photographer and into a happy future together.

Carole had imagined her aunt and uncle would be here forever, both of them, together. Somehow, George's passing seemed to mark the end of an era. She hadn't really noticed her aunt and uncle growing old. Time was an unconscionable thief, she thought. It stole everything from you eventually. Her aunt's forgetfulness was a little worrying. Of course, it might be the after effects of the terrible shock she had experienced. Carole hoped it didn't suggest something a little more serious. Who, she wondered, would look after Aunt Ellen when her niece returned to London?

On the walk to the shops, they met a middle-aged neighbour of Ellen's. Elizabeth Begley was returning from the shops with her own groceries and she recognised Carole immediately.

'I'm so glad you've come,' she said. 'Your aunt's had a terrible shock, so she has.'

'Hello, Elizabeth. I don't suppose you witnessed what happened, did you?' Carole asked.

'No, dear. I was at work. I work three days a week at the supermarket, and that just happened to be one of my work days. As soon as I heard what happened, I came straight over. I hope they get whoever did it though, and soon.'

'So do I,' Carole sighed, 'so do I.'

Chapter 7

Caffrey had explored several ways of travelling to Wexford. Whether he went by train or express bus, or a combination of both, whether direct or changing transport in Dublin, it would take at least five hours. Even driving, it would take as long, if not longer. Never having driven on the left, he didn't relish the prospect of hiring a car and driving himself, and he guessed taking a taxi all the way would be stupidly expensive. He decided he'd better make further enquiries first to establish if there really were any of his relatives still living down there before he committed himself to the trip.

For all he knew, his biological parents might be deceased, or they might have moved away. Since they had elected to put their son up for adoption, they might not even have told other family members or neighbours of his birth. Perhaps that was why his mother had come hundreds of miles north to give birth to him. Perhaps, for some reason, they'd been ashamed of him. Maybe no-one in the whole of County Wexford would have heard of him or his parents. He tried to prepare himself for disappointment.

After breakfast, he took his laptop down to the hotel's lounge area on the ground floor, found a comfortable sofa in a quiet corner and logged on. He signed on to one of the family history websites and began searching for a Wexford marriage record for John and Alice Devereux, beginning the search five years prior to his birth year, then extending to ten years. Disappointingly, there was no result.

He did notice that there was a significantly large number of records in the name Devereux around the county of Wexford, but no marriages recorded for a John Devereux with a wife named Alice. Maybe Alice wasn't her first forename but was one she preferred to be known by. After all, his adopted father's name was Aloysius Patrick Caffrey, but, since nobody could ever spell Aloysius and it was so often mispronounced, he'd always gone by the name Patrick.

Caffrey extended the search to twenty years prior to his birth, but the nearest record he could find was a nineteen fifty-eight marriage between a John Devereux and a woman named Aine whose maiden name was Kenny. He didn't know whether Aine might be the Irish version of Alice. He now noticed that the friendly receptionist who had checked him in was on duty at the front desk, so he took his laptop across to her.

'Excuse me, miss,' he asked, 'would you be able to help me with something? You see this name, Aine, would that be the Irish version of Alice?

'No,' she smiled. 'That's pronounced 'awn-ya' and it would equate to Anne or Annie.'

'I see. Thank you again.'

'You're very welcome. How's the research going?'

'Very slowly, I'm afraid,' he said ruefully. 'I was born here, you see, and sent to America for adoption. I'm trying to track down my birth parents, but it isn't straightforward.'

'Are you thinking of obtaining an Irish passport whilst you're here?' she asked. 'Many Americans do.'

'Well, I hadn't thought of it. Would I be entitled to one?'

'If you were born in Northern Ireland, you would qualify for an Irish passport, and indeed for a British one also, if you wished.'

'You know, I might just do that – the Irish one, I mean. Though I'm not sure how I'd go about it. Would I have to go to Dublin?'

'No. You can pick up an application form at any major post office here in Belfast. You'll need your birth certificate and maybe a few other documents. It'll tell you all you need and how to go about it on the application form.'

He glanced at the receptionist's name badge.

'Well, once again, Zoe, you've been very helpful. Thank you.'

Returning to the comfortable sofa, he pondered on the idea of having an Irish passport to go with his Irish birth certificate. Supposing his birth parents had owned lands or a fine, big farmhouse down in Wexford. He might just be heir to all that. Of course, he'd probably need to take out Irish citizenship in order to take up residence on his estates. He laughed to himself at his fanciful notions. The family farm might be the size of a postage stamp, and it might have been rented. John and Alice Devereux might have been tenant farmers. Alternatively, any land they might have owned might have been sold long ago.

On the other hand, if there were some land or a house, he might just be entitled to it. He reminded himself he would need to check Irish inheritance law, though, since he knew that, in many countries, children who were adopted out lost the right to inherit from their birth families. Whatever the case, it wouldn't hurt to have an Irish passport and it might be an advantage. Besides, it was his heritage, his birth right, but, first things first.

Turning back to his laptop, he decided to check out the records for births occurring between that nineteen fifty-eight marriage and his own date of birth. However, he could find only one child born to Aine Devereux. In that record, Aine's maiden name was again given as Kenny, and the child was a girl named Alice. That birth had occurred two years after the marriage, in nineteen sixty. Was it likely, he wondered, that John and Aine would be having one child in nineteen sixty and another, himself, more than fifteen years later? Well, it was possible, he supposed. The Irish did tend to go in for big, spread-out families, though not usually with such big gaps. Perhaps John Devereux had been absent for a few years – in the army, maybe, or in prison?

He wondered if Aine might have died and John re-married an Alice. He searched for death records for Aine Devereux, from the date of their marriage. He found only one match. It seems Aine Devereux had died in nineteen sixty. Now, he was really confused. If Aine had been the mother of the Alice who had been born in nineteen sixty, and Aine had died the same year, perhaps in childbirth, she could not have given birth to another child – himself – in nineteen seventy-six. It seemed likely, therefore, that John Devereux would have remarried, yet Caffrey could find no subsequent marriage record for John, either to an Alice or to anyone else. Well, it had been the nineteen seventies. He considered it possible the couple might have lived in sin, but, then again, would that have been likely in a Catholic rural area?

Confused, he decided to check out the online telephone directories for any subscribers named Devereux. He found many, but only one listed in the Ballyglass area, and she was named Alice. He felt there was a good chance she might be a relative of his birth family. She might even be his sister. Jotting down her telephone number, he decided to retreat back to his room before calling the number. After all, he would need to think carefully about what he would say before making the call. He had no wish to upset anyone or stir up any hornets' nests.

He was pleased to find the hotel cleaning staff had been and gone already. His bed was neatly made and his room was pleasantly fragranced. Taking a seat at the desk, he got out his mobile phone and dialled the number. A woman answered.

'Hello, Alice Devricks,' the voice informed him.

For a moment, he was thrown.

'Oh, I'm sorry. I'm not sure I have the right number. I'm trying to contact an Alice Devereux.'

'Yes, that would be me, but it's Miss Alice Devricks.'

There was a brief silence, as Caffrey was still unsure he had the right number. She continued.

'Some people do pronounce my name 'Dever-*oh*', but here, in Wexford, it's pronounced Devricks.'

'Oh, I see. Then I may have the right number, after all. I hope I'm not bothering you, Miss Devricks, but I'm calling from Belfast. I'm doing a bit of family history research and I'm hoping to contact some of my Devereux – or Devricks – cousins in and around Ballyglass. Would you be the daughter of John and Awn-ya Dever ... icks?'

'Yes, that's me.'

'Oh, wonderful. Then I think we might be related. Would it be possible for me to travel down to meet you?'

'Where did you say you were from? From Belfast, is it?'

'I'm in Belfast now, but I'm actually over from Boston – in the USA.'

There was a protracted silence at the other end. It occurred to Caffrey that this Miss Devricks might live alone and might not welcome a visit from a stranger. He felt he should reassure her.

'If you feel it's an intrusion, I wouldn't have to come to your house. We could meet somewhere nearby, for coffee maybe. It'll take me around five hours to get down there, so maybe I could buy you lunch somewhere?'

Still there was silence. Yet she hadn't hung up.

'I may be barking up the wrong family tree, Miss Devricks, but you might be able to point me in the direction of other Devereux or Devricks families.'

'No,' she said eventually. 'It's all right. You must come.'

Chapter 8

Carole Murray caught the train from Donaghadee to Belfast. Soon, she found herself sitting in the reception area of Musgrave Street Police station, waiting to speak to a member of the Major Investigation Team. Eventually, a weary-looking detective appeared.

'Miss Murray? I'm Detective Sergeant Dan McKittrick. What can I do for you?'

'Good morning. I'm the niece of George Murray, the retired judge who was murdered last week out at Donaghadee. His wife, my aunt, is elderly and distressed. She isn't up to enquiring herself, so I'm here to find out what progress you may have made in establishing who killed him.'

'My condolences, Miss Murray. We've our crack team working on the case at the minute. Given the years your uncle served in the judiciary, there's a very long list of potential suspects. It'll take us some time to go through them.'

'I imagined that would be the case,' Carole agreed. 'Presumably, you'll look at all those he put away who might have uttered threats against him, and eliminate those who are deceased?'

'Yes, and we can also eliminate those who have emigrated or are still in prison,'

'But not their relatives or associates … I hope,' she added.

He breathed in deeply, raised his eyebrows and gave her one of those fixed smiles, the kind of smile that says *'oh, here we go, another armchair detective'*.

'Sorry,' she said, 'I don't mean to interfere, but I … have a background in investigation myself. If there's anything I can do to help …'

'Thank you. Well, you can take over the investigation, if you like, and me and my team will go to Donaghadee and look after your aunt. We're good at making tea.'

Carole did not appreciate the detective's sarcasm.

'We won't be needing your tea, or your sympathy, Detective Sergeant. It was a serious suggestion. You might just consider the fact that, since his killer knew where he lived, he might also have known he had a niece who works for MI5. The motive may not be as straightforward as you think.'

'We'll bear that in mind, thank you. But we do have our own branch of MI5 here in Northern Ireland, you know. If we need their help, we'll go through the proper official channels. Now, if you'll excuse me, I've a couple of murders and several cases of arson to investigate.'

Meanwhile, around three miles away, at his hotel, the more Caffrey considered the idea of obtaining an Irish passport, the more it appealed to him. He had purchased online a return coach ticket to Wexford for the following day. He thought the drive through the villages along the route might be better than just seeing railway platforms. He now walked three streets over to the Bedford Street post office and picked up an application form. Perusing the instructions that came with the form, he was dismayed to note that, in addition to the birth certificate, he would be required to show evidence of use of the identity in which the passport was sought. This could be difficult since, despite the fact that this was who he really was, he had never actually lived as Killian Devereux. Naturally, aside from his newly issued birth certificate, he didn't have any other documents in that identity.

Reading through the form more carefully, he saw there was a list of suggested documents which would help establish use of the name. One of these was a student's identity card. It suddenly occurred to him that, when he'd been at Stranmillis to visit GRONI, he had passed a college which offered beginners' classes in the Irish language. Enrolling on such a course ought to enable him to obtain a student's identity card, and he wouldn't actually have to attend the course. Well, why not? He checked he still had in his wallet the spare passport photographs from the batch he'd had taken for his US passport application. That was decided, then. He would walk down to Stranmillis again right after lunch.

Later that afternoon, as he left the college with his authenticated photographic student ID and the receipt for the fees he had just paid, he decided to sit on a nearby bench to complete the passport application forms. He would then be able to post off the application before returning to his hotel. Concentrating on the task of completing the form, he did not immediately take notice of a scuffle which had broken out just outside the college, where students were emerging from their end of day classes. It was only as the altercation seemed to be nearing the bench where he was sitting that he looked up and saw a young man being chased down the street by two other youths. Nobody seemed to be intervening as the young man, whose features suggested he might be Chinese, was grabbed by his two pursers, who began to beat and kick him quite violently.

Caffrey was put in mind of similar scenes he had seen on television back home when men, and indeed women, of far eastern appearance had been attacked by passing strangers, purely because the former US President had kept referring to the Covid pandemic as 'the Chinese virus'. Whether it was Chinese or it wasn't, and whether the virus had been released deliberately or not, the attacks on

Chinese Americans, some of whom hadn't been Chinese at all, but Singaporean or even Japanese, had been wholly unfounded and, in Caffrey's view, cowardly. He couldn't believe, though, that Donald Trump's xenophobic outbursts would hold sway here in Northern Ireland.

As the attack on the young man became more and more savage, a couple of local men, seemingly workers on their way home, now stepped in to help the youth. Caffrey felt he had to intervene himself and he, too, rushed to the young man's assistance. On seeing that they were outnumbered, the two attackers ran off. Caffrey and the other two passers-by helped the youth to his feet, led him over to the bench and sat him down. One of the workmen produced a clean handkerchief and handed it to the youth who used it to dab his now bleeding nose. A young female student retrieved the young victim's study notes which had been dropped during the incident and placed them next to him on the bench.

'Did anyone call the police?' she asked.

'What was all that about?' one of the workmen asked the youth.

'I don't know,' he said. 'I never saw them before. I didn't say a word to them.'

'That's right,' the young woman agreed. 'It looked totally unprovoked to me.'

'Mebbe they don't like Chinese,' one of the workmen ventured.

'I'm Malaysian,' the youth protested.

Chapter 9

The following day, Caffrey took the express bus from Belfast's Europa bus station for the long journey down to Wexford Town. From there he took a taxi out to Ballyglass. The driver had to stop at a farmhouse to enquire as to the precise location of the Devereux place. Caffrey prompted him to enquire after 'Devricks', as the name might be better known with that pronunciation, and indeed it was.

Soon, Caffrey found himself at what appeared to be a very modest smallholding in what his Bostonian adoptive father might describe as 'the back of beyond'. He took the precaution of asking the taxi driver to call back for him in a couple of hours, as he thought it unlikely there was much transport to be had locally.

The tiny, modest farmhouse seemed to be in dire need of repair, though the small garden in front of the property seemed to be well tended. This was far from the grand country estate he had allowed himself to imagine might be his birth right. A small, slightly-built woman met him at the door and he introduced himself. This particular Alice Devereux was not the elegant beauty of his imagination, swathed in rustling silk taffeta. Dressed instead in an unfashionable, knee-length, floral polyester dress, lace-up shoes and sensible pale blue cardigan, she ushered him inside and directed him to one of the fireside chairs.

As she made the obligatory pot of strong tea, he glanced around at the equally old-fashioned and well-worn furniture and the various religious bits and pieces. The downstairs seemed to consist of just a sitting room-cum-kitchen with a practical scullery beyond. The place looked as though it hadn't had a lick of paint in several decades. The ubiquitous Palm Sunday cross was pinned to one wall and a framed picture of the Sacred Heart adorned the chimney breast. He was disappointed to note the absence of any family photographs.

When Alice handed him his tea and settled into the other fireside chair, he quickly took in her features, looking for some semblance of himself. Caffrey wasn't tall, but Alice was quite short. She had the same pale blue eyes and dark brown hair as he, though her hair was well streaked with grey. She proffered a plate of buttered tea bread cut into small finger-sized pieces. He took one and placed it in his saucer.

'So,' she said, 'you've found me.'

'Yes. I hope my coming here hasn't upset you at all. It was only recently I learned I'd been adopted, and I wanted to find my roots. At first, I couldn't figure out how you and I might be related, but, now that I see you, I think I'm right in guessing … I mean … you're my mother, aren't you?'

'Yes, I would be your mother, right enough. I'm sure you'll have lots to ask me, but let me ask you this first, for it has haunted me long enough, did you have a happy life?'

'Yes. I did. The Caffreys were good parents. I got a good education. They looked after me well and I wanted for nothing.'

'Well, nothing is what you'd have had if you'd grown up here. So, it was the right decision to give you up, even though it wasn't my decision.'

'Why *did* you give me up? You and John had this place, didn't you? Did you not want to raise a son here?'

She looked up at him sharply, then turned her gaze to the fire before she spoke again.

'I was a single girl when I got pregnant.'

'But the father's name? On the birth certificate. It's given as John Devereux.'

'Sure, I had to put something. 'Twas the first name came into me head.'

40

Caffrey sensed his paternity was a sensitive issue, and one he might return to later.

'So, Shearwater Point. I went to see it. It's a stunningly beautiful spot that you went to have me.'

'It is indeed, though I didn't get to see much of the place. I was put to working in the laundry. That was down in the cellars. I worked there up until I went into labour. The work was terrible hard. Long hard days, they was. But nothing was as hard as giving birth. We had no doctors attend us, you see, and the nuns was awful cruel. As soon as we was back on our feet, it was back to work in the laundry. We mothers was allowed to see our babies for one hour each evening. That was all.'

'Gee, that was tough,' Caffrey said, though he almost wished he hadn't spoken at all, for he knew that whatever he said would sound greatly inadequate.

'I was just fifteen when I had the baby.'

'Fifteen?' Caffrey was shocked.

He now realised that this was indeed the Alice Devereux who was born to Aine in nineteen-sixty – some fifteen and a half years before his own birth.

'The parish priest arranged for me to go up north to have the baby,' she continued. 'My father told the neighbours I'd gone to Dublin to do a typing course. Typing! Little use for typing in this place. If I hadda been able to type, maybe I'd have run away. Maybe I would've run off to Dublin and got a job. Maybe I'd have been able to keep the boy.'

He gazed into the fire again. Though it was a warm day outside, Caffrey supposed a fire was necessary to light and heat the dark little farmhouse all year round. The fire gave off a sweet smell. He guessed it must be turf that was glowing in the grate, though he'd never experienced a turf fire before. Looking around the small room, he felt sad at the realisation that Alice had spent her entire life here. This little room, and the fields outside, and the farm work, had been all she had known, all her life – apart from that brief escape up to Shearwater Point.

He noticed the way she spoke of her baby, as 'the boy', as though it had nothing to do with him. Well, in her memory, it was a little baby she'd had. How would that little baby have anything to do with this comfortably off, middle-aged American man sitting before her? Her baby might as well have died, for all the joy he had brought her. He suddenly felt unaccountably sad for the young girl that Alice had been. The woman before him was his mother, and yet she was a stranger to him, and he to her. Even so, he was surprised at how her history moved him.

'It wasn't my choice, you know,' she spoke again. 'I didn't realise I wouldn't be allowed to take my baby home. I went up to the nursery one evening after work to cuddle him, but he'd gone. The other girls told me the nuns had sold him to an American adoption agency. I cried myself to sleep that night. Eventually, I was allowed to come home … alone.'

'What was your mom and dad's reaction when you got pregnant? Did they support you? Were they kind to you?'

Alice gave a wry smile.

'My parents? My mother died giving birth to me. In that front room upstairs, it was. I came into the world up there just as she left it. I never knew her nor even saw a photo of her. An old aunt helped raise me, but, when she died it was just my da and me. He was a terrible strict man. Brutal, really. I didn't cry when *he* died. At least he left me the farm. 'Twas all he ever gave me. Well, pretty much all.'

Caffrey realised he had tapped a seam of deep unhappiness. He thought it politic to move the story on.

'Why Killian?' he asked. 'What made you choose that name for me? Was that my father's name?'

'No. There was a men's college just up the road from Shearwater Point. Saint Killian's. I used to wash the sheets and shirts sent down from the college. Sometimes, I'd look out the window in the evening and see the young college fellahs passing on their way out to town. They looked like such young gentlemen, in their starched white shirts. 'Twas me starched those shirts. I hoped my baby boy might be a gentleman one day, too. I thought if I called him Killian … they gave you the name Dominic in America, though. That's a good name, too.'

'I went to a good men's college, too. In Boston. I graduated magna cum laude.'

'What's that mean?'

Caffrey smiled. He realised that he and his mother inhabited two very different worlds.

'Oh, it just means with honours.'

'And what do you do now? Did you fall into a good trade in Boston?'

'Well, I run my own legal company. I'm an attorney at law.'

'Oh?'

He judged from her blank expression that it meant nothing to her. He might as well have said he ran a barber's shop.

'So, tell me about your farm,' he asked. 'Is it arable or do you raise livestock?'

'Would you like to see?'

'Yes please.'

He popped the slice of tea bread in his mouth. It looked and tasted home-made. His stranger-mother had gone to the trouble of baking it especially for him, so he felt obliged to eat it. She rose from her seat and led him out through the back door. The patch of back lawn was pretty bare, a state he thought was probably due to the chickens which were strutting about all over. The place smelled like empty egg shells do when the boiled egg within has been eaten. He guessed the chickens were responsible for the smell, too. As a city boy, he found the farm smells wholly unfamiliar.

A short walk further on, they came to a field of lusher green grass. There were four calves grazing in the field. An old galvanised tin bath filled with drinking water for the cattle stood by the fence.

'I buy young cattle, weaners, and I rear them on. Then when they're big enough, I sell them on at a profit. That's my living,' she explained.

'Is it a good living?' he asked, wondering if he ought to be offering her some money to help out. She was his mother, after all. He suddenly felt guilty that he hadn't thought to bring her anything, flowers or a gift or something.

'It pays the bills. It puts turf on the fire and bread on the table.'

She walked him around the field as they chatted, and they climbed a small hillock to have a look at the district. It was a nice enough place, very rural, comprising very green fields dotted with neat little white-washed farmhouses. The remoteness of it told him Alice could not have had much of a life here. Maybe, though, somewhere in that green landscape, there would be a small village with a small dance hall, somewhere she would have met the boy who would become his father. Maybe, with that boy at least, she had experienced love and tenderness, however short-lived.

Alice pointed out the various other houses they could see and told him who lived in them. It was clearly a small community where everyone knew everyone and all their business. Though perhaps they didn't know all of Alice's business. He asked if there were shops nearby, but she told him the nearest ones were up in the town. He recalled having passed through the town which was little more than a crossroads with a small convenience store. He asked where she had gone to school, but she smiled sadly and said she never had. She'd had no need of schooling to tend cattle, she explained.

Back in the dim little farmhouse, they had more tea and more of the buttered tea bread, which Alice informed him was called *Barm Brack*. All too soon, they heard the taxi driver sounding his horn at the gate. It was time for him to leave. She offered him her hand. He'd worked out that, if she'd been fifteen at the time of his birth, she must be around sixty-one years old now, and yet she looked older. The hand that slipped into his was wrinkled and work-coarsened. She was his mother, and yet they had absolutely nothing in common. He wanted to say he would come and see her again, yet he doubted that he would. He could see the weariness in her face, and she expressed no desire to see him again. What sort of conversation could they have? How might they even be friends? What sort of relationship could they possibly have?

'Thank you so much for the tea and the wonderful tea bread. And thank you for the information. It's greatly appreciated,' he said, awkwardly.

He didn't know whether he ought to embrace her before he climbed into the taxi, but, somehow, it didn't seem appropriate.

'Thank you for coming, Mr Caffrey,' she called out, as the taxi pulled away.

Something inside him suddenly gave way. Mr Caffrey? He was her son, the child to whom she'd given birth in such awful circumstances when she was just a child herself, and yet she had called him Mr Caffrey – not Dom, or Killian, but Mr Caffrey. It was as if she thought him above her, as if she knew her place. He was the big-shot American lawyer and she was a little country woman who raised cattle but wasn't allowed to raise her son. Yet, without her, he wouldn't have existed at all. He couldn't help himself. Tears began to flow down his cheeks.

He kept his head bowed, lest the taxi driver should notice. He wouldn't be able to explain the cause of the sudden pain in his heart. He felt grief for the girl whose happiness was the price paid for his existence. He felt guilty that he'd had an easy and comfortable life, whilst she'd had no life at all. As they drove past the farms of this little rural community, he also felt anger rising within him. How dare they treat the young Alice so heartlessly? What sort of Christian community would send a young, pregnant girl off to the other end of the country to work as a slave for the nuns? What hypocrisy. What callousness. How unfair it all was. And he was angry at himself. Maybe he shouldn't have come. Alice Devricks was a complete stranger to him, yet he wept for her.

On the long coach journey back to Belfast, he had much to think about. He would long hold in his head the image of her, all alone on that little farm, in that tiny room into which no sunlight came, making tea and warming herself by the turf fire. There was no television, just a battered old radio, no-one to talk to, no-one to look after her if she became ill. Clearly, she had never married and she'd had no more children. There were no family photographs; no happy family memories. Time must pass very slowly there for Alice.

Of course, he, too, lived alone, and he'd done so ever since his marriage had failed. Yet he had many friends. He had family, even if they weren't his blood family. He didn't have children himself, but that didn't mean he wouldn't one day. He had some Caffrey cousins of his own age, and also many business associates. He had his career. He had dinner parties and occasional dates, as well. Yes, he lived alone, but his life was far from empty. He thought that, if he'd had to live in that little shabby house in Ballyglass, he would have gone mad with the tedium of the place.

Of all the unhappy thoughts that bounced around in his head, though, the one that bothered him most was the question of who his father had been. Clearly, Alice had not wanted to disclose that. He hadn't pushed it as he felt he'd intruded enough into her quiet little life. He hadn't felt he had the right to blunder into her peaceful existence and disturb it. He hadn't wanted to drop a pebble into a still pond.

The more he thought about her past situation, though, a teenaged girl living alone with just a strict and brutal father, and the fact that she had named his father on the birth certificate as John Devereux, the same name as her own father, the more he kept arriving at a hugely repugnant but inescapable conclusion. It was a conclusion which disturbed him greatly. Had Alice's father, John Devereux, fathered his daughter's baby? Was that why she had given her father's name as the baby's father's name on the birth certificate? Was the father of Dominic Patrick Caffrey, Bostonian and attorney-at-law, his own grandfather?

Chapter 10

Mike Malone was waiting for Carole when she reached the café on Belfast's Royal Avenue. She hadn't been there in years and, judging by the clientele, it was now a favourite haunt of the university students. Mike rose to kiss her on the cheek.

'Mike, how lovely to see you. I hope you haven't been waiting long. The train took longer than I expected.'

'Not at all, Carole. Great to see you, too. I'll get the coffees. Are you still a cappuccino and no sugar?'

'Do they do tea, Mike? I've got to cut back on the caffeine these days. The old blood pressure, you know. Earl Grey would be great. No milk or sugar.'

Malone ordered their drinks and returned to the table.

'How's Angela and the boys?' she asked.

'Oh, they're grand. Angela's teaching and we got the boys into a really good school.'

'So, you don't regret making the move?'

'Not in a million years. The quality of life is so much better here than in London, and as for the property prices, well, wait till you come and see our place.'

'And how about the work? Is it as exciting as it was at Thames House?'

The waitress brought their drinks and set them down, and they paused their conversation until she had departed.

'It's different, I'll say that. There's a lot bubbling under the surface here, especially since this contentious Northern Ireland protocol was mooted. The Unionists aren't happy with it, and the nationalist factions are just waiting for the wheels to come off before they kick off again with their demands for Irish reunification. We could have nineteen-sixty-nine all over again.'

'I wonder things haven't kicked off already, though.'

'Well, the thing is, the bad boys have plenty of criminal enterprises on the go at the moment, you know, drugs, kidnappings, extortion, bank robbery. The men who commanded terrorist units and held the power of life and death during the thirty years of the troubles were never going to go back to hod-carrying or driving milk floats. We're keeping an eye on the main players at the moment, although there's a helluva lot of them. But what brings you back here? A family visit?'

'Well, sort of. You heard about the retired judge that was gunned down out at Donaghadee?'

'Yes, but I wouldn't have thought Thames House would be interested in what seems to be a revenge killing.'

'They're not. George Murray was my uncle. I've come to bury him.'

'Oh, Jesus! I'm so sorry, Carole. I heard about it but I had no idea...'

'Why would you? But look, Mike, I went to Musgrave Street police station and I spoke with one of the detectives in the case, a DS McKittrick. I wanted to be sure they weren't going to write this off as just another convict's revenge scenario. I think the DS and I got off on the wrong foot, though.'

'Ah. I know McKittrick. Dan can be prickly, but he's a good detective. They get a lot of stick, you know. The old RUC was mainly Protestant and, rightly or wrongly, they were often accused of bias. The new, reformed Police Service of Northern Ireland now recruits right across the sectarian divide. But they have a hard job policing across that divide. You know as well as I do what it's like here. Your surname and the way you pronounce your 'aitches' instantly places you on one side of the community or the other.'

'Well, I wanted to be sure they didn't discount the possibility that there might be something more sinister behind my uncle's murder.'

'Do you think there might have been?'

'Well, I don't know for sure, but you see Dave and I were going to come over to visit last Christmas ...'

'Dave?'

'Oh, you won't have known. I got married. Dave's my husband.'

She leaned forward and dropped her voice to a discreet whisper.

'I'm over fifty now, Mike, and I've been single too long to change my surname.'

'No, I hadn't heard. But that's wonderful. So, who's the lucky chap who finally walked our confirmed bachelor girl up the aisle?'

'Dave Lloyd. He's with the firm, too. He's a former detective. We head-hunted him from Gloucestershire Constabulary to be one of our agent handlers. You'd like him.

'Thing is, though, is he Catholic or Protestant?'

'Give over!' Carole chided, as she knew her former colleague was joking.

'Anyway,' she continued, 'I was on the phone to Uncle George and he said an odd thing. He said maybe we should wait till Easter or the summer to come over. He said things were not safe at the moment.'

'Did he say what he was worried about specifically?'

'He said he'd been getting threats from some sort of political group.'

'Well, I imagine he would have had such threats before, during the troubles, but why would they start threatening him now, so long into his retirement?'

'He wasn't sure. He thought they were some kind of right-wing fascist group. I think he used the term Another Ulster or maybe Alternative Ulster, something like that.'

50

Mike Malone's face fell suddenly. Carole noticed.

'Does that ring a bell with you?' she asked. 'Have you heard of them?'

'Yes, I have. This isn't the best place to be discussing such things, though. Tell you what, Carole, what are you doing tomorrow? Supposing you come over to my office in Holywood? We can explore this in a bit more depth.'

'Yes, I'd like that. I need to know if my aunt is in any danger, and whether I should consider moving her to London to be near us.'

Chapter 11

At three o'clock the following morning, some thirty-six miles south of Shearwater Point, off County Down's Lecale Peninsula, Jim McKillop and his crew were approaching Ardglass harbour. They had been out all night, trawling for the nocturnal Dublin Bay prawns and had bagged a fairly good haul. Jim hoped there would be enough of a return from the catch to pay the wages of his Filipino and Ghanaian deckhands, and to make the monthly repayments on the quarter of a million-pound loan on his trawler, as well as putting some food on his family's table.

He was contemplating the fact that, although Britain's exit from the European Union had removed the crippling fishing quota system which had so reduced his income year on year, it had simply replaced it with equally crippling export tariffs. France, Spain and the Netherlands were still the biggest customers for what would become known as langoustines once they left the UK for the continent but, by the time the catch had been auctioned off electronically and the EU's duties added, the fishermen's return on this highly prized seafood would be substantially reduced.

The thirty-six-foot pelagic trawler *Ocean Star* was within sight of the harbour and had slowed to four knots for the approach when, suddenly, McKillop heard an almighty bang. He felt the collision reverberate right throughout the vessel's superstructure. Almost immediately, the onboard generator failed and all the electrics blacked out. Glancing quickly around him into the darkness, he couldn't see what he could possibly have hit. There had been no other boat in sight and he wasn't aware of any submerged wrecks or other underwater hazards in this particular area.

Moments later, the emergency generator fired into life and McKillop immediately activated the radio and put out a 'mayday' distress call, reporting his position and the fact that he'd had some sort of collision. He heard half the response from the Kilkeel coastguard station before the back-up generator also cut out. The loss of power and propulsion was worrying enough, but his crewman Francisco suddenly appeared in the wheelhouse to announce he had checked the diesel tanks to find they were contaminated with seawater. As an experienced mariner, Francisco could tell just by the smell.

Kwame, too, appeared in the watchhouse to announce that the crew's accommodation, where he'd been making a pot of tea, was knee-deep in water. The words had hardly left his lips when the *Ocean Star* was jerked backwards violently. McKillop and his two crew members were instantly hurled down onto the deck. Rising quickly to his feet again and steadying himself by holding the wheel, McKillop saw the harbour lights were now receding into the distance rapidly. To his horror, he realised that something was dragging them backwards out to sea. In all his years at sea, he had never experienced an undertow of such power and speed.

He began to realise the *Ocean Star* must be hooked onto something. Another vessel must be dragging them backwards, and yet he could see no other vessel out there in the pitch darkness. Next, he felt the trawler being spun around as whatever had seized them from below now turned sharply northwards. He and his crewmen now found themselves pitched sideways. Then, as suddenly as the encounter had begun, the *Ocean Star* was free of its grip but was now left floating on its side in the water. The brief spark of hope McKillop felt at the trawler having been freed was immediately quenched by the realisation that they were sinking, and rapidly.

The Portaferry lifeboat had already been launched in response to an alert from the coast guard and the RNLI crew sped with all haste towards the *Ocean Star*'s last position. The 'mayday' call had also been picked up by the coastguard station thirty-two miles away at Peel on the Isle of Man. There, watch officer Paul Kelly scrutinised his radar screen. Amongst the small green dots which represented the flotilla of returning fishing boats, he spotted something bigger. To his trained eye, this appeared to be a submarine and it was heading away from the flotilla in a northerly direction at a speed of around ten knots.

Kelly immediately rang the Royal Navy Intelligence Branch and advised the duty officer of the apparent collision between a submarine and a fishing trawler just off the County Down coast. Armed with the co-ordinates of the incident, the naval officer assured himself there was no Royal Navy submarine known to be in the vicinity and he quickly put out an alert.

An hour and a half later and fifty miles further north, the Russian *Akula* class nuclear submarine found herself confronted by two Royal Naval *Astute* class subs in the narrow neck of water between Rathlin Island and the Kintyre Peninsula. The Russian vessel, over thirty years old and twice re-conditioned, would have been no match for the modern *Astute* subs, had their instructions been to attack the interloper. However, they had been despatched solely to identify it and warn it off.

The Royal Navy's submarines boasted not only a low noise signature, giving them the advantage of stealth, but they were also equipped with world beating sonar to detect the incursion by enemy vessels and establish their type and point of origin. After issuing a warning by radio, the British vessels allowed the Russian sub to continue its passage north but would follow it all the way around the coast of Scotland towards Norwegian waters.

Meanwhile, the Lifeboat had picked up a lone Filipino seaman treading water in the pitch darkness of the Irish Sea. Francisco had been visible only by his lucky white cotton baseball cap which never left his head. However, of the *Ocean Star,* her master Jim McKillop and crewman Kwame Boateng, there was no trace.

Chapter 12

The next day found Caffrey at PRONI, Belfast's other records repository. The smart building on Titanic Boulevard was a relatively recent home for the Public Records Office. The clerk, with white cotton gloved hands, bestowed the registers upon him with all the reverence of an altar boy handling the patten and host at holy communion.

'There y'are. *La Mère du Bon Pasteur*. We get a lotta people asking for these,' he commented.

'Are they all Americans?' Caffrey asked.

'Not all, but I'd say most would be.'

Caffrey opened one of the registers and turned the well-thumbed pages until he found those relating to his date of birth, then he worked backwards a couple of months until he found the handwritten admission record for Alice Devereux. He saw she had been admitted from Ballyglass, County Wexford, so he knew this was the right entry. The name of the Wexford priest who had arranged her admission to the home was included, though that was of no interest to Caffrey.

There, though, was her age. She was, indeed, just fifteen years and five months old, and her parents' names were given in the penultimate column on the page. John Devereux and Aine Devereux (deceased). Of the birth and despatch of Alice's infant son, however, there was no mention, much to his disappointment. He supposed there would be another register, perhaps destroyed long since, which would have recorded the fee the nuns had received for the sale of Alice Devereux's baby boy.

At the final column of Alice's entry, was the date of her discharge from the home. He noted this was four months after his birth. So, altogether, the nuns had got six months' unpaid work out of Alice before sending her back to a different form of enslavement on her father's smallholding. It occurred to him that viewing the entry in the register was like seeing a prison record, and he had seen a number of those during his legal career. Alice had been given over to the cruel custody of the nuns for her crime, a crime which, legally speaking and given her age, had not been her crime, but someone else's. She had undergone half a year's penal servitude, hundreds of miles from home, and then had been returned to her community.

It made him so angry. He slammed the register shut suddenly. The sound reverberated around the quiet reading room, attracting glares from the other users. Instantly, the clerk was by his side.

'Is everything all right?'

'Yes. I'm so sorry. It's a heavy book. I didn't mean to let it close so heavily. But, can I ask, would it be okay if I used my camera phone to take a photo of the page where my own birth is listed.'

'Yes, you can, but, please, be careful. These registers are getting more fragile as the years go by.'

Afterwards, Caffrey wandered outside and sat by the River Lagan. There were tourists enjoying the spring sunshine and queueing for *The Titanic Experience*. The big modern museum was an impressive monument to Belfast's glory days of shipbuilding. He supposed he might like to see the museum himself, but not today, perhaps. Today, he wasn't in the right mood to enjoy himself. In any case, it now seemed he had no family connections with the city and its industrial past. It was just a fluke that his birth came to be registered here in Belfast. His being born out on that beautiful Down coast, too, was a fluke. It seemed that his proper place was down in the less exciting rural farming community in Wexford.

The more he thought about his fifteen-year-old mother and what she had been through, the more his heart ached. He didn't feel any kind of kinship to her, and, oddly, he resented the fact that he didn't. His having been snatched away from her so soon after birth meant there would never be an emotional mother and son bond between them. However, he did feel outrage on her behalf. The more he reflected on her experience, the more outraged he felt.

He now wished he had spent longer at the maternity home. Now that he had an idea what it had been like there for Alice, he decided he wanted to return, to get the feel for the place. He wanted to see the cellars where she had worked. He also wanted to banish from his mind the stifling image of the dingy little farmstead in Ballyglass, and replace it with the big skies and sea air of his beautiful birthplace out on the coast.

He took out his phone and Joe Doyle's business card and called the number.

'Joe? It's Dom Caffrey. How are you fixed for another run out to Shearwater Point? Tomorrow? Great.'

Six miles further east, out on the Old Holywood Road, Mike Malone met Carole Murray outside Palace Barracks and escorted her through the security barrier.

'Welcome to MI5 Northern Ireland,' he grinned as he handed her the visitor's pass and escorted her into his office.

From his jacket pocket, he produced a few sealed sachets containing tea bags and waved them at her.

'Earl Grey,' he said. 'Angela found some and made me bring them in for you. She says you must come back with me for dinner tonight. I'll drive you home afterwards.'

'How thoughtful. I'd love to, Mike.'

Malone took his keys from his pocket, unlocked the security cabinet behind his desk and removed a file.

'Now, have a seat while I make us some tea. Black, no sugar, wasn't it? Here, take a look at this while you wait. I'll be back in a tick.'

Carole put on her reading glasses and picked up the file. It was marked 'Alternative Ulster'. She began to read the briefing notes within. Soon, Malone was back with their tea.

'So, Alternative Ulster does exist,' she remarked.

'Oh yes, and we're very interested in it. They have floating affiliations with other groups here in Ulster, such as the Red Hand Commando, and with some individuals within the UVF. And they've established links with other right-wing groups in England, such as Combat Eighteen, the National Front and the British Nationalist Socialist Movement. But they also have much wider connections abroad. They're closely involved with Russky Obraz, a Russian fascist group, and with their Serbian equivalent, the Serbian Obraz, and many more. You'll be familiar with some of these?'

'Oh, yes. So, what sort of activities are Alternative Ulster into?'

'They're a shadowy group, believed to be behind most of the racist attacks and gay-bashing in the province. Their clarion call is for ethnic cleansing. They also want to see a re-partition of Ireland, with a wholly white, Protestant Ulster, taking in all nine northern counties, not just the six that make up the province of Northern Ireland. They're transphobic, homophobic, anti-Semitic. You name it, they're anti-it.'

'They sound a thoroughly nasty bunch.'

'They are indeed.'

'So, do you have eyes on their membership?'

'No, I'm afraid we only have snippets of intel about the organisation. It's also believed to be an organised crime group, probably involved with drugs, the club scene and a bit of robbery and fraud, and those activities help fund their political agenda.'

'Do you have any names?'

'We only have one name, so far. Sources tell us the organisation was formed around four years ago by a man who used to run with the UVF. See, we arrested a local thug for a serious assault on a Jewish cabbie and he was willing to give up a certain amount of info about the group's activities and connections, in return for a lighter sentence. But he was too scared to divulge many names.'

'Could he be pressed to reveal more?'

Mike shook his head: 'Afraid not. That thug died in prison. Fell in the showers and banged his head – several times. The rumour mill also says the head of Alternative Ulster has been seen having meetings with a senior member of Russky Obraz. That's a Russian named Ilya Kirasov.'

'We've been looking into Russky Obraz back at Thames House. I'm sure you're aware that Putin's regime is operating something they call 'managed nationalism'. They're not just turning a blind eye to the right-wing groups in Russia, they're actively encouraging them to forge links with similar groups in other states. It's part of Putin's plan to de-stabilise western liberal nations. He's had great success galvanising the far-right groups in Hungary, Belarus and Poland. Neo-Nazism is also growing in Belgium and Portugal. Seems he's interested in Northern Ireland now, too.'

Malone nodded, thoughtfully.

'Carole, the death of your uncle is quite shocking, but it's not without parallels elsewhere. It's believed Russky Obraz killed three members of the Moscow judiciary recently, too. They'd been handing out long prison sentences to some of the nationalist thugs. And one of the Moscow lawyers involved in the prosecutions was beheaded. His head was left in a city centre rubbish bin.'

'Dear God, Mike! So, what name do you have? Who's this former UVF man who's running Alternative Ulster?'

'Intelligence suggests he's called Killian Devereux.'

Chapter 13

In London, Sir John Hooper, Chief of Britain's Defence Forces, was at Thames House, headquarters of the Security Service, for an informal meeting which he had requested with MI5 Director General Helena Fairbrother. At Sir John's suggestion, Helena's head of Counter-espionage, Adrian Curtis, was also included.

'Thank you for seeing me, Helena. Good to see you again, too, Adrian. I'll be as brief as possible. These incursions by Russian aircraft and submarines into our sovereign airspace and territorial waters, well, they're getting out of hand. There was last year's serious air collision in which the crew of one of our Voyager refuelling aircraft were killed, and, this year, we've had several more near misses in the Irish Sea. This week, one of their antique nuclear subs sank a fishing trawler off the Northern Irish coast, drowning the skipper and one of the crew.'

'And the Russians had the bare-faced affrontery to fire warning shots at our naval vessel just for passing the black Sea coast of Russian occupied Crimea,' Helena added. 'Has there been any apology or explanation from the Russians over the fishing boat?'

'No. No response at all. As you know, our strategic assessment on the situation has recommended, in the strongest possible terms, that a major joint initiative be set up with the Irish authorities.'

'How do you see that initiative working?' Helena asked.

'Well, you may know that the Nordic countries combine their sea and air resources to conduct joint patrols of their airspace and their waters. Similarly, the Benelux countries have joint patrols. We're putting pressure on the Prime

Minister to seek a treaty with the Irish aimed at a more formal defence relationship. That would include joint patrols in the Irish Sea and in our adjacent air space, possibly also off the west coast of Ireland, and also increased intelligence sharing.'

'Forgive me, Sir John,' Adrian said, 'but do the Irish have much of a defence capability to add to our own?'

'They don't at the moment,' the Defence Chief conceded, 'but I believe there is a will on their part to demand more funding from the EU to boost their defence capabilities. The UK no longer has access to EU funding, of course, and there may be some resistance from Brussels to an EU state co-operating with a 'third country', as they now see us, but I believe the Irish are very keen.'

'Why do you think they've suddenly warmed to the idea, John?' Helena asked.

'Well, over the last couple of years, the Irish have reported significantly increased activity by Russian spy ships in their waters. There are four communications cables beneath the sea off the west coast of Ireland connecting Ireland with the US. They've a further eight cables off the east coast connecting Ireland with Britain and they're planning to sink more cables to link Ireland directly to France and other European states, too. They've been monitoring one ship in particular, the *Yantar*, a known spy ship, which is moored directly above one of the transatlantic cables. The Irish are aware of other spy ships in the area, too, but they can't monitor them all.'

'Why not?' Adrian asked.

'Lack of resources, basically. Under Ireland's maritime legislation, responsibility for their subsea defences falls not to the navy but to the gardai – the police – but the Irish sea mass is ten times as big as their land mass and the police have just one police boat.'

'One boat?' Adrian was shocked. 'But we know the Russians are actively trying to access the data that passes through our cables and, no doubt, through the Irish links to the US, too. Shouldn't they get their navy involved?'

'Well, unofficially, they have, but their navy is not very big and not very well funded.'

'That's right, Helena added. 'And the Irish have little in the way of signals intelligence and have to rely on ours, which we're happy to share. Their airspace is adjacent to ours and we also share the Irish Sea. It makes sense to have a joined-up response to hostile Russian activity, whether in the air or in the sea or, indeed, in cyber-space. So, is the treaty being enacted?'

'No. I'm afraid it isn't,' Sir John frowned. 'Whilst the Irish can see the advantages in it, Brussels aren't keen, and our own PM is highly resistant to the idea.'

'Is that because he's unwilling to upset the Russians?'

'Yes, Helena. That's exactly why. So, I wondered whether your people could come up with a way of convincing Ivan Thompson, not only that the Russians are the biggest threat that we and the Irish face, but also that it would be to everyone's advantage for us to join forces.'

Helena glanced sideways at Adrian and raised her eyebrows. She knew that, if anyone could come up with a plan to influence the PM, however unorthodox that plan might have to be, it would be Adrian and his Counter-espionage team.

Chapter 14

Joe Doyle turned off the coast road and headed, once again, up the steep driveway that led to the semi-derelict *La Mère du Bon Pasteur* home. He and his passenger both got out of the taxi and had another look at the amazing sea view. Caffrey thought it was still a most pleasing sight, despite his discovery of the cruelty and misery visited upon the unfortunate women and girls who had passed through these rusting gates.

'Do you know how long this place was in operation, Joe?' he asked.

'I'm not sure when it started up, probably early twentieth century, but it definitely closed in the 'nineties. There was a lot about it in the papers.'

'So almost a century. There must have been thousands of frightened young girls taken in here during that time.'

'Did you manage to trace your birth mother?'

'I did. She's living down in County Wexford. She told me what it was like here. It seems the nuns were exceptionally cruel. My mother was made to work in the basement laundry, right up until the time she went into labour with me. And there was no medical attention. Even after she'd had me, they put her back to work in the laundry. She was here for half a year in total.'

'Yes, they had a good racket going here. The nuns got paid for taking in laundry from the local hotels and the girls got paid nothing for washing it. Nowadays, that'd be called slave labour and they'd be put away for it. 'Course, the nuns made even more money from the adoption agencies when they sold their babies to them rich and childless American fuckers. Oh, no offence, Dom.'

65

'None taken, Joe. You're absolutely right. What a racket. It's kinda ironic that the nuns were known as Mother of the Good Shepherd. Nothing motherly about them. She was just fifteen, you know, my mother, when she gave birth to me here.'

'Jesus! That musta been rough. The poor wee girl. I don't suppose she could've kept you.'

'She wasn't given the choice, Joe. She didn't even get to say goodbye to me. She came to the nursery one evening, for the single hour in the day they were allowed access to their babies, and I was gone.'

'*Jee-sus!*' Joe cursed again. 'But at least you found her. I suppose it was important to you to know where you came from.'

'You're right, Joe. I mean, I know *what* I am, but I guess I needed to know *who* I am. Anyway, I'd like to try and get into the building. I'd like to see the inside, to see where my mother had me, and where she worked. Do you mind waiting whilst I have a look around?'

'No, I don't mind. Technically, you'll be trespassing, but I don't suppose anyone will know. I don't imagine anyone cares about this place anyway. You go ahead. I'll wait here.'

Caffrey tried the big front doors of the abandoned home, but they were firmly locked. He went around the back and walked the length of the building until he noticed that one of the small cellar windows down at ground level appeared to be loose. It had been propped shut with an old rain barrel. He pulled the barrel away and pushed at the window frame. It gave way and opened inwards, allowing him just enough room to clamber in.

Wandering around, he found himself in a warren of dim basement rooms. One cellar room held numerous broken metal bedframes. They were of the old-fashioned, single, hospital bed type. He wondered how many young women had suffered unrelieved agonies of labour on those beds. It occurred to him that he'd probably been born on one of them. He passed on to the next room which was piled high with plain wooden benches of the kind usually found in chapels. There were old enamel chamber pots stacked in one corner and broken wooden cots in another.

Eventually, in the dingiest recesses of the cellars, he came to what was obviously the laundry area. Naïvely, he expected it to have rows of washing machines, like an American laundromat. Instead, there was a row of deep ceramic sinks along the exterior wall, and several huge metal cylinders dominated the middle of the room. He guessed these were for boiling up the water to wash the bulkier laundry items. Wooden laundry paddles were stacked up on the floor. He instantly thought of Alice's coarse hands, doubtless roughened by six months of washing shirts and sheets by hand. He hadn't noticed a washing machine in the little scullery of the farmhouse back in Ballyglass, either.

There was a bank of huge cupboards along the back wall. One stood open and inside were drying racks. The next large cupboard along was padlocked. This struck him as odd. He wondered why they would have left the cupboard locked. Surely the nuns wouldn't have left behind anything of value? It crossed his mind that there might be paperwork in the cupboard. Maybe there were more registers and ledgers. Perhaps there were accounts books with the details of all the nuns' transactions, of their history of human bondage and child trafficking. The lawyer in him suddenly had the urge to search for these documents.

He thought that maybe it was time the sisters were brought to account for their wicked exploitation of those helpless young girls and unworldly young women. Maybe women like Alice Devereux should be compensated by the Catholic church for the awful cruelty meted out to them. If the cupboard did contain evidence which might support a class action against the nuns, then maybe it needed a lawyer to secure and evaluate that evidence.

Fired with a sudden desire to discover the truth, he pulled at the padlock, which looked surprisingly new and which, disappointingly, held fast. He noticed, however, that the door hinges were well rusted and the right-hand cupboard door was loose where it met the door frame. He pushed his fingers into the gap between door and door frame and felt it give a little. He decided, though, that he needed something solid which he might wedge into the gap and force the door off its hinges.

Returning to one of the cellar rooms he had passed through earlier, he found a broken strip of metal bedframe. He took it back with him to the laundry room and jammed it into the gap. Bringing all his weight to bear, he levered the bar against the door until, eventually he felt it give way.

The door now hung from just one fragile hinge. Pulling it open as far as he could, he gazed into the darkness. He saw shelves before him. There was lots of stuff on the shelves, but it was too dark to see exactly what the stuff was. Taking out his mobile phone, he used its light to illuminate the darkness. To his disappointment, there didn't appear to be any registers or paperwork on the shelves. To his surprise, however, there were weapons. He saw stacks of hand guns, rifles and semi-automatic weapons. There were also piles of boxes of ammunition of various types. For a moment, he had a strange vision of the nuns using the weapons to maintain discipline amongst the young mothers.

'Nuns with guns?' he thought to himself, *'don't be silly.'*

Yet he couldn't imagine what the weaponry was doing here, in this abandoned building. Perhaps he had stumbled upon an IRA arms cache. He realised he had only uncovered half of the cupboard's interior. Perhaps the other half contained the documentation he had hoped to find. Using the metal bar again, he jemmied off the door at the left-hand side of the cupboard, too. He had to quickly step aside as the two doors, still firmly padlocked together, crashed heavily to the floor. Stepping over them, he made to lift his phone to shine a light into the left side of the cupboard.

Before he could do so, however, something toppled out of the darkness and landed against him. It caused him to overbalance. He fell backwards onto the wooden cupboard doors and whatever it was that was in the cupboard fell on top of him. It felt wet, and it shed dust and shreds of damp bits onto his face and chest. He pushed it off him and jumped to his feet. Shining the phone's torch beam downwards, he saw, to his profound shock, that what had fallen onto him was a dead and decomposing human corpse. It had been stuffed tightly into the cupboard in an upright position, and, clearly, it had been there some considerable time. For one horrible moment, he wondered if it might be the body of a young woman who had died at the home.

He poked at the now prone body with his foot and saw that it was covered with maggots. His stomach turned over. Shining the light on himself, he saw that he, too had maggots on him. Retching, he quickly swept them from his hair and from his shirt. His clothes felt unpleasantly greasy where he had come into contact with the rotting cadaver. He retched again, as he realised he even had one of the maggots in his mouth. He quickly spat it out. Stepping away into the dim light cast by the window that was set at ceiling height, he heaved several times before throwing up on the floor.

He now heard footsteps. He suspected Doyle must have heard the doors crashing to the floor and was coming to see if he was all right.

'Joe!' he shouted, 'Come here, Joe! Come quick and look at this!'

The footsteps came quickly. He turned around, but it wasn't Joe who came running into the room. It was half a dozen uniformed officers of the PSNI's armed response unit, and their guns were pointed at him.

Chapter 15

That afternoon, Carole returned to Musgrave Street Police Station, but this time she had Mike Malone with her. Thanks to Malone's intervention, the senior investigating officer handling the murder of George Murray had agreed to see them. DS McKittrick appeared to collect them from reception.

'Hi Dan,' Malone greeted him. 'I believe you've met my colleague, Carole.'

The detective looked sheepish.

'Yes, hello, again Miss Murray. Apologies if I was a bit short with you last time you were here. So, you really are a spook?'

'Yes, Detective Sergeant. Well, I'm no James Bond. I'm simply an intelligence analyst, and I'm sure I owe you an apology, too. I was probably a bit pushy. As you can imagine, I'm still shocked and upset about what happened to my uncle.'

'Well, never mind, now. Come upstairs and meet my boss, Detective Chief Inspector Thomas O'Keeffe.'

The DCI rose from his seat to greet them as they entered his office. There were numerous foreign police plaques arranged on the walls around the room and Carole noticed a framed photograph in pride of place. In it, the DCI was pictured accepting the Queen's Police Medal from Her Majesty in person. She suddenly felt reassured.

'Hello Mike. Miss Murray. Please take a seat. And may I offer you my sincere condolences, Miss Murray. Now, I expect you want to know what we've uncovered so far about the murder of your uncle.'

'Yes, please,' Carole said.

'Well, as you know, in his days on the bench, your uncle put away a lot of terrorists. These were mainly IRA, Provos and INLA, but also a fair few loyalist extremists. He gave out hefty sentences, but it's my impression he was even-handed. No-one could say he favoured one side or the other. We're working our way through a very long list of possible suspects, as I'm sure Dan here told you.'

'That's reassuring to hear,' Malone agreed. 'Carole works in MI5's Counter-espionage section over in London, as did I before I left Thames House to transfer to our Holywood office. So, Carole has a couple of ideas she'd like to throw into the pot, that's if you don't mind.'

'Not at all,' the DCI said affably, 'anything you can add will be welcome.'

'Well,' Carole began, choosing her words carefully. 'My uncle retired from the bench quite a few years ago, now. Most of those he sent down were released from prison back in nineteen ninety-eight, following the Good Friday Agreement. It would seem odd for any of them to have waited till now to take their revenge.'

'True,' the DCI agreed, 'though they do say revenge is a dish best eaten cold, don't they?'

'Indeed, but it might be my uncle's more recent activities which led to his murder.'

'Recent activities?' the DCI looked puzzled.

'He was acting as a legal advisor to the Northern Ireland Human Rights Commission. As I'm sure you know, the Commission is funded by UK government but is an independent public body. It holds the accreditation of the United Nations.'

'And what was your uncle's exact role with the Commission?' the DCI asked.

'His was an unpaid role which involved working with the Commission's lawyers, helping them to check existing laws to ensure they uphold human rights, and advising on amendments, as well as helping to draft new laws, such as the Bill of Rights for Northern Ireland. He was instrumental in securing changes to Northern Ireland's abortion laws in two thousand and nineteen, and he influenced the introduction of the province's same sex marriage legislation in two thousand and twenty.'

'So, he wasn't just growing roses in his retirement, then?' the DCI said.

'Indeed, he wasn't. He was also advising lawyers who are pursuing individual human rights abuse cases through the courts. Two of those lawyers quit when they began receiving death threats.'

The DCI flashed a look of displeasure at DS McKittrick, who shrugged. It was clear to Carole that neither policeman had been aware of her uncle's more recent connections with such controversial initiatives.

'To be fair, his recent activities probably weren't reported in the press,' she consoled. 'He had also agreed recently to serve on the proposed Truth and Reconciliation Committee. You'll be aware that the Committee was recently set up to carry forward the work of the disbanded and ineffective Historical Enquiries Team. You'll also have heard there's been a lot of controversy surrounding that initiative, too.'

'Indeed, there has,' the DCI agreed. 'In some quarters, the committee's purpose has been lauded as encouraging victims of the thirty years of troubles to forgive and forget. However, other elements in our society fear it will uncover a good deal of truth and guilt which has remained hidden all these years. Not everyone wants the truth to come out. Well, it's helpful to know all this, though I imagine this will quadruple the number of potential suspects we need to consider.'

'Well,' Carole continued, 'last December, I spoke with my uncle on the phone. He said he'd been receiving threats from someone he believed was connected with a proscribed political organisation'

'Which organisation are we talking about?' O'Keeffe asked.

The DCI's expression was one of deep and genuine concern. It was Malone who answered his question.

'Alternative Ulster.'

'I've heard of them, of course,' The DCI confirmed. 'They're believed to be neo-Nazis, aren't they? Is there anyone in particular in that organisation we should be looking at?'

'Well,' Malone continued, 'intelligence suggests the head of the organisation is a loyalist, a former UVF man who has a reputation for extreme violence, although he has no criminal record, so we don't know what he looks like or where he is. His name is Killian Devereux.'

DCI and DS exchanged surprised glances once again.

'What?' Mike asked, noticing their expressions.

'Killian Devereux?' the DCI said, 'well, as it happens, we have Killian Devereux in custody right now. He's being interviewed by my DI as we speak.'

Chapter 16

In the station's custody suite, McKittrick's immediate superior, Detective Inspector Sarah Lawrence, had just commenced her interview of the suspect.

'So, how long have you been using this identity?' she waved the American passport at Caffrey.

'How did you get that?' Caffrey asked.

'Found it in your hotel room. Clumsy of you to give the Europa as your address on the Irish passport application.'

The detective flipped open the US passport.

'Dominic Caffrey from Boston, eh? I don't suppose you've even been to Boston, have you?'

'Of course I have. That's where I live. I *am* Dominic Caffrey. At least I have been since the Caffreys adopted me as a baby.'

'So why the Irish passport application in the Killian Devereux identity? And the student ID? And why have you decided to come back to Belfast now? Or, have you been here all along?'

'Come back? I'd never been to Belfast before this trip, at least, not as an adult. See the name on the Irish passport application, that's my birth identity. I was born Killian Devereux. I came to Belfast because I wanted to ... I dunno, reconnect with my heritage. I came to find my birth mother.'

'And did you find her?'

'I did. She's down in County Wexford. Alice Devereux. Except she pronounces it Devricks. You can ask her about me. She'll tell you I *was* Killian Devereux, but I'm now Dom Caffrey.'

The detective shook her head.

'That's the feeblest story I ever heard. And that's before we get to your explanation for the guns and the murder victim.'

'Murder? Look, I never murdered anyone. And I don't know anything about the guns and stuff. I'm sorry about breaking into the home ... except, legally speaking, I didn't actually break in. The window was unlocked. I was just looking for documents about what those nuns did to my mother and the other girls who gave birth there.'

'Just looking, were you?'

'Yes, and anyway, that cupboard had a new padlock on it. If I was responsible for what was in the cupboard, I'd have had a key, wouldn't I? Those old hinges just gave way when I pulled on the doors. You can't charge me with criminal damage. It was damaged already.'

The detective laughed suddenly.

'Criminal damage? You're looking at more serious charges than that, Devereux. I'll grant you, though, that's a passable Boston accent. We'd been wondering where you were hanging out. I can believe you've been living in Boston. But as for the rest of your story ...'

'Wait a minute. That ... maggoty body in the basement, it's obviously been there quite some time. I only arrived here on Monday. Check out the stamps in my passport. Anyway, look, I'm a lawyer and I'm pretty sure I have some rights here. I'm not saying another thing until you get me legal representation. And I believe I have a right to phone the US Consul.'

'Oh, you're a lawyer now, are you, as well as a law breaker? Well, we've already asked the US consul to check you out. I see this passport was only issued recently, and there's no reference in it to any previous US passport.'

'There wouldn't be,' Caffrey protested. 'That's because this is my first US passport. Oh, what's the point? You clearly don't believe anything I say, so there's no point in my saying anything more.'

'As you were told earlier, you do indeed have the right to remain silent, but …'

The detective broke off as a uniformed policewoman entered the interview room and handed her some papers.

'For the benefit of the tape,' the detective spoke towards the recorder, 'Constable Eileen O'Neill has just entered the room with documentation. And we'll take a break here.'

Switching off the recording device, the detective perused the paperwork. She frowned as she scrutinised the image on the US passport application which had just been faxed across directly from the US embassy in London. She looked quizzically at Caffrey. He noticed she did not switch the recorder back on.

'Well, Mr Caffrey,' she said, at length, 'it seems you're not who we thought you were. You're not the real Killian Devereux.'

Caffrey felt relief flooding over him, and yet he was baffled. He had not a clue what was going on.

'Detective, I don't understand. What do you mean the *real* Killian Devereux?'

'It seems you've applied for an Irish passport using the identity of a man who's wanted for questioning – a man we suspect is behind a number of brutal killings. The name Killian Devereux was flagged up three or four years ago on the Europol and Interpol databases. That's why the Irish passport office in Dublin called us when they checked your application. I don't know what it is you're up to, but why on earth would you try to take on the identity of a wanted man?'

'But, I didn't. That's *my* identity. I really am Killian Devereux. At least I was when I was born. Nowadays, I'm Dominic Caffrey.'

'Okay, well, we'll see about that. If we need to speak to you again, we'll contact you at your hotel.'

'Does that mean I can go?'

'Yes, for now,' she waved the American travel document at him. 'But your passport stays here until I'm sure you had nothing to do with the body out at Shearwater Point.'

Joe Doyle was waiting for Caffrey when the American eventually appeared in the reception area. Caffrey had forgotten all about his taxi driver.

'Joe, I'm so sorry I got you into this mess. Did they give you a hard time, too?'

'Yeah, well, they always do. I had a bit of bother with the police back in my youth. Nothin' serious, but, as you'd expect, they gave me the third degree in there. But, what's all this about guns and a dead body? What did you find down in those cellars?'

'Oh, God knows what's been going on up at that place, but I'll tell you all about it later. Meanwhile, what about your cab? Is it still out at the coast?'

'Yes, it is. No worries though. My nephew's a cabbie, too. He'll drive me out later to fetch it back.'

Caffrey took out his wallet and removed a handful of notes which he stuffed into Doyle's hand.

'Oh, this is too much Mr … Dom. You don't owe me this much.'

'No, please, take it for your trouble, Joe. And if today's experience hasn't put you off, I might call on you again.'

'Sure thing, Dom. Anytime.'

Chapter 17

DCI O'Keeffe led his visitors down the corridor to the DI's office, where Sarah Lawrence was writing up her case notes.

'Sarah,' he asked, 'what's the story with this Killian Devereux?'

'It wasn't him, sir. Not the Killian Devereux in which we have an interest. I had to release him.'

'Really? Well, I think you know Mike Malone from MI5's Holywood office, and this is his colleague from Thames House in London, Carole Murray. Miss Murray's here about her uncle, you know, Judge George Murray who was shot dead out at Donaghadee. They're interested in Devereux and the Alternative Ulster organisation, and they think there might be a link with Judge Murray's murder.'

Sarah rose to shake their hands.

'DI Sarah Lawrence. Pleased to meet you. Do take a seat, and may I offer my condolences Miss Murray?'

'Thank you,' Carole said, as she and Malone sat down and the DCI took his leave of them. Malone was puzzled.

'You say the man you just had in custody wasn't the Devereux you're interested in? He's not the one connected with Alternative Ulster?'

'That's right. It's very odd. Same name. And from what our intel suggests, he'd be about the same age. He was born in County Down, too, but, judging by the info from the American embassy, it's definitely not the same man. The man we just brought in is an American visitor. He's only been here a few days. He says he was born over here, as Killian Devereux, but was adopted by a family called

Caffrey and taken to the US as a baby. The US Consul just confirmed he's a US citizen who arrived there on an adoption visa in nineteen seventy-six. He's a lawyer and he's been paying taxes in the US for the past twenty-odd years.'

'Devereux isn't a common name in County Down, though,' Carole said, 'and Killian isn't that common a Christian name. Wouldn't it be an unlikely coincidence that there would be two men of that name born around the same time in the province? My husband's a cynical ex-cop and he always says there's no such thing as coincidence.'

The detective inspector nodded.

'Yes, there's a lot of people named Devereux in southern Ireland, but, you're right, hardly any recorded at this end of the island. I've got a constable checking out the birth records to see if there might have been two infants of that name born in Northern Ireland back in the 'seventies.'

'What did you make of the American Devereux?' Carole asked.

'Well, since his adoption, he's been known as Dominic Caffrey. He says he came here for the first time this week from Boston to research his family and locate his birth mother. Says he's actually found her living down in County Wexford.'

'So, why was he arrested?' Malone asked.

'He suddenly appeared on our radar when he decided to obtain an Irish passport in his birth identity, as Killian Devereux. The Irish passport authorities saw the name had been entered on the Europol database by us and they gave us a call. We went to check his room at the Europa Hotel and the woman on reception told us he'd taken a taxi out to the former mother and baby home at Shearwater Point. That's where we arrested him.'

'What was he doing out there?' Malone asked.

'He says he was looking at the place where his mother gave birth to him. However, when our ARU boys got there, they found him in the cellars, and Caffrey wasn't the only thing they found down there. There was a dead body and a cache of arms and ammunition. He disclaims all knowledge of that. Says he was having a nosey around and simply stumbled across the stiff and the shooters.'

'Do you believe him?' Carole asked.

'Actually, I do. His story about stumbling over a body when looking for historical documents is far-fetched enough to be true. The body has obviously been there a long time, anyway. And there's nothing adverse known about him as Dominic Caffrey. It'd be pretty bad luck if, for some reason, he'd decided to assume a false identity and just happened to pick the ID of someone who's wanted for questioning.'

'What if ...,' Carole began.

'Yes?' Sarah said.

'What if it's the case that your suspect has assumed *his* identity?'

'How do you mean?' Sarah asked.

'Well,' Carole reasoned aloud, 'it's a common pattern with identity fraud, isn't it? I mean, all over the UK and Ireland, there are birth certificates in dormant identities. The certificates were issued to children whose births were registered in one name, but who were later adopted and given a different name and a new certificate in the new identity.'

'That's right,' Malone chipped in. 'Criminals like to use what they call 'clean skins'. Those birth certificates represent unused or virgin identities. What's more, they're usually just filed away in local adoption authority offices, and not in particularly secure cupboards. It often happens that these original birth certificates are stolen and used to acquire passports and other documents for use by criminals and terrorists.'

'So, you're suggesting that, maybe, Killian Devereux, the man we want to speak to, isn't Killian Devereux at all.

81

He's somebody who stole the adopted baby's identity?' Sarah asked.

'That would make sense,' Malone added. 'That might explain why we he doesn't have any convictions in the Devereux identity. But he might have a CRO in his real identity.'

'Yes,' Carole agreed. 'Like we saw in the film 'Day of the Jackal', imposters used to use dead infants' identities, but then registrars got wise and they got computerised. They began linking infant deaths with their birth records, so that's one scam that's not so easily done any more. What better identity to steal than that of an infant who isn't registered as dead but who hasn't been using his birth identity?'

'Don't the adoption authorities notice when those birth certificates go missing?' the detective asked.

'No reason why they would even check,' Carole said. 'Those certificates just remain on file indefinitely. They're just put away to gather dust. And fraudsters know that.'

'Your suspect, the man who intelligence suggests goes by the name of Killian Devereux, he will almost certainly have committed offences in his true identity,' Malone suggested.

'But, as he hasn't been arrested in the Devereux identity, you wouldn't know,' Carole added. 'If he should be arrested, though, his true ID would come up when he's fingerprinted.'

'Not necessarily,' the DI shook her head. 'If it was just a juvenile record, it would have been wiped when he reached adulthood. Even if it was an adult CRO, under the Rehabilitation of Offenders Act, he may well have had his record expunged – especially if he hadn't re-offended using his real identity for a few years. And, don't forget, there was that unfortunate incident last year when over a hundred thousand prints and records were accidentally wiped from the police national computer. At least, so far as we know, it was an accident.'

'Of course, the first hurdle is that we'd have to catch him first to get his dabs to check against the PNC records,' Malone added. 'But we don't even know what he looks like.'

'Do we know whether an Irish passport had already been issued in the name Killian Devereux – to the fake Devereux, I mean? If it was, there'll be a photo of the fake Devereux on the Irish Passport authority's file, won't there?' Carole asked.

'No,' Sarah replied. 'There hadn't been an Irish passport application in that ID until the American submitted his this week. I will get our constable to check the UK Passport Agency's records, though, just in case there's been an application for a British passport in the Devereux ID.'

The detective sat back in her seat and tapped her lip with her pen, thoughtfully.

'So, if Alternative Ulster's Killian Devereux isn't really Killian Devereux, then who the hell is he?'

Chapter 18

It was getting on for midnight and things were really throbbing at The Rainbow Room, the newest disco club in Belfast's gay quarter. Ryan Donovan wasn't really fond of dancing, and he wasn't too keen on loud music and crowds. It had been his partner, Will Gibson, who had really wanted to dance the night away. Ryan was in awe of his lover, however, so naturally, whatever Will wanted to do was what they would do.

Will was two years older than Ryan and had been two years above him in the science faculty at Queen's University. Ryan had watched and adored him from afar but hadn't dared to hope they would ever date. He was just a fresher back then, and he worried that Will would have thought him a squirt.

The taller of the two, Will exuded confidence, from his well-coiffed black hair down to his fashionably shod feet. He was as dark as Ryan was fair. He was also a gym-bunny and he loved showing off his toned and tanned abs. Ryan had had to pinch himself when Will had approached him in the college refectory. He couldn't believe this handsome hunk wanted to get to know him. They'd been a couple for four years, now, and Ryan couldn't remember a time when he'd been happier.

'Will, can we please split now,' he pleaded, as yet another sweaty body collided with his on the dance floor. 'I'm dying on my feet.'

'Okay, love. C'mon, then. Let's go home.'

Will grabbed Ryan's hand and led him through the throng of couples who were slowly gyrating to the eighties' sound of Bronski Beat's 'I Feel Love'. Evenings at The Rainbow

Room always seemed to wind up with Bronski Beat. That meant dancing was likely to end soon anyway. They collected their jackets from the cloakroom.

'Thanks for indulging, me,' Will said. 'It's been a fun evening, and I know it's not your scene, but thanks. I love you lots.'

They got to the top of the stairs that led to the ground floor bar. Will paused and, pulling Ryan to him he kissed him.

'I really do love you, you know,' Will said. 'I mean it.'

'I love you more than you love me,' Ryan pouted.

'No, you don't. I love you more than you love me,' Will grinned.

'No, I love you more than you love me,' Ryan laughed childishly. 'But what I'd really love most right now is a pee. Wait for me downstairs,' he said as he thrust his jacket at Will and disappeared into the gents.

Draping both their jackets over his arm, Will wandered downstairs. The bar area was almost as crowded and hot as the upstairs disco. He glanced around at the crowded tables and bar. This was certainly the in-place these days. However, He'd promised that, next weekend, they'd go wherever Ryan wanted. An intimate supper for two at a nice restaurant, maybe, or a quiet night in. That was more Ryan's scene.

He caught sight of his reflection in the window glass and he ran a hand through his hair. Flexing his bicep, he was aware a few of the guys seated around in the bar were staring at him admiringly. He could see their reflections as their heads turned to look at him.

All was dark outside in the street, save for the white transit van parked in front of the club. He now saw the silhouette of a slightly-built man standing looking in at him. He couldn't see the stranger's face, just the outline of his hooded jacket. The stranger was staring straight at him. Will supposed he might be a young guy just exploring his true nature. Sometimes, guys like that stood outside watching the scene, afraid to venture in. Will smiled encouragingly at the young man.

After a few moments, the stranger took several steps back towards the van. Will could see his face now, illuminated by the street lamp. The stranger wasn't smiling and didn't look particularly curious. His expression was actually quite unpleasant. He produced what looked like a bottle of wine. To Will's surprise he lit the top of it. Realisation hit Will immediately. It was a bloody Molotov! He turned around and screamed as loud as he could.

'Get out, everyone! Fire bomb! Get out now!'

His first thoughts were of Ryan who was still upstairs in the gents. He ran for the stairs and was half way up when he heard the bar window smash and he smelled the petrol fumes. He ducked down and looked back over his shoulder. The carpets were already alight and people were on their feet, shouting and rushing for the exits.

'Ryan!' he screamed. 'Ryan, where are you?'

He continued to run up the stairs again but the music had stopped. Immediately, he was met by the stampede of disco revellers charging down the stairs towards him. He flattened himself against the stair rail and clung on, but the wall of people surging against him was too great. The pressure of bodies caused him to lose his grip and, seconds later, he was flat on his back and feet were trampling all over him.

'Ryan!' he called out, 'Ryan!' but then someone stumbled and fell on top of him. A knee collided with his head. He felt himself losing consciousness as the thick, hot, acrid smoke began to sear his nostrils and fill his lungs. Then, all the lights went out.

Ryan sat on the damp pavement by the open doors of the ambulance. Everywhere he looked, there were people with varying degrees of injury. Paramedics worked their way around silently, tending to the injured. There were bodies lying motionless on the pavement and in the road. Some people were moaning. Others were coughing. The walking wounded were meandering around, shocked, dazed and looking for friends. Ryan shivered, partly from the cold and partly from the shock. Eventually, the paramedic came to tend to his hands. They'd been burned. He could see that. Yet, oddly, they didn't hurt. He suspected they would tomorrow.

'Your hands are a wee bit burnt, so they are,' the paramedic reassured him as he applied dressings and bandages, 'but I don't think there'll be any lasting damage. Did you see what happened in there?'

'No, not really,' Ryan said. 'I'd gone to the gents at the top of the stairs and, when I came out, the whole place was on fire. I went to look for my partner who'd gone downstairs but I couldn't see him. I came outside, thinking he'd got out, but he wasn't here. I ran back in, searching for Will, and I called out his name, but I couldn't see him anywhere. I couldn't see anything at all. There was so much smoke. I worried that maybe he'd gone back upstairs looking for me, so I tried to go up there, but everyone else was coming down. I got knocked over and the carpet was alight. That's when I must have burned my hands.'

'Did you find your friend? Is he out here?'

'No. I can't see him anywhere.'

Ryan suddenly pushed the paramedic aside and jumped to his feet.

'Will!' he screamed. 'Will!'

Holding a half-bandaged hand aloft, the bandage trailing on the ground behind him, and with tears running down his cheeks, he set off, stepping over bodies and bouncing off the same sweaty individuals who'd bumped into him earlier in the evening.

'Will!' he called out.

'Will!'

He called again and again, until he was hoarse. His call would go unanswered.

Chapter 19

Caffrey was comfortably settled on one of the hotel bar's sofas, once again. A pint of stout sat, untouched, on the table before him, next to his laptop. He was preoccupied with the information he had just turned up on the internet. As he scrolled further and further through the lengthy conclusions of the Republic of Ireland Judicial Commission's investigation into Ireland's mother and baby homes, he found the scale of the mental, physical and sexual abuses almost unbelievable. The more he read, the angrier he became.

He saw, however, that the Commission had only looked at those homes which were situated in the Republic of Ireland. When he searched under mother and baby homes in Northern Ireland, he found a similar report which had been issued only weeks earlier by the Northern Ireland Executive but which wasn't so detailed.

Press reaction to the latter report suggested it had only come about as a grudging response to accusations by Amnesty International that their own enquiries into Northern Ireland's homes had turned up evidence of arbitrary unlawful detention and ill-treatment of women and girls. Amnesty had also highlighted the issues of forced adoption and trafficking of the women's babies. The Catholic church had been asked to comment on Amnesty's findings regarding the Northern Ireland homes, but had yet to do so.

Two further highly respected bodies, the United Nations Committee Against Torture and the United Nations Committee for the Elimination of Discrimination Against Women, had ruled that the Northern Ireland Executive should, with all haste, establish a full official enquiry into their mother and baby homes. They had also demanded an enquiry into the associated laundries which had exploited young women.

To Caffrey's great disappointment, he saw that the UN ruling had actually been made a couple of years earlier, even before the most recent NIE report, but it had been put on hold because of the power-sharing disagreement which had led to the province's parliament being shut down. Now that Stormont was up and running again as Northern Ireland's seat of government, and despite the recent report having identified several hundred cases of prosecutable abuses, historic wrongdoing still had to take a back seat to the pressing needs of the here and now.

The anger he had felt since leaving Wexford, and the growing resentment he now felt building up within him at this latest piece of research, caused him to sigh. He took a long draft of the stout and sank back into the sofa. He didn't know how much more of this he could take in. His impression had always been that things were more progressive here in Northern Ireland than they were down in the conservative Republic, and yet, from his reading, it seemed that, in terms of some issues, quite the opposite was true. Abortion had been legalised in the Republic before it had been here in the north, and so had same-sex marriage.

The last of Northern Ireland's mother and baby homes had closed in the nineteen-nineties. In the years since then, though, there had been not a single prosecution. What were the lawyers doing, he asked himself? What would it take for them to get their damned act together and to acknowledge these historic wrongs, even if, in some cases, it was too late for them be put right?

He wondered how many Americans like himself had been born here and their mothers forced to surrender them, for the financial benefit of religious orders and adoption agencies? Doubtless, there were those who would say the trafficked babies were better off being snatched from their natural mothers and raised in America. But who would know? Had anyone researched that? Who had the right to make such a Goddamned lofty and inhumane decision anyway?

Caffrey was beside himself with indignation, so much so, that he didn't notice the dark-haired, middle-aged woman enquiring at reception then being pointed in his direction until he was suddenly aware of her standing by him.

'Mr Caffrey?' she asked.

'Yes?' he looked up.

'My name's Carole Murray. I hope I'm not intruding, but I was at the police station yesterday when you were there.'

'Are you with the police?' he asked, warily.

'Oh, no. I'm over here from London, on a private visit. You see, my uncle was murdered over here last week and I came over to arrange his funeral.'

'Oh, I'm real sorry to hear that. Did the police catch his killer?'

'Not yet, but they're looking for someone they believe might have had him killed. The man they suspect, well, his name might be familiar to you. His name is Killian Devereux.'

Caffrey stared at her for a few seconds, before closing his laptop.

'Would you like to sit down, Miss Murray? And can I get you a drink?'

Chapter 20

Dave Lloyd brought his coffee and two thickly-buttered slices of toast to his desk in the Counter-espionage section at Thames house. He had just sat down when his desk phone rang. It was Carole calling from Northern Ireland. He was delighted to hear his wife's voice. So far, she had only given him one quick call shortly after her arrival to confirm she had got there safely so he was relieved to hear from her again.

'Hi, love. How's your aunt? Is she bearing up okay? And how are the funeral arrangements going? … Who? ... Ilya who? Ilya Kirasov?'

Dave grabbed a pen and began writing down Carole's information. Overhearing Dave's side of the conversation, his colleague, Harry Edwards, raised his head and stopped to listen.

'Who's he? … He's Russian? … Russky Obraz? Why do you want me to check him out?' Dave asked. 'What's this got to do with the funeral?'

As Dave listened to Carole's explanation of what had transpired thus far with the two Killian Devereux characters and the Alternative Ulster organisation, her husband's happy expression turned to one of concern.

'Wait a minute. What are you getting yourself into over there? You went there to support Ellen and to help her with the burial arrangements, not to investigate your uncle's murder. Leave that to the local MIT, love.'

He didn't feel any less alarmed by Carol's assurances that she was simply taking a behind-the-scenes look at some of the dubious organisations who might have gained some advantage from her uncle's death. He looked at the digital display on his phone but he didn't recognise the number from which Carole was calling.

'Well, fair enough, if they haven't released the body yet, I suppose you can't do much arranging till then. But, love, where are you calling from? You're not ringing from your aunt's phone.'

Carole admitted she was calling from Mike Malone's office.

'The MI5 office? Carole, what the hell are you doing over there? Is the Security Service arranging funerals now? … Okay, okay. I'll do some checks for you, but you shouldn't be getting involved when you're on compassionate leave. Don't worry, I'll call you back. Missing you, love.'

'Was that Carole? Is she okay?' Harry asked when Dave had put the phone down.

'Yes, but you know our Carole. Not content with burying her uncle, she's on the trail of his killer now.'

'I didn't mean to eavesdrop, but did I hear you mention the name Ilya Kirasov?'

'Yes. He's some Russian she wants me to check out.'

'I know about Kirasov. Did she say what her interest is?'

'Well, it seems he's connected with Russky Obraz, and he's in Belfast right now, making connections with one of their right-wing organisations.'

'He's in Belfast?' Harry seemed shocked. 'I wonder how he got there without us knowing. He's flagged up as a person of interest to us and we knew he was in the UK. He was clocked arriving at Heathrow a couple of weeks ago. Every time he passes a border control or fills out a landing card, we should get a report. Not sure why we didn't know he was in Belfast.'

'He wouldn't have generated a landing card travelling between here and Belfast, though. It's a domestic destination,' Dave reminded him.

'Oh, of course, it is,' Harry conceded. 'And Special Branch stopped checking passengers on flights to and from both ends of Ireland years ago, didn't they?'

'Yes, ever since peace broke out,' Dave said. 'I take it he's not under surveillance, then?'

'No. So far, he's just a person of interest. But, if he's visiting a neo-Nazi group in Belfast, then maybe that level of interest needs to be raised.'

Their section head, Adrian Curtis, was on his way to the office kitchen to top up his own coffee when he heard Carole's name being mentioned. He paused by Dave's desk.

'Have you heard from Carole? How's she getting on over there?'

'Well, she can't sort out the funeral until they release her uncle's body,' Dave grimaced, 'so she's now sticking her nose into the investigation, instead.'

'What? In Northern Ireland? I don't like the sound of that.'

'Nor do I, boss. She's even found a Russian connection. She thinks one possible suspect is linked with that neo-Nazi outfit Russky Obraz. Seems even Northern Ireland has its own neo-Nazi group. Something called Alternative Ulster.'

'Really? Well, that would tie in with what we know about Putin linking up Europe's right wing extremist groups. I presume, though, she's leaving it to our Northern Ireland branch to check out?'

'Not our Carole. She can't *not* get involved. I'm wondering if I ought to go over there myself and keep an eye on her. That's if there's any possibility of my taking leave.'

'I don't see why not. After all, Kirpal's back from leave now. Harry will be in the office all week, and Jo is fully up to speed now. Keep me in the picture, though, won't you? If two of my best people are running round Belfast chasing villains, whether Irish or Russian, I need to know exactly what's going on.'

'Will do, boss.'

Dave was chuffed to hear Adrian refer to him and Carole as two of his best people. Before he gave any thought to booking himself a flight to Belfast, however, he thought he'd better pick Harry's brains a bit further about this Ilya Kirasov and the Russky Obraz. He didn't feel easy about Carole being involved in the investigation. He didn't feel easy at all.

Chapter 21

'Good morning, Mister D,' Alistair called out cheerily as he emerged through the French windows onto the terrace at Ardmore House. Killian Devereux, clad in pale blue cotton sateen pyjamas and a pristine white towelling dressing gown, stood by the terrace balustrade, staring out to sea, his binoculars firmly trained on the magnificent avian theatre which was playing out before him. There were arctic terns and guillemots, as well as several varieties of seagull, circling, soaring and dipping in the blue spring skies, all energised with the sheer joy of being.

'Morning, Alistair,' he said, without looking around. 'Help yourself to coffee there.'

The slightly-built youth found a clean china cup on the white wrought iron table and poured himself some coffee. He, too, gazed at the view.

'That's a grand spectacle right there, Mister D.'

'It is indeed. This is the best time of year to see the biggest variety of birds. And what better place to see them from than here at Shearwater Point. This place is well-named, so it is.'

'Which ones are the shearwaters, then?'

'Oh, you won't see the shearwaters out there this morning, Alistair. They'll be in their burrows. They only fly out at night to feed. There's too many predators around during the day, so that's when they tend to lie low. A bit like myself, in fact.'

'So, how are you settling in here, Mister D?' Alistair asked.

'Oh, grand, thanks. I'm only renting to start with but, if the place comes on the market, I may make them an offer.'

'Are you pleased you came back?'

'Naturally. The missus and I have a nice wee place on the Lancashire coast, and it's convenient for tripping back and forth to Belfast on business. But there's nowhere as beautiful as the Down coast. I mean, just look at all of this. The missus will love this when she joins me.'

Devereux sat down at the table and exchanged his binoculars for his own coffee cup. Alistair took this as a sign that he might sit also.

'So, what news have you?' Devereux asked.

'Well, I didn't want to say over the phone, but Hughie's police contact told him they found the stuff we had stored at the old maternity home.'

'So, they'll have found the bodies, too, then?'

'Only one, so far, though I suppose they'll continue poking around till they find the rest.'

'Well, that's a shame. That home was a handy hiding place. Still, there's nothing to tie us in with that, and the arms can be replaced. There's another shipment due in the next few weeks. I want you and Hughie to find somewhere else to stow it. Not around here, though. Not now I'm living out this way. Don't want tha poliss sniffing round here.'

'Right you are. Oh, and I've another bit of news. They arrested some other fellah named Killian Devereux, thinking he was you.'

'Really?'

'Yes. Some American tourist. They gave him a grilling and then let him go.'

'So, they *are* looking for me, then. That confirms it. Maybe it's time I got myself a different identity. Will you not have a drop of milk and sugar in your coffee? And do help yourself to a saucer, son.'

Blushing with embarrassment, for it seemed he was neither used to, nor comfortable with bone china, Alistair slipped one of the delicate saucers under his cup and poured some milk into his coffee, followed by two large spoonsful of sugar. Stirring his coffee vigorously, he placed the wet spoon back into the sugar basin. His host raised a critical eyebrow.

'After all,' Devereux added, 'we're not savages, are we?'

'No, Mister D.'

'Anyway, tell me about this American. You say he's called Killian Devereux?'

'Yes. He's the one who led the police to the guns we'd stashed at the old mother and baby home.'

'Is he, by God? So, what else do you know about him?'

'Well, he's some kind of lawyer, and he's staying at the Europa.'

'I'm not sure I like the sound of that. Well, maybe you and Hughie should go and have a look at him.'

Chapter 22

The following afternoon, DS Dan McKittrick and his DI, Sarah Lawrence, arrived at Shearwater Point. Driving up the steep driveway and into the grounds of the former maternity home, McKittrick eased their unmarked saloon into the space between the large mortuary vehicle and the equally large white van marked *Forensic Science Northern Ireland*. They could see half a dozen or more of the FSNI personnel on the scene, all clad in white forensic suits and black plastic overshoes.

One of the police constables who was guarding the site pointed the detectives around to the back of the building. There, they were greeted by the head of the forensic team Dr Mairead Mulroney.

'What's the body count, so far?' Sarah asked the scientist.

'Six adults – four males and two females. There's the man whose remains were found in the cupboard down in the cellar and the other five adults were buried out here in the grounds, in fairly shallow graves. But they weren't all buried at the same time. They're at different stages of decomp. We'll know more when a full examination has been carried out.'

'From the message passed to me earlier, I'd got the impression there were more cadavers than that,' Sarah said.

'Oh, indeed, there are. That's just the adults. We saw, from the plans of the place, that there was a large, redundant septic tank situated roughly below the spot where we'd found disturbed earth and where we dug up the adult remains. This place wasn't always on mains drainage, you see. It was one of the few areas in the grounds that hadn't been concreted over, and the earth had been excavated decades ago for the tank to be installed. That's probably why whoever buried the bodies there chose that particular spot. Easier to dig.'

The scientist replaced her face mask firmly over her nose and mouth and led them over to the main site where digging was still going on. She pointed to a large spoil heap which contained not only soil but also a highly pungent sludge which had been drawn out of the tank. The top of the tank had been peeled back like the top of a giant sardine can, and more of the sludge could be seen within.

'We broke into the tank and that's where we found more bodies. I suspect there are still more to be found,' she told them gravely, 'but, so far, we've brought up the remains of forty-two infants. We're going to need another mortuary van to accommodate them all.'

The detectives were stunned into silence momentarily. McKittrick suddenly turned pale. He covered his mouth with the back of his hand to try to keep the awful odour at bay. His DI pulled a tiny bottle of lavender oil from her handbag, unscrewed the top and dabbed some of the oil on her upper lip before offering it to McKittrick, who did likewise.

'Doctor, are you telling me there were forty-two children dumped in that septic tank?' Sarah asked

'Yes. They're babies and very young infants. They've been there a long time, decades probably. We won't know the causes of death until the post-mortem examinations get under way. To be honest, given the lack of soft tissue, we may never be able to say how they died.'

'Why's that?' McKittrick asked.

'Well, the deaths could have been pre-natal, or peri-natal. They could have been born dead, or died during childbirth. If we find any broken bones, though, broken hyoid bones in the neck, for instance, we could infer they were beaten or strangled. But, in the absence of soft tissues, something such as suffocation or poisoning would be impossible to detect, as would any number of natural causes of death. And we won't even know who the children were until we check the death registration records – that's assuming their deaths *were* actually registered. Then, we'd have to hope people might come forward to offer DNA for comparison.'

'Dear God!' Dan McKittrick exploded. 'The poor wee souls died and weren't even buried in consecrated ground. I wonder if they were even baptised. This has to be down to the nuns, I suppose. I mean … Jesus God almighty!'

'Dan, will you follow up on the sisters of *La Mère du Bon Pasteur*?' Sarah asked. 'See where they re-located to and who's in charge nowadays. Hopefully, they'll be able to tell you who was in charge over the years they were operating here. Maybe you could get Eileen to have a look at the local infant death records, and cross-check against births recorded at the home, too.'

'I'll get right on it, gov.'

Deeply affected, McKittrick turned away from the site of the excavation and walked slowly back to the car, shaking his head. Sarah Lawrence turned back to the forensic head, who was apologetic.

'Perhaps I shouldn't have put that so bluntly. I think I've upset your sergeant.'

'No, not you, doc. Tragically, Dan and his wife lost three babies of their own – all stillbirths. They've given up on the idea of having children. And the adoption agencies they approached don't consider police service to be a respectable occupation for prospective adopters.'

'Oh, my. No wonder he's upset.'

'Well, I'll leave you to it. I think this is going to take your team a very long time to process, and I don't envy you the task.'

'We'll start with the adults. Their deaths are more recent. We should have more to work with than we have with the infants. I'll call you as soon as we have anything to report.'

Chapter 23

Caffrey walked several blocks eastwards until he found Alfred Street. The headquarters of the Northern Ireland Human Rights Commission was housed within a reassuringly solid looking edifice with a red brick façade and ornate stone window arches. He was a little dismayed, however, to find the HRC only occupied a part of the building. Somehow, he had expected it to be a much bigger organisation, as its name might suggest.

Up on the fourth floor, he was greeted by the lawyer who had agreed to meet with him.

'Good morning, Mr Caffrey. I'm Aminullah Miah. Can I get you a coffee, or a tea perhaps?'

'Oh, no thank you, Mr Miah. I just had the full Irish breakfast over at the Europa. I may never need to eat or drink again.'

Miah smiled and bade him take a seat in the office. Caffrey noticed there were three desks in the room though only Miah's desk appeared to be in use. Miah shifted to one side a large stack of casefiles to better see the Bostonian who had sought his help.

'On the telephone, you said you had concerns over historic abuses at a mother and baby home?'

'That's right,' Caffrey nodded. 'I was born at a mother and baby home at Shearwater Point, on the County Down coast. That was in nineteen seventy-six. My mother gave birth to me there when she was just fifteen, without any medically qualified person in attendance and without anaesthetic. I was taken from her by the nuns and sent off to America for adoption, and she was made to work at the home as an unpaid laundry worker. She was kept there for half a year in total. No wages. No contact with the outside world. The modern definition would be slave labour.'

'I have no doubt what you say is true, Mr Caffrey. Abuses in those homes was widespread and there have been many witness statements taken. I take it you've heard about the recent historic institutional abuse enquiry?'

'Yes, I see they issued a report on the homes, but why is no-one taking any action on behalf of those victims? Why isn't the Human Rights Commission involved?'

Miah pointed to the stack of files on his desk.

'The simple answer is we have so many *live* cases of human rights abuses to investigate that we don't have time to even begin to consider the historic cases. Human Rights covers a huge panoply; disability equality, gay and lesbian equality, children's rights, the elderly and 'right to life' cases, and that's before we even get to the religious discrimination issues.'

'Are you the only lawyer working on these cases?' Caffrey asked.

'No, there are two of us but my colleague is on maternity leave. Two other colleagues quit recently and haven't been replaced. We did have a retired judge helping out, too, but he died recently. Our funding has been cut several times over the past decade, and our staffing level nowadays is just half what we started out with. Working right across the broad spectrum of HR issues, we can only take on the most blatant and easily resolvable cases.'

'Well, I'm an attorney, too, Mr Miah. I run a large law practice in Boston. For obvious personal reasons, I feel very strongly about this particular area of historic abuse. Many of the women who passed through the gates of those homes are still alive. My own birth mother is. Suppose I offer to help you investigate this? *Pro bono*, of course.'

'That would be wonderful, Mr Caffrey, but they wouldn't allow it.'

'Why not?'

'A few years ago, a very philanthropic American foundation offered us a source of additional funding. That foundation was backed by the fortune of a wealthy Irish-American businessman. It does great work all over the world. They donate millions to HR projects helping children and the elderly. Unfortunately, the Northern Ireland Office blocked the offer. They wouldn't let us accept it, and the money went to the Irish Republic instead.'

'But why would they turn down free funding?'

'I don't know. We in the commission weren't told the reasoning behind their decision. I just know that a kind offer of help from a US lawyer, however desirable and well-motivated, would probably also be rejected.'

Miah saw the expression of crushing disappointment on Caffrey's face.

'I will, however, take another look at the issue, and I'll look into the Shearwater Point home specifically. I'll also make sure I keep you appraised of any findings. But we have looked into this area of abuse before, and we found there are some legal stumbling blocks.'

'What sort of stumbling blocks?'

'For one thing, the Catholic church was able to prove that the mothers who voluntarily placed themselves into the care of the church-run mother and baby homes, actually signed agreement forms. They agreed to work for no pay for fixed terms, and in some cases indefinitely. The women also signed consent forms allowing the nuns to put their babies up for adoption. I appreciate they would have been desperate, and that no other option was open to them but it's hard to get around the fact that they consented.'

'But you and I both know, Mr Miah, that, for it to be legally binding, consent has to be *informed* consent.'

'Do you have reason to think your mother didn't fully understand what she was signing?'

'Well, I'm not sure how she could have done, considering she never learned to read or write.'

Chapter 24

Carole and her husband Dave arrived at the Malone residence for dinner at seven o'clock. The large house was situated not far out of Holywood on the Old Esplanade and enjoyed uninterrupted views out to sea.

'You weren't kidding about the house,' Dave exclaimed, as they got out of the car. 'I'll bet they got a heap of change back from the sale of their place in London.'

'And you don't get sea views in London,' Carole added. 'Even a Thames view would add thousands onto the price.'

Mike Malone opened the door and welcomed them in. He gratefully accepted the bottle of wine Dave proffered and he shook his hand warmly.

'We meet at last, Dave. Congratulations on your marriage, by the way.'

'Are we okay parked in your drive?' Dave asked, pointing at the vintage orange Volkswagen parked outside.

'Sure. That's some jalopy,' Malone remarked.

'It's my aunt's,' Carole explained. 'I've taken out insurance so I can drive it whilst we're here. My aunt never really enjoyed driving at the best of times. Nowadays, she seems to have forgotten how.'

'Come on into the lounge and make yourselves comfortable. I'll just check on dinner and get us something to drink. Angela will be down in a minute. She's just upstairs issuing death threats to the boys to get them to do their homework. Now what'll you have?'

'Just a soft drink for me, thanks, since I'm driving,' Carole said.

'A glass of red for you, Dave?'

'That would be great, cheers.'

After dinner and some earnest conversation about local house prices, Angela Malone went upstairs again to enforce their sons' bed time, whilst Mike poured the coffee and a brandy each for himself and Dave.

'Dave has been looking into that ultra-nationalist organisation, Russky Obraz, for me,' Carole said.

'Yes,' Dave agreed, taking a sip of his brandy. 'They're a pretty brutal outfit. Russia's the last place where you find skinheads these days, but most of theirs belong to the Russky Obraz. They're pushing Putin's xenophobic policies and they've been implicated in some pretty horrific murders. It's not just ethnic minorities like the central Asians that they target. They go after public prosecutors, journalists, and any moderates who oppose them.'

'Why would they be interested in Northern Ireland, though?' Malone asked.

'Well, they've worked their way across Europe. They engage with local mobs in other states and fan the flames of any existing resentment. No offence, Mike, but there's always been a lot of home-grown resentment over here. It's probably a fertile ground for these neo-Nazis to establish a toehold. It's all part of Putin's grand plan of fomenting unrest and destabilising other states.'

'And that's not all we know, is it, Dave?' Carole urged.

'Indeed. It seems one of Russky Obraz's lieutenants – a chap named Ilya Kirasov – arrived in the province recently. He's staying at the Europa, apparently.'

Just then, Angela Malone appeared. She gave Carole a hug and was introduced to Dave. Mike poured her a glass of wine.

'We should have got some champagne in, Mike,' she said. 'We should be celebrating Carole and Dave's marriage.'

'Speaking of champagne,' Carole said, 'have you heard about Vladimir Putin's latest law he's introduced?'

'Which one?' Malone asked. 'He's churned out a lot, lately.'

'I meant the one banning French champagne from being labelled as champagne in Russia,' Carole said. 'Seems only Russian sparkling wines can call themselves champagne. French champagne now has to be labelled as sparkling wine instead. So, naturally, the French have stopped exporting their champagne to the Russian Federation.'

'The man's really lost it, hasn't he?' Dave declared. 'I mean, his country's still being ravaged by the Covid virus, over two hundred thousand Russians have died from it and fewer than fifty thousand have been vaccinated. On top of that, he has trouble with Dagestani separatists and the failure of his ageing infrastructures, but all he's worried about is French champagne.'

'If he'd been on Titanic,' Angela declared, 'he'd have been the guy re-arranging the deck chairs.'

'I hear he's also changed the law to render outgoing presidents immune from prosecution for criminal activities, and also to ensure he can now serve a further twelve years in office,' Malone added.

'He has indeed,' Carole agreed, 'but he may not benefit from either of those changes. It seems there may be a medical reason for his recent odd and reckless behaviour. There have been allegations in the press that he's suffering from an inoperable brain tumour. In Moscow, the political vultures are circling, hoping to steal his crown.'

'Then I really do wish we'd got some champagne in,' Angela added.

It was Guinness, rather than champagne, that Dom Caffrey was about to enjoy in the Piano Bar at the Europa Hotel. He was watching the generous, creamy head on his pint gradually reduce and darken like the skies over the

Irish Sea. He checked his watch and worked out that his office back in Boston would be open. He dialled the number of his associate, Brad Spence. He didn't have to hold long.

'Brad? Hi it's Dom. Yeah, yeah, great, thanks. No, it's not raining. In fact, the weather here is fabulous. And that's one of several reasons why I've decided to extend my stay. I'm booked to head back end of next week, but I think I'll change my booking and stay another coupla weeks. Is there anything urgent that needs my attention or do you think you could manage without me?'

Brad's response was reassuring.

'Good. But there's something you could do for me, Brad. Would you check if there are any groups or organisations in the US that are interested in Americans who were adopted from Northern Ireland as infants, and maybe anyone who has an interest in the maltreatment of their mothers in the province's mother and baby homes? You know the kinda thing, pressure groups and so on.'

Caffrey expected his associate to be baffled by his request, and indeed Spence was.

'Why? Well, it seems there's some major issues over here with abuses in those homes, and also with whether or not the babies born there were legally surrendered or were trafficked. Nobody's doing anything about it. Since many of those babies are Americans now, I think there might be something here which our firm could get into, you know, blanket state compensation claims and that kinda thing. Hell, we might even get to open an office here to deal with the historic cases. There could be thousands of them.'

Caffrey's assistant digested the details of the request but had some exciting information of his own to impart.

'What? Who's coming to Belfast?' Caffrey thought he had misheard.

'You're kidding. Our President's coming here? When? … Why? … Yeah, I knew he had family connections in County Louth, and that's just down the road from here, but

I thought he was going to be on a state visit to London next month … Oh, I see. Yeah, I guess it makes sense he'd come here straight after that. Well, now, that could be to our advantage.'

The import of Brad's news struck Caffrey immediately. His legal mind whirred with the possibilities the presidential visit might afford him in connection with his new quest.

'Say, Brad, didn't you tell me your brother Rich was offered a position in Joe Biden's new cabinet office? Wasn't that in the office of the US Ambassador to the UN? … So, did he take it? … Well, that's great. Could you also get me Rich's contact details? I haven't thought it all through yet, but that could be very useful, very useful indeed.'

Chapter 25

Ellen Murray shivered in her black crepe dress and thin black coat as she stood in the front pew in the little Catholic church. It was a bright sunny day outside. Shafts of strongly coloured sunlight filtered through the huge stained-glass window of the church's south transept and floodlit the catafalque which stood within the altar rails, ready to receive the coffin. Despite the warmth of the day outside, for those standing in the dark nave of the church, it was cold. Carole grasped her aunt's gloved hands and rubbed them between hers to warm them slightly. Her aunt seemed somehow detached from the proceedings.

'Carole,' Ellen whispered, as they awaited the arrival of the hearse, 'have you kept up your faith?'

'No, auntie. I no longer go to mass.'

'You'll not remember the words of the hymns, then, I suppose.'

'I'll do my best, auntie.'

Carole was surprised that, at a time like this, her aunt should concern herself with something as unimportant as whether her niece would be able to join in with the singing. However, it seemed to be just one of a set of recent odd behaviours which were symptomatic of what Carole suspected was her aunt's mild dementia. She gained the impression her aunt thought this was simply another Sunday mass.

Carole was also surprised to see a lot more people than she had expected gathered into the little church. Theirs wasn't a large family, George and Ellen having had no children of their own, and Carole being their only niece. Carole's own parents had both been dead some years now and, as she reflected, Uncle George's wasn't the first funeral she'd had to arrange. She guessed many of those assembled to pay their respects would be George's former colleagues from the legal profession. Others would be from the golf club or the fishing fraternity, or any of the clubs and societies to which her uncle and aunt had belonged.

'You okay?' Dave whispered.

Carole nodded. She was pleased Dave was there to support her and Ellen. She was touched that Mike and Angela Malone had turned up, too. She wasn't surprised, either, to see DS Dan McKittrick slip into a pew at the back of the church, along with a tall, reddish-haired, woman who wore sensible lace up-shoes. Though the redhead wore a plain navy quilted jacket, Carole guessed the unfashionable shade of dark green trousers visible beneath the jacket would be standard police-issue uniform. It was normal, she knew, for the police to attend the funeral of a murder victim.

Hearing a degree of shuffling and whispering up above in the choir loft, Carole looked up and saw, in addition to the church's small choir, around fifteen or more children had filed in and were being kept in order by a woman who, presumably, was their teacher. She now recalled her late uncle enthusing about the occasional little presentations on natural history which he had been asked to give to the children at the local junior school. She imagined that his had been a full and rewarding retirement. She just wished it might have lasted a few more years yet.

She had taken the decision, on behalf of her aunt, not to have the full requiem service, since she guessed many of the guests would not be Catholics. She wouldn't put anyone through that, especially as her aunt didn't seem to fully grasp what was going on and probably wouldn't appreciate it. Soon, the church organ began to play as the priest led the pall bearers down the aisle. They deposited the coffin, with practised respect, onto the pall-draped catafalque and withdrew, as the priest climbed the wooden steps to the pulpit.

As the forty-minute funeral service progressed, Carole's thoughts were elsewhere. From the reading of the funeral liturgy, Old Testament passages and psalms, through to the delivery of the homily and a sincere eulogy read by one of George's friends, Carole was remembering the many happy times she had spent with her uncle and aunt. According to the psalm, he was now walking through the valley in the shadow of death, and she hoped he would, as the psalm promised, fear no evil. It seemed, however, that the evil had already overtaken Uncle George. He had exchanged the blue hills and turbulent Irish sea for the green pastures and still waters of that Kingdom of Heaven in which he and Ellen fervently believed.

As the choir gave a perfect rendition of *Pie Jesu*, and then a pure-voiced soloist sang Schubert's *Ave Maria*, both of which pieces Carole had loved as a girl, she hoped the ceremony and the ritual were bringing comfort to Ellen. She could not be sure that was the case, however, as her aunt seemed distracted, absent almost.

Soon, it was the turn of the children to lead the singing. Carole did, in fact, remember the words of the hymn she had often sung as a child herself. Penned in an earlier century by an anonymous Sister Agnes, the words and the tune were sweet.

> *Hail Glorious Saint Patrick, dear saint of our isle.*
> *On us, thy poor children bestow a sweet smile.*
> *And now thou art high in the mansions above,*
> *On Erin's green valleys look down in thy love.*

She sincerely hoped that the soul of her uncle, after a lifetime's earnest endeavours to promote the cause of justice and to serve his community, had now found repose

112

high in those mansions above, whether or not she believed in them. She joined in enthusiastically with the chorus:

On Erin's green valleys, On Erin's green valleys,
On Erin's green valleys, look down in thy love.

The rite of committal having been conducted at the graveside, once George Murray's body was committed to the black Irish earth, Carole invited everyone back to the house to consume the refreshments she had spent the previous day preparing.

This being an Irish funeral, a large home-cooked ham sat on a big oval platter and was deftly sliced by Dave, as guests helped themselves to salads and to the hot, floury potatoes boiled in their jackets and liberally doused in butter. Copious amounts of whiskey and tea were consumed, as the funeral guests reminisced and exchanged stories about their departed friend.

Ellen passed among the guests, checking that neither plates nor glasses stood empty for long. She displayed the same solicitous manner she had when entertaining her husband's colleagues whenever they would visit him in life. Carole thought it was perhaps something of a blessing that Ellen seemed to have forgotten for the moment that she was supposed to grieve.

DS McKittrick introduced his constable, Eileen O'Neill. Carole noticed McKittrick had knocked back several scotches in quick succession and she guessed the lemonade-sipping WPC had been brought along mainly to act as his driver.

'It was kind of you to come,' Carole told him.

'Well, we wanted to be sure you and Mrs Murray would not be subjected to any unpleasantness today,' he said. 'I mean, we've no cause to think you or your aunt are in any danger, but, then again, we still don't know who killed your uncle. We won't let it rest until we do find out. Let me assure you of that.'

'Thank you, DS McKittrick.'

'Dan, please,' he corrected her.

Carole made to top up his whiskey glass. He did not decline.

'This is going down very well, Miss Murray, thank you. We've had a bit of a bad week, for deaths and such, to be honest with you.'

'Please, call me Carole. And you must meet my husband, Dave.'

Carole waved Dave over and introduced him to the Belfast detective.

'Dan, this is Dave Lloyd, my husband. He's an ex-policeman. He was with Gloucestershire's MIT but now he works in my section at Thames House. Dave, Dan here is with Belfast's MIT.'

'How's the investigation going,' Dave asked, as he shook McKittrick's hand, 'that's if you don't mind my asking?'

McKittrick drained his glass before replying.

'Well, we've taken on board what Carole has told us about her uncle's various activities and, commendable as they were, it's possible they may have attracted the attention of some very dangerous people.'

'May I ask which people it is we're talking about?' Dave asked.

McKittrick turned to his constable and handed her his glass.

'Eileen, will you run over there and get yourself another lemonade. Get me one, too, will you?'

The constable dutifully disappeared.

'I didn't want to say too much in front of Eileen, as I think some details of the investigation should be restricted to as small a number of people as possible, but we're exploring links between the judge's killing and whoever it is who's been using the assumed identity of Killian Devereux. We're also looking at a connection with some more bodies we've found buried out at a former maternity home at Shearwater Point.'

'Shearwater Point?' Carole queried. 'That's not far from here. Isn't that the home where the real Killian Devereux, the American, was arrested?'

'Yes. And ...oh well, it'll be all over the papers tomorrow, so I might as well tell you, we've found a whole lot more bodies at Shearwater Point.'

'*More* bodies? Dave asked. 'How many are we talking about?'

'We found another five adults, that's in addition to the one in the cellar, and we've also uncovered the remains of an awful lot of infants.'

'Infants?' Carole was aghast. 'How many infants?'

'So far, sixty-seven. Just imagine, sixty-seven babies. All thrown into a septic tank, they were. I've never seen the like of it.'

There was a shocked silence as Dave and Carole took in what they had just been told. Constable O'Neill now reappeared and handed McKittrick a glass of lemonade.

'Dan, would you like some whiskey in that?' Carole asked.

'Yes, please.'

Carole's aunt now joined them and was introduced to the detectives.

'Did you ever find out who burned down that nice restaurant, the Star of Bengal?' she asked, 'for George and I ate there a few times. George loves a good curry.'

'We're still working on that, Mrs Murray,' McKittrick told her.

Carole was surprised her aunt should have asked about the restaurant fire-bombing and not about her own husband's murder. Since Ellen still referred to her late husband in the present tense, despite the fact that they had just buried George, Carole supposed the fact of his death hadn't fully sunk in as yet.

'Only I heard tell it was attacked with one of those *Mazel Tov* cocktails,' Ellen added.

In spite of the tragedy and solemnity of the occasion, Dave and Dan struggled to supress their mirth at Ellen's gaffe.

'There you are, Dan,' Dave said, 'you might be looking at an Israeli arsonist.'

Chapter 26

Caffrey called at the reception desk at Musgrave Street police station where, as agreed by DI Lawrence, he was able to collect his US passport, student ID card and the Irish passport application form which he had completed a few days earlier. With the DI's assurance that the Irish passport authorities had now been advised this particular Killian Devereux was not the man wanted for questioning in Northern Ireland, he was now able to pursue his application for an Irish passport.

Perhaps it was because the success of his application had been in some doubt following his arrest, that Caffrey now wanted that Irish passport more than ever. Or maybe it was because his biological mother had been deprived of her rights, that his assertion of his own rights seemed to take on greater importance.

Of course, it had also occurred to him that, with an Irish passport and the right of residence it granted, he should have no trouble remaining beyond the extent of the ninety-day entry stamp endorsed in his American passport, should he choose to do so. If he really did decide to set up a sub office of his law practice here in Belfast, he suspected he would find the process easier as an Irish citizen and local resident. Conversely, for all he knew, there might be tax breaks available for a US citizen seeking to do so. He would take the most advantageous options, just as soon as he had worked out what they were.

Having re-submitted his passport application, he next returned to the public records office to have a look at more of the admissions registers for *La Mère du Bon Pasteur*. On his previous visit, he had only asked to see the register covering the nineteen seventies. He was now astonished at just how many registers there were, but he requested only those from the nineteen-fifties onwards, where there was a chance the women who had given birth at the home might still be alive and might benefit from whatever recognition and justice he could secure for them.

Using his camera phone, he photographed page after page after page. He was astonished at the numbers of girls and young women who had passed through those imposing iron gates over the four most recent decades up until its closure. Clearly, the home was always full to capacity and, no doubt, the laundry would have operated at full capacity, too.

He was equally astonished to find that some of the women had remained at the home not for months but for years. In fact, some of them had never left but had died there in relatively old age. He supposed their families would not take them back. Theirs would have been a lifetime of unpaid employment. He could not imagine how it must have been for the women to have absolutely no income, to have to rely on the nuns to provide them with all life's essentials. He didn't imagine they would have had any of life's little luxuries, such as access to books and magazines, clothing they had chosen for themselves, cosmetics or indeed any of the little things that might make a young woman's life worth living.

What he did imagine, though, was that those who had left in their sixties would only have had the basic state pension to support them in their old age. Laundry skills apart, they would have had precious little in the way of education or learning of life skills. They would have been denied personal choice and the chance to develop discernment, judgement and taste. He wondered where they would go in retirement, to hostels, probably. Since the nuns had paid the women no wages, they wouldn't have been obliged to offer them an occupational pension scheme, or a private health scheme. The more Caffrey thought about it, the greater was the number of their rights which had been infringed.

Caffrey's next port of call was the general records office again. He planned to trawl through GRONI's birth indexes and find the registration details for the births which had occurred at the home. By establishing the infants' given names, he hoped he might check where they had gone, so that he could include the children in his crusade for justice as well as their mothers. If he had thought this would be an easy task, however, he was to be disappointed.

'Have you made an appointment to see the indexes?' the same officious GRONI clerk demanded. 'For we only allow a limited number of people at a time to view them.'

'No. I'm sorry, but I didn't know that was necessary. Can I make an appointment to see them now?'

'There's available slots next week,' the clerk said, checking his bookings.

'Next week? Well, that's kinda disappointing. I just flew in from America to try to find my birth parents, you know, and a week is a long time for me to wait.'

The clerk was unsympathetic.

'You should've checked our website before you left America. It tells you on there that you have to book.'

'Well, that's too bad. My flight home is booked for the end of this week,' Caffrey said, and that was true, since, although he intended to extend the booking, he had not yet done so. 'But, if I may ask, how many people are in there at the moment looking at the indexes? Might there be space for one more?'

The clerk looked at his bookings and Caffrey thought he looked uncomfortable.

'Well, as it happens, there's nobody in there at the moment.'

'So, it wouldn't hurt to let me in, then, would it?'

Caffrey flashed his broadest smile at the clerk and watched him squirm with the effort of trying to come up with a reason to deny him access.

'You haven't booked, though.'

'But, surely, there's no need now, as there's no-one in there.'

Caffrey recognised what he termed the 'gatekeeper mentality'. He had often encountered this back home, too, whether from doctors' receptionists, tax office employees or records office clerks. There was always this odd attitude that they were not there to support the patients or the public, but to man the ramparts and keep the castle secure. Caffrey thought it was like old story of the factory storekeeper who wouldn't lend out to the workers any of the tools in his stores because he saw his role as storekeeper being simply to keep the tools in the stores.

'I suppose you can go through, then,' the clerk reluctantly conceded.

Satisfied that logic had defeated the gatekeeper, Caffrey set about his mammoth task.

Chapter 27

DS Dan McKittrick entered the building in Alfred Street and headed up to the fourth floor. Aminullah Miah was surprised to see him again so soon.

'Come in, sergeant. Take a seat. Have you identified who burned out my parents' restaurant?' Miah asked.

'Not yet, although our enquiries into that incident are still ongoing. I've actually come to speak to you about your brother's disappearance.'

'Mohinullah? You've found something? After all this time?'

'We're not at all sure yet, but you may have read in the papers about some bodies that were found out at Shearwater Point, in the grounds of an abandoned maternity home.'

'Yes, but weren't those the remains of children?'

'Most of them, yes. And those appear to be historic remains. But we also found some remains which were placed there in more recent years. They're adults, and mostly males.'

'And you think one of them might be Mohinullah?'

'Well, at the moment, it's no more than a possibility, so I wouldn't want to raise your hopes of a conclusion unnecessarily.'

'I see. Have my parents been told?'

'No. I saw no point in upsetting them, in case we're wrong. I think they've had enough upset this week with the fire and the death of their chef. Having spoken to you the other day, though, I thought it would be better if I came to you for help first.'

'That's very thoughtful of you. How can I help?'

'When your brother disappeared, no DNA samples were taken. We'd normally only do that if we're sure a *misper* is dead – a missing person, I mean. Often, they've just taken off somewhere and they turn up again later. But, since we now have these individuals' remains to identify, I wondered if you'd be willing to submit a DNA sample for comparison. If it turns out your brother isn't amongst them, then we needn't mention it to your folks.'

'Again, that's very considerate of you, sergeant. Of course, I'll be happy to give my DNA.'

'Thank you, Mr Miah. It would be most helpful if you could pop over to the Forensic Science lab at Carrickfergus to give your sample, but, if that's not convenient, I could arrange for someone from the lab to come here.'

'No, I'll be happy to go over to Carrick. But, tell me, there must be dozens of … *mispers* in Northern Ireland. I can't imagine you've had time to approach all their families. Do you have some particular reason to suspect this might be my brother?'

'Not really. Just my gut instinct.'

'Well, clearly, you trust your gut instinct, and I trust you, so that's good enough for me.'

McKittrick's DI, meanwhile, was over at the Palace Barracks in Holywood. It was only Sarah Lawrence's second visit to the MI5 office. The first time had been for a familiarisation visit and security briefing a few years earlier. Now, she had been invited by Mike Malone to have sight of the Security Service's file on the Alternative Ulster organisation. By the time Malone returned with their coffees, she had seen all she needed to see.

'Your basis for suggesting that this fake Devereux is involved with this ultra-right group, it's not exactly A1 info, is it?' she said. 'Like our intelligence on him, it's come mainly from informants. And, useful though it is, intelligence isn't evidence.'

'True, but some of our sources are informants who've proved reliable in the past,' Malone said. 'We'd been copied in on reporting from our regional office in the north west of England that someone named Killian Devereux was in Manchester recently, meeting with a Russian, a man from an ultra-right-wing organisation based in Russia. They met at Manchester's Midland Hotel. And, now, that same Russian, Ilya Kirasov, is visiting Belfast. He's staying at the Europa. If you were able to spare a constable or two to keep an eye on him, it could be just a matter of time before he led us to the fake Devereux.'

'Even if he does, though,' the DI suggested, 'we don't have any hard evidence to link Devereux with Alternative Ulster, or to link Alternative Ulster with any of the racist and homophobic attacks that have happened here over the past year or two. In fact, we don't even have enough evidence to pull him in for questioning. We just need a lucky break, Mike. Just one lousy little lucky break.'

'Did you find out whether Devereux holds a British passport?' Malone asked.

'Ah, yes, we thought we were onto something when my constable found out a British passport had indeed been issued in that identity. However, when she rushed over to the passport office to check out the photo of the holder, it turned out to be an infant.'

'An infant?'

'Yes. Seems it was issued to the real Killian Devereux back in nineteen seventy-six to enable him to be given a US visa to travel to Boston where he joined his adoptive parents. I'm not sure our friend from Boston even knows once held a British passport.'

'So, no more recent UK passport issues in the Killian Devereux identity?' Malone asked.

'No. It'd be interesting to discover what identity documents the fake Devereux has been using. Maybe he's been using docs in his real name.'

'But we still don't know what his real name is. We don't know who he is, and we don't know where he is.'

Chapter 28

It was a quarter to three the following morning, when the white transit van cruised to a halt outside Firoze's Fusion Diner. The diners and drinkers had all drifted home hours since and Belfast's newest and most sumptuously appointed Indian restaurant, which had so recently featured in the press and on the tourism websites, was in darkness.

The slightly-built young man in the hooded jacket emerged from the van and looked both ways up and down the street. Taking a lighter from his pocket, he lit the rag which protruded from the whiskey bottle in his hand. As the petrol-soaked rag caught alight, the man drew back his arm and flung the bottle as hard as he could against the restaurant's large front window.

The arsonist could not have known that Firoze Gul, the proprietor, had given his new restaurant the most expensive toughed plate glass window he could afford. Designed to withstand being collateral damage in any sectarian brick-throwing protests or even bomb blasts, the window glass now proved its worth.

To the astonishment of the window's assailant, the Molotov bounced off the plate glass and hurtled right back at him. It hit him in the chest before landing at his feet, where it smashed. Immediately, the young man was engulfed in flames. To the accompaniment of the restaurant's loud burglar alarm, activated by the vibration of the window glass, the young man beat at his petrol-soaked burning clothes with his bare hands and tore the blazing hood from his head. He turned to run back to the van and, still alight, he made a grab for the door, but the crop-haired driver hit the accelerator and took off, leaving the now fallen fire bomber still alight and writhing helplessly on the pavement.

It was a good few minutes before a couple of local residents, roused from sleep by the ceaseless alarm, stumbled from their apartments and came to the rescue of the burning man. A police patrol car was next on the scene and, a little later still, the ambulance which had been summoned came screeching to a halt. Soon, the casualty was speeding on his way to the Burns Unit at the Royal Victoria Hospital.

Awoken by the sirens of, firstly, the ambulance, and then the police vehicles which zig-zagged across the city all during the early hours, Caffrey gave up the struggle to sleep. He arose and began his packing. By eight o'clock that morning, he had showered and breakfasted, so he took his luggage down to reception and awaited his turn to see Zoe, his usual helpful receptionist. She was busy checking out the departing guest ahead of him. Caffrey didn't mean to eavesdrop but he was intrigued to hear the man's strong eastern European accent. The man produced a credit card to settle his bill but was informed by Zoe that it was not necessary to pay. Caffrey's interest was further aroused.

'That's all settled, Mr Kirasov,' Zoe smiled. 'Mr Maharg has paid your bill. I hope you've enjoyed your stay. Your taxi is waiting outside.'

The man nodded, put away his credit card and, scooping up his bags, he left the hotel.

'Good morning, Mr Caffrey,' Zoe smiled. 'Are you leaving us already?'

'Leaving the Europa, yes, but I'm not leaving your beautiful city just yet. In fact, I've decided to stay a few more weeks or so on business, so I've found myself a small rental apartment. But I've promised myself I'll come back soon and treat myself to the afternoon tea in your piano bar. It looks sumptuous.'

Zoe smiled warmly as she printed out the invoice and took Caffrey's credit card. Caffrey was still somewhat intrigued by the eastern European guest whose bill had been paid by someone else.

'Say, Zoe,' he asked, 'that guy who just checked out ahead of me, did I hear you mention the name Maharg?'

'Yes, that's right.'

'That's kind of a strange name. Is it an Irish surname, only I'd never heard it before, but I think I've seen it somewhere recently during my family history research?'

'Maharg? Yes, it's said to be a reiver name, and one which originated in Northern Ireland.'

'A reiver name?'

'A few hundred years ago, the reivers were bands of robbers who lived around the border areas between England and Scotland. One of the big reiver families was the Grahams. They were into horse stealing and cattle rustling, and a lot of them got caught and were banished over here to Ulster. There's a wee bit of a legend surrounding the name Maharg. They say the Mahargs were originally Grahams and they wanted to shed their notoriety. So, when they came to Ulster, they turned the name Graham backwards and started calling themselves Maharg.'

'That's a heck of a story. But the guest who just left, I'm not too good on accents but he didn't sound like a Maharg.'

'Mr Kirasov? No, he's a Russian gentleman.'

'Ah, I suppose he's heading home to Moscow, then.'

'No. Like you, he's decided to stay on a while longer, but he's gone to stay with a business associate out at Shearwater Point.'

'Well, I'm not surprised. It's a beautiful spot.'

'Of course, you went to Shearwater Point, didn't you? Did you find what you were looking for there?'

'I did indeed. And a whole lot more,' he said ruefully.

'I'm so glad that business with the police was resolved, Mr Caffrey.'

127

'You and me both, Zoe. You and me both.'

Caffrey retrieved his credit card and pocketed his copy of the hotel receipt, then he stepped to one side of the hotel lobby to make a brief call on his mobile phone. He dialled the number on the business card Carole had given him.

'Miss Murray? Dom Caffrey. Hello again. Look, you mentioned a Russian name in connection with that group you think was responsible for your uncle's death? ... Yes, Kirasov, that's it. Well, a man named Kirasov just checked out of the Europa where I've been staying, and ...'

Caffrey paused and looked around the lobby. There were a fair few people coming and going and others just sitting around reading newspapers.

'Listen, I'm probably not in the best place right now to be discussing this. I'm just checking out of my hotel and I'm about to head off to an apartment I've rented. Maybe I could phone you later when I'm settled there? ... Oh, well, if you're up in town right now, why don't we get together for coffee? Do know Great Victoria Street? Yeah? Well, there's a coffee shop just a block down from the Europa ... yes, that's the one. I'll be in there. Okay, see you there in around ten minutes.'

Caffrey exited the hotel and, pulling his wheeled suitcase along behind him, headed down the street to the café. He didn't notice the crop-haired man and the youth who'd been seated in the hotel lobby now following him at a discreet distance. Hughie McCalmont and his new young henchman, Billy Boyd, followed Caffrey into the café and seated themselves a couple of tables away from the one at which Caffrey parked his suitcase. Caffrey bought himself a coffee at the counter. McCalmont sent the lad over to the counter to get them a couple of coffees, too.

Soon, Carole appeared and greeted Caffrey. She declined his offer to buy her a coffee but took a seat at his table.

'So, I mentioned that a man named Kirasov was staying at the Europa,' Caffrey explained, 'and that he checked out just ahead of me. The hotel receptionist told me he's gone to stay with a business associate over at Shearwater Point.'

'Do you know where at Shearwater Point?' Carole asked.

'No, I don't know the address. But, if it helps, his bill was paid by a Mr Maharg.'

'Maharg, you say?'

'Yes. That's Graham spelled backwards, or so I'm told. Maybe this Maharg character lives out that way. If it turns out he has anything to do with the man who's using my identity, perhaps you'll let me know. I might just decide to sue the ass off him.'

McCalmont strained to hear what was passing between them but he could not. Squinting over his accomplice's shoulder, he tried to lipread, but lipreading was not one of his skills. Soon, however, Carole was on her feet and shaking Caffrey's hand. She left the café, but Caffrey remained, sipping his coffee.

'You follow the woman, Billy,' McCalmont ordered. 'I'll see where the American goes.'

Billy drained his coffee and followed Carole out of the café. He followed her at a discreet distance to the multi-storey car park on Grosvenor Road. Since he was on foot, and Hughie had the keys to their vehicle, he saw no point in following her up to the floor where she had left her car. Instead, he positioned himself by the exit ramp, took out his mobile phone and began to draft a text to McCalmont. A few moments later, a distinctive vintage orange Volkswagen appeared. Billy saw that Carole was at the wheel, so he added the car's index number to his text and hit 'send'.

Still seated in the coffee shop watching Caffrey, McCalmont received Billy's text, took out a pen and copied the car number onto a paper napkin. He thought about

129

calling his tame police contact for a subscriber check, but then he decided it would be quicker to call a contact he had within the Driver and Vehicle Licensing Authority over in Armagh. His contact there could pull up the details of the vehicle's keeper on his computer immediately. His contact did indeed provide the information instantly, and McCalmont scribbled the details onto the napkin.

He sat back, shocked to learn that the woman he had sent Billy to follow was driving a car licensed to one George Murray at an address in Donaghadee – the address of the late Judge George Murray, the man McCalmont himself had killed. How was she connected with George Murray, he wondered, and what was she doing talking to the American? He looked up and saw that, whilst he'd been on the phone to the DVLA, the American had left. He put away his phone, pocketed the napkin and headed out into the street. Looking up and down the street in both directions, he could see neither hide nor hair of the real Devereux. He would have to explain to the other Devereux, the fake Devereux, that he had lost sight of the real one. Damnit!

Chapter 29

That evening, out at Ardmore House, McCalmont made his excuses to his employer, explaining that it had been his judgement call to concentrate on trying to identify the unknown woman, rather than keeping an eye on where the American had gone.

'Not sure who she is, Mister D, but she's staying at the judge's house and driving his car, and it wasn't clear what she was talking to the American about. She might be police.'

However, his boss was less perturbed by this than was McCalmont.

'Sounds more like she's a relative of Murray's. A policewoman wouldn't be driving Murray's car, now, would she? And it makes sense that a family member would be in Donaghadee helping out the widow with the funeral arrangements and all that there. And, if you think about it logically, the Yank found our weapons cache at the ma and baby home, and, the woman's relative has been murdered just up the road from there. It stands to reason she might link the two events and want to speak to the guy who found the guns. Don't sweat it, son. She's mebbe just a relative trying to find out what happened to the auld fellah.'

'D'ye think we should keep an eye on her, though?'

'Aye. Well, it wouldn't do any harm. Anyway, off you go now, for I've a house guest waiting to meet the committee.'

McCalmont left, and the man who was known as Killian Devereux collected his house guest from the lounge and ushered him into the dining room to introduce him to his associates.

'Gentlemen, may I present Mr Ilya Kirasov. Ilya, let me introduce you to Mr Eamon Kennedy, our propaganda campaign manager, and Mr James Maharg, our treasurer.'

Kirasov shook the hand of each man around the table in turn.

'Mr Dermot McCluskey here is over from County Londonderry. He runs our branch over there. And this is Mr Donal McKenna from the Letterkenny branch in Donegal. We have representation also in the counties of Cavan and Monaghan, but we five are the administrative committee for the organisation.'

Kirasov took his place at the table next to Devereux and accepted the glass of whiskey Devereux poured him.

'Good evening, gentlemen,' Kirasov began in good, though heavily accented English. 'I am looking forward to hearing all about your organisation and to exchanging ideas with you. Devereux has given me a brief outline of your aims and objectives, but I should like to hear how you are going about achieving them.'

Devereux nodded at Kennedy, who kicked off the discussion.

'In my city of Belfast, Mr Kirasov, as in most UK cities these days, we're seeing huge numbers of in-comers and refugees. No-one wanted to come here during the troubles, and, indeed, the troubles damaged our economy very badly. That conflict left many people without work. Since our city found peace and prosperity, though, that's when the poor of other nations started flooding in. They're taking up jobs and housing, and those who can't or won't do the jobs on offer are taking advantage of our benefits system. It is our aim to discourage them from remaining here.'

'That's right,' Maharg cut in. 'There's whole families of Syrian refugees in the city, and Romanians. Then there's the Poles and there's Afghans, Somalis, and the Roma. You name it, we have them here. They've outstayed their welcome and it's time we showed them the door.'

Devereux nodded in wholehearted agreement. He would add his own four pennorth.

'The thing is, Ilya, there's many of us feel we can't call this province our own, these days. I don't know how much you know of our history, but, exactly one hundred years ago, the island of Ireland was partitioned. The southern counties became an independent and mainly Catholic republic. Here in the historic northern province of Ulster, a separate British province of Northern Ireland was created, but only six of Ulster's nine counties were included. Three of the nine counties were arbitrarily given to the Republic. Well, we want them back.'

'Yes,' Kirasov nodded, 'that seems an odd division. I have always wondered why they didn't just draw the border as a straight line between north and south. This whiskey is excellent, by the way.'

'There was pressure from Rome, and also from America, not to include the counties with a high Catholic population,' Devereux explained. 'So, what we in the Alternative Ulster movement are committed to is to make the whole nine counties of Ulster a single unity, and an entirely white Protestant state. We don't want diversity. We want a more homogenous society where priority for jobs and housing is given to *our* community.'

'So, you have been taking a stand against foreign individuals, I understand,' Kirasov said, 'just as my organisation is doing in Russia. But it doesn't seem to be having any great effect over here. Have you considered taking your protest to the next level? Perhaps you need to do something to make the British and Irish governments sit up and take notice.'

The others all looked to Devereux so see whether it was all right to reveal their intentions. Devereux nodded his assent. It was Kennedy who took it upon himself to explain the plan.

'Mr Kirasov, the Anglo-Irish treaty came into effect in nineteen-twenty-two. So, this year being two thousand and twenty-two, it's the centenary of the implementation of that treaty and of the partition of Ireland. Now, it seems likely there'll be celebrations of that centenary down in Dublin, but we don't feel it is a cause for celebration. We have something different in mind to mark the event. We're planning a few little events of our own.'

'Is that why you want us to send you more guns and explosives?' Kirasov asked.

'Yes. We would appreciate your sending all you can,' Devereux smiled, as he briefly removed his dark tinted spectacles and polished the lenses with his handkerchief, before continuing.

'You see, our own events to mark nineteen twenty-two are due to start next month, to coincide with the arrival in Northern Ireland of the President of the United States. An American president was instrumental in the partition of Ireland back in nineteen twenty-two under pressure from the Irish-American lobby. So, it seems only fitting that an American President should be instrumental, albeit unwittingly, in the *re*-partition of Ireland in twenty-twenty-two. More whiskey, Ilya?'

Devereux re-filled his guest's glass.

'It's Bushmills,' Devereux explained. 'A sixteen-year-old single malt, made in County Antrim with the water from Saint Columba's rill. You see, Ilya, the Catholics have their holy water, and this is ours.'

Chapter 30

DS Dan McKittrick returned to the building on Alfred Street and headed up once again to the fourth floor. He could see, via the office door's glass partition, that Aminullah Miah had someone with him, so he waited patiently in the corridor. He made good use of the time by working out exactly what he would say to the young lawyer. He hated this kind of task, but someone had to do it.

Eventually, he saw Miah's visitor rise and, shaking Miah's hand vigorously, make to leave. To his surprise, McKittrick recognised the visitor who emerged into the corridor.

'Mr Caffrey. What brings you here?' he asked.

'Detective sergeant. I could ask you the same question,' Caffrey replied. 'Human rights issues, in my case.'

'Mine, too, in a manner of speaking. Did you get your Irish passport, by the way?'

'Well, I've re-submitted my application, and they say it will be issued from Dublin quite soon. And it seems I also qualify for a British passport, so I've submitted an online application for one of those, too. It's kinda funny that, last week, I was just an American, next week I'll also be Irish and British.'

'And in which of your identities will your new passports be issued?' McKittrick asked.

'Same as the Irish birth certificate. As Killian Devereux.'

'So, you'll have two identities and three nationalities. Not many people can say that. Well, I wish you the best of luck with your family history research, Mr Caffrey.'

'Thank you, detective. And good luck with your pursuit of the fake Killian Devereux.'

Caffrey left and Miah welcomed McKittrick into his office. It seemed to the detective that the piles of files on the lawyer's desk and on top of his cupboards had increased since his last visit.

'I didn't know you and Mr Caffrey were acquainted,' McKittrick said as he took a seat.

'Yes, Mr Caffrey wants us to tackle the issue of abuses at the mother and baby homes here in Northern Ireland, especially at the home out at Shearwater Point.'

'And are the HRC going to get involved? Only, if you are, our latest discoveries out there are certainly going to be relevant.'

'I'm afraid our casework in connection with recent rights infringements is pressing enough. So far, we haven't had the resources to look at historic abuses. However, Mr Caffrey just told me he's found a much more powerful source of support than I could provide.'

'Oh, yes?'

'No doubt you're aware that the US President is due to visit the province in a few weeks' time? Well, fortuitously, the White House has asked that the mis-treatment of the women at the mother and baby homes, and also the trafficking of local children to America, be included on the agenda for discussion during the President's visit to Stormont. In fact, the American Ambassador to the United Nations has resurrected the UN recommendations for enforcement action, too. Seems Mr Caffrey has some good connections in Washington.'

'Is that good or bad news, as far as you're concerned?'

Miah glanced at McKittrick over the barrier of files that sat between them.

'Well, it'll greatly increase my workload, but, on the plus side, I don't see how the Northern Ireland Office can refuse to increase our resources now. But, speaking of good and bad news, I imagine the reason you've come here in person, rather than telephoning, is that you have bad news for me.'

'Yes. I'm so sorry to have to tell you this, but one of the sets of remains found at Shearwater Point is indeed that of your brother.'

Miah nodded. He had been expecting this to be the case. He sighed deeply.

'Do you wish me to call on your parents to tell them the news' he offered, 'or would you rather break it to them yourself? If you'd want me to accompany you when you do tell them, I'd be happy to do so.'

'No, thank you. I'll tell them myself. I suppose there's no doubt, is there?'

'No. The DNA showed a clear sibling match. Oh, and the deceased was wearing this ring. Perhaps you recognise it?'

From his pocket, the detective pulled a small evidence bag containing a man's gold signet ring and handed it to Miah. Miah gazed at it sadly. Stretching the plastic bag taut to get a better look at the small ruby chip embedded in the ring, he recognised also the smoothly worn edges and the faded engraving on the ring's interior.

'Yes. This was our grandfather's wedding ring. He left each of us boys something of his. I inherited his silver pocket watch. Mohinullah, as the eldest, got the gold ring. He never took it off.'

'I'm truly sorry for your loss, Mr Miah. This isn't the end of the story, though. This is the beginning of a multiple murder enquiry.'

137

Chapter 31

Ten miles away, at the forensic science laboratories in Carrickfergus, Dr Mairead Mulroney was looking for a member of her staff who had recently returned from sick leave. She spotted a young, white-coated woman with her head bowed over a microscope. Harpreet Gill, one of the assistant scientific officers, looked up at Dr Mulroney's approach.

'Harpreet, I just heard that Ryan Donovan came back to work today. Where is he? Have you seen him?'

'Yes, Doctor. He was in really early this morning, but he's just popped out somewhere. He said he'd be back soon.'

'I have to say I'm a little concerned that he's come back to work so soon. I need to see his GP's certificate, just to make sure he's been signed off sick leave. Did he say where he was going?'

'Um, well, he did ask me where the nearest off licence was.'

'Off licence? At nine o'clock in the morning? Did he say why?'

'No, he didn't. But he seemed fine. His hands have been burned but he's wearing special cotton gloves. He said he needed to get back to work, you know, to take his mind off things.'

'Okay, well, when he returns, will you give me a discreet call and I'll come down and see him.'

'Yes, doctor.'

Half an hour later, Ryan was back in the laboratory, carrying a plastic carrier bag. Harpreet watched discreetly as her fellow ASO took a bottle of Bushmills sixteen-year-old single malt whiskey from the bag. He dropped the bag into the waste bin, then, clutching the bottle, he disappeared in the direction of the staff kitchen. Concerned for his well-being, she followed him. Watching through the kitchen door's glass panel, she saw Ryan unscrew the cap from the bottle, then pour the entire contents down the kitchen sink. She quickly returned to the laboratory and picked up the phone.

By the time Dr Mulroney had returned to the laboratory, she saw Ryan was adding water to a quantity of white powder.

'Ryan, welcome back. I'm surprised to see you back at work so soon after … well, if you have a moment, perhaps we could go to my office and have your return-to-work interview.'

'Would you mind if we did that here, doctor, only I've just made up a batch of quick-drying plaster of Paris, and I need to use it now before it sets.'

'All right. May I ask what it is you're working on?'

'This is the evidence collected from the scene of the fire-bombing at Firoze's Fusion Diner, and from the clothes of the suspected arsonist. One of the crime scene investigators dropped this off. They want us to carry out further trace analysis.'

'Okay, well, let's talk while you work. How are you now, are your hands better?'

'Oh, they're good enough.'

'And how are you in yourself? What happened was shocking. I hear you lost a friend in the fire at the pub.'

'Yes. I did. But I wanted to get back to work as soon as possible, doctor. I need to move on from what happened. Work is the best way of doing that.'

The laboratory chief glanced down at Ryan's hands. She couldn't believe his burns would have healed so soon but she couldn't see through the latex gloves which he wore on top of the fine white cotton gloves. He seemed to be concentrating well enough on the task he had taken on, though, so perhaps he was right. Perhaps work was the best therapy.

'Have you given your line manager the doctor's note certifying you're okay to return to work?'

'The surgery said it's on its way,' Ryan said, not lifting his eyes from the task in hand.

'Okay, well, I'll leave you to it. When you've done ... whatever it is you're doing here ... we'll have a chat over coffee.'

Ryan nodded but concentrated on pouring the plaster of Paris into the empty whiskey bottle until it was full to the top. Dr Mulroney left. Ryan's curious colleague, Harpreet, watched him discreetly from her side of the laboratory bench, not having the faintest idea what he was doing.

'I'm making tea, Ryan. Do you want a cup?' she said.

'That would be grand, thanks,' he said, still concentrating on his task.

When Harpreet returned with two mugs of tea, she saw Ryan was bending over the waste paper bin with a hammer, smashing the whiskey bottle to smithereens to release the plaster mould he had made. She put down his mug of tea and returned to her side of the bench. Still curious, she watched as Ryan shook every shard of glass from the plaster mould into the waste bin before using a dry paint brush to brush the mould free of fine splinters.

Harpreet continued to watch Ryan as he gently tipped the contents of a forensic evidence bag out onto a large sheet of white paper. The contents consisted mainly of many fragments of smoke-blackened glass and charred bits of a paper label. To her amazement, she watched her colleague begin fitting the tiny pieces of glass onto the plaster mould. Using long tweezers and working from the bottom up, he began painstakingly glueing the pieces together onto the mould, as if it was a thousand-piece jigsaw.

'That looks like it'll take you a week or two,' she suggested.

'It probably will,' he agreed. 'But it'll be worth it.'

Ten miles away, at Belfast's Royal Victoria Hospital, the general and emergency wards were as busy as ever that morning. Things were slightly less hectic in Ward 2E of the Burns Unit when the crop-haired man in the blue surgical gown, blue surgeon's mask and disposable latex gloves, entered the ward. Carrying a clipboard, and with a stethoscope draped around his neck, he waved a casual greeting to the duty nurse who was on the phone in earnest conversation. She nodded in response.

Checking the patients' names written on the whiteboards above each of the beds, the man paused beside the one above which the name 'John Feenicks' was written. Walking to the head of the bed, he stared down at the sleeping patient. Despite the patient's severe injuries and the bulky dressings which had been applied to them, the man in the surgical gown appeared satisfied this was the casualty he was seeking. Drawing the wheeled privacy screens around the bed, he roughly yanked the pillow out from under the sleeping patient's head.

The jolt awoke the patient. His eyes brightened at first in recognition of the masked man hovering over him. Then those eyes grew big with confusion and fear as he saw his visitor raise the pillow and press it down firmly over his face. Burnt flesh, dressings and breathing tubes, all were brutally squashed as the masked man brought all his weight to bear on the pillow. The casualty made a feeble attempt to struggle but soon was still. Leaving the screens and pillow in place, the man in the surgeon's gown stepped away from the bed and left the ward.

Chapter 32

The following day, Mike Malone ushered DI Sarah Lawrence and DS Dan McKittrick into his office at Palace Barrack's regional MI5 office and seated them around his desk.

'Thank you for coming over,' Malone began. 'You said on the phone there've been some developments in your investigation which you felt we need to know about?'

The detective inspector nodded.

'Yes, Mike. One of the sets of adult remains found at Shearwater Point has been identified as being those of a young Belfast man of Bangladeshi origin. Mohinullah Miah went missing, believed abducted, three years ago. He was the son of Joytul and Aliyah Miah, the couple whose restaurant, The Star of Bengal, was burnt out recently in an arson attack.'

'Is that likely to be just a tragic coincidence?' Malone asked.

'We don't believe so,' McKittrick replied. 'The Miah's other son, Aminullah Miah, is a lawyer working with the Human Right's Commission in Belfast. I've advised him to take extra security precautions, just in case someone is targeting his whole family.'

'Do you think the two incidents could have something to do with his work for the HRC?'

'Unlikely,' McKittrick said. 'He got into that field of work after, and probably because of his brother's abduction. And he doesn't seem to have worked on anything contentious, so far as I can see. Both incidents could simply be racially motivated.'

'Has the cause of his brother's death been established yet?' Malone queried.

'Not definitively,' Sarah Lawrence said, 'though the post-mortem exam showed a few broken bones which hadn't had time to heal. He was almost certainly badly beaten just before he died.'

'Anything turn up on the other adult cadavers?' Malone asked.

'So far, all the pathologist has been able to establish is that none of them grew up around here,' Sarah advised. 'DNA and bone content tests suggest two of the males were from the horn of Africa. The other corpses, male and female, were from central Europe. We've had cases of women trafficked from Romania to work in the sex industry. Romanian pimps, too. It's not been possible to establish who these dead foreigners were, though, since there are no DNA samples on file for family comparison purposes.'

'But the pathologist also found bullets in two of the bodies,' McKittrick added. 'They were compared with the bullets taken from the body of Judge Murray, and they were a match. All those bullets were fired by the same weapon. So, now we know that the deaths are all connected to the same weapon and probably carried out by the same killer.'

'You'll maybe have heard there was another fire-bomb attack on another curry house,' Sarah added.

'Yes. That wasn't owned by the Miah family as well, was it?' Malone asked.

'No,' McKittrick replied, 'though it was owned by a Pakistani entrepreneur. But there's been a worrying development in that case. The arsonist bungled it and managed to set himself on fire. Youngish chap, in his twenties. We haven't identified him yet. He was admitted to the Burns Unit at the Royal under a pseudonym, John Feenicks, but, yesterday, someone killed him. He was smothered in his bed.'

'Why 'John Feenicks'?' Malone asked.

'That was Dan's idea,' Sarah said, nodding towards McKittrick. 'You know, like the Phoenix, rising from the ashes. Seems his killer was dressed like a surgeon and, although the ward nurse was busy and didn't get a good look at him, she noticed he went straight to the right bed. It may be that someone on the hospital staff tipped off the killer that Feenicks was the arsonist.'

'Or someone in MIT,' McKittrick added.

The DI flashed McKittrick a warning glance before she continued.

'CCTV shows the killer arrived at the hospital in a white transit van. An identical white transit was caught on CCTV near the fire-bombings of the two curry houses and The Rainbow Room night club. In each case, false number plates were used, but not the same plates each time. We've got our team checking back through CCTV for vans with those index numbers, to see if they can trace the van's routes on the nights those attacks occurred.'

'So far, then,' Malone summed up, 'the incident at The Rainbow Room was presumably a homophobic attack. All the other victims have been from ethnic minority groups. Could those be racially motivated attacks?'

'All except for the dead arsonist,' McKittrick explained, 'and although we haven't identified him as yet, the hospital staff say that, when he was admitted, he was conscious but delirious, and he was speaking with a local accent. It's possible the motive for his murder was that whoever sent him to burn the restaurant didn't want him to talk.'

'There's quite a high rate of attacks on ethnic minorities and members of the gay community here, these days,' Malone said, 'higher even than in London. Any idea why that should be?'

'I'm sorry to say you're right,' Sarah admitted. 'On average, there are two racist attacks a day in Belfast alone. An elderly Chinese man was attacked in the street

144

yesterday. Last week it was a Romanian selling copies of *The Big Issue*. We've even had two cases of pipe-bombs exploding outside Syrian refugee-occupied houses of multiple occupancy – one here and one in Londonderry – and a fire bomb at a Belfast hostel housing Somali and Afghan families.'

'Growing up here, though, I don't remember Ulster folks being less tolerant of ethnic minorities,' Malone opined. 'So, what's changed?'

'Well, you're right,' McKittrick said, 'It wasn't always like this. Racially-motivated violence has definitely been increasing over the last few years, so much so, it looks more like ethnic cleansing, to me. And attacks on the LGBT community are also on the rise, as you say. And people here have seen so much violence in the past, perpetrated under the badges of various para-military groups and sectarian dissidents, they've become inured to it. It's all too easy to shrug it off as gang violence. But we believe it's something more than that.'

'Yes,' the DI agreed, 'this is more than random street attacks and attacks on refugee hostels. It now looks like individuals from ethnic minorities are being abducted, taken out into the countryside, killed and disposed of. Dan's not exaggerating when he suggests it's ethnic cleansing. We've been liaising with the Salvation Army and the National Missing Persons' Helpline to find out how many *mispers* are from ethnic minority backgrounds. The numbers are greatly disproportionate to the number of ethnic Irish who go missing. It looks like the killers were using the old mother and baby home out at Shearwater Point as one of their dumping grounds, but it's possible there are more bodies buried elsewhere.'

'Sounds like you're looking at something significant, systematic and well-organised,' Malone said, ominously. 'Are you, by any chance, considering the involvement of Alternative Ulster in all this?'

'Yes, we are, Mike,' the DI said, 'We're looking at them very seriously indeed. We just need to know who they are and where they are.'

Chapter 33

Dom Caffrey was in good spirits as he headed along Victoria Street. Law Society House, home of Belfast's UK Passport Office, was a modern, glass-fronted building. He presented himself at the reception desk.

'Good morning. My name is uh … Killian Devereux. I've been called in for interview in connection with my British passport application. My appointment is at ten, so I'm a little early.'

The desk clerk checked the list of appointments and nodded.

'Ah, yes. I'll just let them know you're here. If you wouldn't mind waiting a wee minute,' he indicated a vacant seat and picked up the phone.

Clutching his file containing his Irish birth certificate and his American passport, Caffrey sat down and, as he waited, he thought over the reasons why he had decided to pursue an application for a British passport. He hadn't considered doing so initially as he hadn't seen what advantage there might be, especially since the UK was no longer part of the European Union. However, the more he had thought about it, the more he had come around to thinking that, in fact, it could well be advantageous.

He'd been weighing up the pros and cons of opening a branch office of his law practice in Belfast, and another down in the Republic of Ireland, to deal with the rights of people who had passed through the mother and baby homes on both sides of the Irish land border. He now thought that, if he had offices in Dublin and Belfast, why not open a London office, too? Caffrey's Boston law practice could then truly describe itself as an international firm. He could employ bright young legal minds, like that Aminullah Miah, for instance. Lawyers with knowledge of local law and practice would be very useful. Having a British passport might be conducive to that plan also. So far, he'd been too busy to look into the tax advantages, but he suspected there might just be some.

He thought it was ironic that Alice, his birth mother, had been deprived of so many of her rights, and yet here he was, her son, discovering rights and entitlements he hadn't known were his. It seemed right and proper that he should grasp those rights. So deep in thought was he that, at first, he didn't realise someone was calling his name – the name by which he was not used to being addressed.

'Mr Devereux. Mr DEVEREUX.'

Caffrey glanced up at the civil servant standing before him. Oddly, he saw there was a uniformed policeman standing there also. He rose to his feet. To his surprise, the policeman stepped forward and grasped him by the arm.

'Killian Devereux, or whatever your real name is, I am arresting you on suspicion of seeking to obtain an identity document with improper intention. You do not have to say anything, but it may harm your defence if you do not mention when questioned ….'

'Oh, no,' Caffrey groaned, 'not again.'

Half an hour later, upstairs in the passport office's interview room, Caffrey had explained, several times over, the reasons why he was using two identities and why he had applied for a British passport to add to his American and Irish ones. His interlocutors did not look convinced.

'I can assure you that I had no improper intention whatsoever. I understood that, having been born here in Northern Ireland, as Killian Devereux, I am entitled to a British passport. I am simply seeking to exercise that entitlement.'

'But you've submitted your form as a first-time application. You've crossed through the section requiring details of previous British passports held. You've written 'none'. However, a passport was issued to an infant Killian Devereux with the same date and place of birth. The passport was issued back in nineteen seventy-six, and there have been no further applications in between times. That suggests identity theft to me,' the passport officer insisted.

'But I didn't know I'd been given a British passport when I was a baby, not until you just told me. I'm guessing that first passport was issued so a US visa could be stamped in it. That was to enable me to go to America for adoption, and that's where I've lived ever since. I was born to an unmarried mother, Miss Alice Devereux, at the mother and baby home out at Shearwater Point, in County Down.'

The passport officer glanced again at his printed record.

'What was the name of the home?' he asked

'It was *La Mare doo Bon Pastooer.*'

The passport officer turned to the policeman.

'Well, that does appear on the original application. That application was indeed submitted by the home.'

'Yes,' Caffrey agreed. 'It would make sense that they would have applied for the first passport on my behalf. Then I was despatched to the States to join my adoptive parents.'

'That's not the only issue, though,' the policeman chipped in. 'If you really are Killian Devereux, then your name and date of birth are flagged up with Interpol. It seems you are wanted for questioning.'

Caffrey turned to the policeman.

'Ah, no, that's not me. I mean, you're right, someone has been using the Killian Devereux identity fraudulently, but it's not me. In fact, he's being investigated by your MIT cops over at Musgrave Street police station. They know me there, and Detective Inspector Sarah Lawrence there will vouch for me. She'll corroborate what I'm telling you. If you check with her, she'll tell you it's the guy who's using my birth identity who is the subject of the Interpol notice. I had some difficulties because of that when I applied for my Irish passport, as well.'

'Well, that sounds far-fetched enough that it just might be true,' the passport officer said. 'So, constable, do you have a number for MIT?'

Chapter 34

Mike Malone caught up with Carole and Dave as they sat in the sunshine outside a small café overlooking the harbour at Donaghadee. Once the waitress had taken their order for coffee and cakes, Malone began to update Carole on the progress in her uncle's case as the MIT detectives had related it to him.

'There isn't a lot of CCTV coverage around here, as you can imagine,' Malone explained, 'but a black BMW with three men in it was clocked on a couple of domestic security cameras as it sped past a couple of properties. It's not possible to see clear detail, or to be sure they were your uncle's killers, but the timing is about right, and a burnt-out, stolen BMW of the same model was found on the outskirts of Belfast later that night. There's no forensics, unfortunately.'

'Are you still thinking there might be a connection with that Alternative Ulster group?' Carole asked.

'We certainly can't rule them out. We've established that the gun that killed your uncle was also used to kill some of the bodies we found out at Shearwater Point. There's been an inordinately high number of abductions and murders of people from minority ethnic groups in Northern Ireland, and Alternative Ulster are reputed to be opposed to the idea of diverse communities. Forensic testing revealed that the adult bodies found buried at the former mother and baby home were all people born and raised overseas. It's likely they were victims of Alternative Ulster, and so was your uncle.'

'Sounds like they're not much different from all the other neo-Nazi groups around Europe,' Dave added.

'That's right, Dave, and some of these groups in Europe have been implicated in assassinating members of the judiciary and lawyers, which is another reason for thinking there's a connection between Alternative Ulster and the death of Carole's uncle.'

'So, are they any nearer finding this fake Killian Devereux character who's reputed to be the head of the organisation?' Carole asked.

'Well, they still don't know his real identity or what he looks like,' Mike said. 'Your uncle's murder is still being given high priority, naturally, but it would help if the police had sufficient resources to look at the wider picture. If they had more intel analysts looking at some of the other crimes they think may be down to Alternative Ulster, they might find evidence to identify who's in the organisation. As you know, that's often how the breaks occur. You crack a small case or two and that leads to cracking the bigger one.'

'Are MIT short on resources, then, Mike?'

'Not normally, but their big priority for the coming weeks – and ours, too – is going to be the US president's visit. He's flying in from London to address the legislative assembly at Stormont during his official visit, but then he's also undertaking a private family visit just over the border in Louth. It's a logistical nightmare, with us, Special Branch, and the British and Irish police forces all involved in security for the visit. It'll be a case of all hands on deck and all casework on hold.'

'Heaven preserve us from Americans checking out their Irish roots,' Carole grinned. 'Oh, and, speaking of which, did Caffrey's information about the Russky Obraz man's hotel bill being paid by a Mr Maharg turn out to be useful?'

'Well, the Europa receptionist has given us details of the account used to pay the bill, and it's that of a James Maharg. All I've had a chance to do is check out the name. There's no James Maharg known to us, and the police confirm no CRO and nothing adverse known on his address.'

'Caffrey said he'd seen the name Maharg recently, in another context, but he couldn't remember where,' Carole added.

'I'm sure Caffrey's well-intentioned, Carole, but he's certainly making work for us and the police, and also for the Human Rights Commission.'

'Is he? Why, what's he done?'

'He's only managed to get the historic abuse issues at the province's mother and baby homes tabled for the presidential discussions at Stormont. The Northern Ireland Office aren't too happy about that. Caffrey's mounting a one-man crusade over the issue. Seems he's got a lot of influential American adoptees on board, as well as the US President *and* the UN. I'm just awaiting a call from God.'

Carole smiled to herself.

'What does he seek to gain out of this?' Dave asked. 'Do you think he's going to be taking a cut out of any compensation pay out?'

'I'm not sure. I suspect his main motivation is personal. Then again, it wouldn't do his legal reputation and his business any harm if he's seen to successfully tackle such an emotive humanitarian issue, especially an issue with a trans-Atlantic remit.'

Just then, the waitress appeared with a tray on which were two very large cappuccinos, a pot of Earl Grey and three large scones with butter and strawberry preserve.

'Oh dear, Dave,' Malone grinned, as he took one of the very large coffee cups. 'This'll keep me awake all afternoon.'

Carole poured her tea whilst she took in all Malone had said.

'You know,' Dave grinned, his mouth full of buttery crumbs, 'this is the best scone I've ever had. How do they make them this good over here?'

'Buttermilk,' Carole said. 'That's your cholesterol shot through the roof, Dave. So, Mike, you won't mind if I give

153

Caffrey a call, will you? If he's conducting his own investigation, it might be worth me tapping into it – as a murder victim's relative, that is, not as an intel analyst.'

Seeing her husband's look of disapproval, Mike urged caution.

'It probably wouldn't do any harm to ask, but you will be careful, won't you, Carole? Your uncle's killers are clearly extremely nasty individuals, and Dave would never forgive me if any harm came to you.'

Carole thought better of telling them she had already met with Caffrey.

'Don't worry, either of you,' she reassured them. 'It's just one phone call. That can't hurt, can it?'

Chapter 35

Dom Caffrey was pleased with the outlook from his serviced short-let apartment on the ninth floor of one of Belfast's tallest buildings. He had a wonderful view over the River Lagan, and the internet signal was good. As a newly refurbished building, it had good sound insulation, too, so he was able to work undisturbed on his latest project.

He was pleased that his Boston-based associate, Brad Spence, had pulled out all the stops for him. Brad had secured the involvement of both an international anti-child trafficking organisation and a major pressure group whose aim was to make it easier for US citizens adopted from overseas to trace their birth families. Also involved was a well-funded, Boston-based group dedicated to challenging child abuses perpetrated by Catholic clergy and nuns.

Having enticed all these agencies on-board and achieved his main goal of getting the Northern Ireland Office to the discussion table with White House staff to re-consider the United Nations' recommendations, Caffrey felt he could now relax a little and have another look at his own family history research. Before he put them to one side, he took a last look through the images he had taken of the admissions register of *La Mère du Bon Pasteur* home. The names of the unfortunate young women made sad reading as he scrolled through the pages he had photographed and which were now uploaded onto his laptop. Some of the girls were so very young, he noted

One surname suddenly caught his attention. One of the girls who had passed through the home was a Marie Maharg. Of course, *that* was where he had seen that unusual surname before. As with his own mother's entry, there wasn't a great deal of information in the register, but he noted down the date on which Miss Maharg had given birth.

Having recently been informed by a more helpful clerk at GRONI that, for the princely sum of fifty-pence per name, he could conduct online searches of their indexes, he now logged on to the GRONI website and paid the fee with his Amex card. He proceeded to enter the search details for the Maharg infant born on the date shown in the admissions register.

There was only one Maharg birth record which came up in response to his search. The record was for a male child named James Maharg. The mother's maiden surname in the record was also Maharg, confirming that this James had most likely been born to an unmarried woman. Caffrey took out his mobile phone and called a number which he had now committed to his phone contacts list.

'Miss Murray? Dom Caffrey. This may be of no interest to you but, do you recall we spoke about that mysterious Mr Maharg, the man who paid the hotel bill of that Russian guy you were interested in? … Yeah, well I knew I'd seen that surname recently. I was just checking the photos I took of the admissions register for the home at Shearwater Point, and it looks like, back in the nineteen seventies, a young single girl gave birth there to an infant named James Maharg. If you think it's relevant, I could e-mail you all the images right now.'

Carole had been contemplating calling Caffrey, so it was a coincidence, perhaps even an omen, that he had suddenly decided to call her.

'Actually, I don't have access to my e-mails or a printer,' she told him. 'Would you e-mail them to an address I'll text you? It's that of a colleague of mine named Mike Malone.'

'Sure thing,' he assured her.

Ending her call with Caffrey, Carole immediately called Malone.

'Mike, it's Carole. Look, Dom Caffrey's just found something during his family history research which may be interest to you. He's found an infant birth for a James Maharg, born at *La Mère du Bon Pasteur* in the mid nineteen seventies. That baby is very likely to have been adopted. I guess most babies born there were given up for adoption. Well, I suppose it's just possible this is the same James Maharg who paid Ilya Kirasov's hotel bill. And, if this identity was stolen in the same way we think the Killian Devereux identity was, there could be more such stolen IDs. There could be more of them connected with Alternative Ulster… Yes, if it's okay, I'll text him your e-mail address and he'll send you details.'

Feeling pleased that she might have passed on information which could move the investigation on a little, Carole hung up and went into her aunt's kitchen to check out the contents of the fridge. Its meagre contents persuaded her she needed to visit the shops again. Checking that her aunt was happily chatting with Dave, she picked up Ellen's car keys, left the house and started up the Volkswagen. As she pulled out of the driveway, she noticed a blue Mazda with two occupants parked a little way along the coast road. She found nothing remarkable in this, since tourists, especially birdwatchers, occasionally stopped there to gaze at the sea and sky, the view being especially lovely at that point.

Continuing along the road, she arrived at the shops and parked near the Co-op. Entering the supermarket, she picked up some lamb chops and vegetables, a fresh loaf of bread and some milk and butter. As she emerged, she caught the irresistible aroma from Pooley's fish and chip shop just across the street. Deciding that cod and chips would make a good lunch with the bread and butter, she went in and joined the queue. As she leaned on the warm stainless steel counter top, awaiting her turn, she checked out her reflection in the large mirror at the back of the shop.

157

She saw something else reflected in the mirror. The blue Mazda was now parked up across the street. Perhaps bird-watching and sea gazing had given the tourists an appetite, she thought.

Leaving the chip shop, a little while later, with three warm parcels tucked into the crook of her arm, she waited to cross back over the road and, as she waited, she glanced casually left and right. Discreetly, she took in the appearance of the crop-haired driver of the Mazda and his younger passenger. She also clocked the car's index number. Climbing back into the Volkswagen, she took a pen from her handbag and wrote the car number on a corner of a fish wrapper then started up her engine.

Back at the house, she parked the car and walked back down the driveway to the gate to see if the blue Mazda had followed her home. There was no sign of the car, however. She told herself she was letting her imagination run away with her. The murder of her uncle had made her unduly wary, she decided.

Chapter 36

Ryan Donovan sat back and admired his handiwork. It had taken a lot of time and energy, and it had proved to be a most frustrating task, but he had at last succeeded in reassembling the many tiny shards of glass from the fire-bomber's Molotov. On the bench before him, there now stood an almost entire whiskey bottle, its hundreds of constituent parts reconstructed and adhering to the bottle-shaped plaster mould.

The largest pieces to have survived the damage almost intact, when the blazing petrol-filled bottle had broken, were the neck of the bottle and a chunk of the base. The latter had the letters 'shmi' embossed into the glass. It had not taken much imagination for Ryan to work out that the word moulded into the glass was the name of the distillery, and that the name would be 'Bushmills', makers of Northern Ireland's best-known brand of whiskey. He congratulated himself on having bought the right bottle to create his mould.

Also on the base, as Ryan's magnifier now revealed, were some traces of black ink. This was hard to see, owing to the sooty deposits on the glass, but he took the reconstructed bottle into the nearby dark room and subjected the base to various kinds of light. Eventually, he realised this was a production batch number which had probably been printed onto the glass at the time the bottle had been filled at the distillery. He duly copied out the number.

Next, he dusted the entire bottle for fingerprints. Unsurprisingly, nothing showed up on the crazed and splintered main body of the bottle. However, on close inspection, he spotted a partial print on the mainly intact neck of the bottle. To his trained eye, the print, though partial, represented the major part of a thumb print. He now took several photographs of the print, before lifting the impression from the glass, onto a piece of clear adhesive film which was then sealed down onto its backing paper and labelled.

Half an hour later, back in the Specialist Fingerprint Unit, Ryan found himself in front of the fingerprint comparator screen, looking at two thumbprint images, one partial and one which was complete. According to the Automated Fingerprint Identification System, the partial was a match for the complete thumbprint. Studying the points the two separate prints had in common, he nodded to himself, satisfied that AFIS had made an accurate identification.

A few more key presses on the adjacent computer, brought up the record of one Samuel John McClure. McClure's was the face of a man in his early twenties. That face wore the classic expression of defiance of the just arrested thug. Ryan had seen that same expression before in criminal records mugshots. It was often accompanied by the greasy, tousled, just dragged out of bed hair, or the scuffed forehead or bruised cheek sustained during the arrest. Always, though, there was that look of defiance, never defeat, always defiance.

Ryan noticed a couple of unexpected things about this particular criminal, besides the several arrests for violent assault. Firstly, he was surprised to note the subject's date of birth. This particular violent criminal was born in nineteen seventy-four. That would mean he would now be in his late forties, and yet there were no more recent criminal convictions listed. McClure's final conviction, however, had been for murder. In two thousand and one, he had been sentenced to fifteen years for a murder. The last note on the record showed he had actually been released in

160

two thousand and eleven, having served three quarters of his sentence. Ryan wondered why McClure, whose record suggested he was a cold-blooded killer, had not come to adverse notice since then. Perhaps he had gone straight. And yet, here was his thumb print on the neck of a bottle used to fire-bomb a restaurant.

It now occurred to Ryan that McClure could not be the bomber who had thrown the Molotov at the upmarket Indian restaurant. The hospitalised arsonist, who had been caught immediately after the act, was estimated to be only half this man's current age. So, if McClure hadn't thrown the bomb at Firoze's Fusion Diner, why was his thumbprint on the whiskey bottle? Could this mean that a different fire-bomber had been responsible for the burning of The Rainbow Room and for the deaths of Will and the other pub-goers? Were there two fire-bombers? Or had the hospitalised man committed both incidents, and possibly the burning of the Star of Bengal too, but the bottle had been supplied by McClure? Of course, it was possible McClure had nothing to do with the arson attacks. After all, the bottle could simply have been picked up from his trash. Maybe it was mere coincidence that the man whose discarded whiskey bottle had been used by a fire-bomber had a murder conviction himself.

Ryan stared hard at the face of the owner of that thumbprint. No, he told himself, there was definitely nothing innocent about that face. This was no coincidence. The other unexpected thing he saw in the mugshot concerned the subject's eyes. At first, he couldn't work out what was different about them. Then he scrolled down to the subject's physical description and there he found the explanation. Most unusually, it seemed Samuel John McClure had one blue eye and one green eye.

Chapter 37

Twenty-six-year-old news reporter Clare Topping had just completed her piece to camera in front of the long sweeping road that led up to the Stormont parliament building, and the film crew were just about to pack up when their sound man spotted a black Limousine approaching up Stormont Hill.

'Hey, look at that,' he said. 'It'd be great to get that in the backdrop, wouldn't it? It'd give an idea of how it'll look when the President's motorcade actually does arrive.'

'Yeah, that's great, Vince.' Clare agreed. 'Let's roll without sound. Just me looking to camera and the car passing us and heading up the hill. Okay?'

Every inch the professional, Clare stood still, a neutral expression on her face and the light breeze gently stirring her hair, as the camera rolled once again. The Limousine came into view and rolled slowly past the crew and on up the hill. The shot was perfect.

'And ... cut,' Clare's producer called out.'

The camera stopped rolling and Clare lowered her microphone, but, just at that instant, there was a loud retort. The crew whirled around to look at the trees behind them, from where the noise had apparently emanated. There was no-one to be seen. However, when they turned their attention back towards the parliament building, to their horror, they saw Clare lying, motionless on the ground.

Vince McAndrew, the sound man, dropped his boom and rushed forward. Dropping to his knees, he grasped Clare's hand. Deeply alarmed, he looked into her lifeless eyes.

'She's been shot!' he gasped. 'Clare's been shot! She's not breathing. Get help someone. For God's sake, get help!'

The main item to make the local news on that otherwise quiet Tuesday lunchtime wasn't Clare's routine piece on what route the US President's motorcade would take and how long he was expected to spend at Stormont. It wasn't even her explanation of the contentious issues Joe Biden and his team intended to raise once the talks began inside the parliament building. The main breaking news story was the shooting dead of this popular young television news reporter and the speculation as to what possible motive there could have been for her murder.

DS Dan McKittrick joined the forensics team who had completed their fingertip search of the area but who had found no evidence left behind by the sniper. The incident made no sense to him. His first thoughts were that the bullet had been intended for the occupant of the Limo but had hit the reporter by mistake. Then, he learned that the vehicle had been on its way to the parliament building to collect three Canadian trade officials who'd been attending a meeting at Stormont and who were to be taken back to their hotel. The Limousine had only the driver on board at the time of the shooting.

Given the distance involved, McKittrick reasoned a trained sniper must have been involved. His weapon would have had good sights. He would have seen exactly who was in the vehicle and who was filming on the pavement, and therefore it seemed unlikely that the wrong target had been shot. There had been no-one else on the spot apart from the reporter and her regular film crew. But who could have wanted this popular young woman dead? He cast an eye over the crew. They were clearly in shock. The one most affected seemed to be the sound man, Vincent McAndrew. McKittrick decided to speak to him first.

'This is my fault,' Vince faltered.

'How is it your fault?' McKittrick asked, gently.

'We were just about to pack up when I saw that Limo coming. It was my idea to take a wee bit more footage with the Limo in the background. If I hadn't suggested that, we might have been leaving. Clare wouldn't have been standing where she was.'

'There's no way that was your fault, Mr McAndrew. What we need to quickly establish is whether Miss Topping was the killer's intended target. Then we can begin to fathom out why she was killed and by whom. What can you tell me about her? Has she run any stories recently that might have upset anyone? She mainly does political stories, doesn't she?'

'Yes, she does,' Vince agreed. 'Oh, it's just tragic, so it is. The poor wee girl was about to get married, too. The wedding's set for June. Her fiancée will be devastated.'

'Her fiancé, what's his name?' McKittrick asked.

'She,' Vince corrected him. 'Fiona Walsh is her fiancée. She's on our production team back at the TV station. Oh, God. I don't know if anyone's called her. I'd better see ...'

As the victim's devastated colleague wandered off, clutching his mobile phone, McKittrick was thoughtful. So, the murdered woman's partner was female? Could her sexual preference have been a factor in her murder? Might this have been her killer's motive? Of course, there would be much delving to be done into her political reporting and into what grievances her past interviewees might have had. As with the assassination of Judge George Murray, there would probably be a long list of potential motives and suspects, but, at this stage, McKittrick decided he certainly wouldn't rule out anything.

Chapter 38

MI5's head of Counter-espionage, Adrian Curtis, joined his journalist friend Ronan Rogers at the latter's favourite bistro in St Thomas Street, not far from The News Building at London Bridge. *The Times* editor, Ronan, was already browsing the menu when Adrian arrived.

'Sorry I'm late, Ronan,' Adrian apologised. 'Been watching the footage of that young reporter shot over in Belfast.'

'Yes, outrageous,' Ronan put down the menu. 'In broad daylight and right outside Stormont. That poor girl. She was only in her twenties. Another black day for journalism.'

'What's the story behind it, do you know?' Adrian asked, as he checked the label on the bottle of red wine from which Ronan had already poured himself a glass. Adrian poured some into his own glass.

'I was hoping you chaps would know,' Ronan replied, raising his glass to his friend. 'Well, here's to a speedy resolution of the case.'

'Cheers,' Adrian clinked his glass against that of his journalist friend and took a welcome draught of the wine. 'Mmh, that's good.'

Adrian opened the menu and quickly scanned the daily specials insert.

'Ah, the Boeuf en Croute's back on the menu, I see. Would it be too unhealthy to have frites with that? What do you think?'

'I think you're holding back, Adrian,' Ronan chided.

'Yes, you're right. Frites it is, then.'

'No, I mean on the Clare Topping shooting. You know something, don't you?'

'I'm not sure I should say, Ronan. It's nothing absolutely concrete as yet ...'

'Now, don't be coy, Adrian. You know you want to tell me. And I'm prepared to run to a crème brûlée, as well.'

Adrian laughed. He knew this was just a little game between them, and he knew that Ronan knew this, too. Adrian would disclose the odd snippet of information which might, or might not be *entirely* accurate, but it would be an exclusive. It would also, of course, be unattributable. He would never give Ronan anything wholly untrue or likely to cause him embarrassment, but the publication of it would be a scoop for *The Times* and, at the same time, its disclosure would suit MI5's purposes.

'Sold to the man with the generous expense account,' Adrian joked. 'Well, intelligence suggests this may have been a dry run for something the bad boys have planned for the US President's Belfast visit. They may have been testing how easy it would be to deploy a sniper at Stormont, or, on the other hand, they may be intending to have us think that's where an attack *might* take place.'

'And you believe there will be an attack, but you don't think it will take place at Stormont?'

'That's right. I think it will happen near the border, when the presidential motorcade is heading down to County Louth. You see, that would serve to embarrass two governments at once, wouldn't it? We don't know which side of the border the attack may occur. It could be in County Down, or it could be in Louth. It's all very rural down there and there's a lot of countryside to police.'

'But it will be policed, I take it?' Ronan put down his glass, the better to concentrate on Adrian's disclosure.

'Well, you see, that's problematic.'

'How is it problematic?' Ronan's face fell.

'It's all to do with border protocols. You see, the Down and Louth border isn't just the border between the UK and the Irish Republic. It's the border between the UK and the

166

European Union. And the UK is now what the EU terms 'a third country'. It's all highly political. It was okay when we were in the EU and our police and the Irish police were a part of Europol. Nowadays, though, cross border co-operation between us and the one EU state we share a land border with – the Republic of Ireland – is a very sensitive issue.'

'Good Lord! I see what you mean.'

'Gone are the days when the police in Northern Ireland could work side-by-side with their Republic of Ireland counterparts on operations. It now needs all sorts of memoranda of understanding and EU orders in council. These issues have to be debated in Brussels. The enforcement agencies' hands are tied with red tape.'

'But, do you really think there might be an attack on Joe Biden? I mean, why?'

'Have you forgotten what year it is?'

'What do you mean?'

'This year sees the centenary of the implementation of the Irish Free State agreement. In nineteen twenty-two, the Anglo-Irish treaty was enacted. That treaty led to the partition of Ireland and to the creation of that very border. A hundred years down the line, it's still not acceptable to all affected parties. There's almost certain to be demonstrations, or perhaps worse.

'Oh, dear.'

'Yes, oh dear. The Irish-American lobby was heavily involved in Irish nationalism. Indeed, American dollars helped fund the Irish war of independence. Despite President Woodrow Wilson's reluctance to get involved, Irish-Americans encouraged it. In some quarters, the Americans are considered as much to blame for partition as the British.'

'So, what's to be done? *Can* anything be done?'

'Well, the MOD had a great idea recently. They proposed a bi-lateral treaty with the Irish – an agreement for us to share army, navy and air force resources to jointly patrol our respective land, sea and airspace. It was mainly intended to thwart the Russian incursions, of course. But the Cabinet Office Secretary and the Parliamentary Intelligence and Security Committee have suggested it be expanded to include the enforcement agencies, too, to combat cross-border crime.'

'Well, that sounds eminently sensible, Adrian. When will that be implemented?'

'It won't. It seems the PM isn't at all keen.'

'Why on earth not?'

'Thompson's inexplicably reluctant to upset the Russians. I imagine he also harbours a vain hope of doing trade deals with the EU. He knows the EU don't like individual states making bilateral agreements, and Brussels is still being difficult over the Northern Ireland protocol. I suspect he's prepared to sacrifice our national security and the safety of the US President simply to avoid upsetting Brussels and Moscow.'

'But that's ridiculous.'

'I know. It's a shame, because the Irish are very keen on the treaty. You see, if such a treaty were to be signed, they could then ask the EU for greater funding for their military and police in order to protect the EU's western borders jointly with us.'

'Do the western borders need protecting, Adrian?'

'Oh yes. the Russians aren't just a threat on the EU's eastern borders. They've been rattling their sabres ever since we sailed one of our warships into the Black Sea past the disputed Crimean Peninsula, in support of the Ukraine. They've stepped up their incursions into our waters and airspace. They've even got spy boats anchored over undersea communications cables off the Irish coast.'

'Good God!'

'Oh, yes. The treaty would be in everyone's best interests. Just think what could be achieved for us and the

Irish with closer co-operation between our intelligence and security agencies and theirs, our armed forces and theirs, our police and theirs. And the treaty has already been drafted. It just needs the PM to change his mind and sign it.'

'Or he needs someone to change his mind for him,' Ronan suggested.

The waiter appeared, ready to take their order.

'I'll have the Boeuf en Croute, please. And some frites. How about you, old man?' Adrian smiled, enthusiastically.

'Well, I think you and I have reached a bi-lateral agreement, Adrian. Same for me, please. And what about a side order of Vichy carrots and Brussels sprouts – just to keep the Europeans happy?'

Adrian smiled to himself. If there was one thing more satisfying than a splendid lunch, it was the prospect of getting one over on the bumptious oaf of a Prime Minister.

Chapter 39

Ryan Donovan walked into Cleery's Vintners and Spirit Dealers in Belfast's Donegall Place. The old-fashioned bell atop the shop door gave a nostalgic tinkle as he entered. Ryan gazed around at the floor-to-ceiling shelves of wine racks and attractive wine boxes. He imagined much of Cleery's business would be conducted via repeat orders placed online by local restaurants and hotels, since his research had confirmed that this long-established dealer handled both wholesale and retail sales. He produced his staff identity card.

'Good morning,' he smiled pleasantly. 'I'm with Forensics Northern Ireland. I'm here on a sensitive matter. Is there somewhere private we could speak?'

The surprised young salesman ushered Ryan into the back office.

'I've been tasked by HM Revenue and Customs to make some discreet enquiries in connection with their investigation into cross-border smuggling of dutiable goods, specifically whiskey produced here in the province.'

'Oh, yes?' the young man's curiosity was piqued.

'The production manager at Bushmill's whiskey distillery informs me that thirty-two crates of their sixteen-year-old single malt, bottles bearing this batch number, were delivered to you last month. Some of them have found their way into the Irish Republic without the import duty having been paid. Would you be able to tell me to whom those bottles were sold?'

The young man took the paper bearing the batch number from Ryan and turned to his computer.

'Yes, I should be able to print off a list of the customers who received bottles from that batch.'

Five minutes later, Ryan left the premises clutching the printed list. Happily, it wasn't as long a list as he had expected, but it was long enough. He would start tomorrow, with the hotels and restaurants based in the city and would establish how and where they disposed of their empties, before he checked out the more rural recipients of that particular batch of bottles. This was likely to be yet another protracted exercise and it might not lead to those behind the fire-bombings, but he had to try. For Will's sake, he had to try.

On his way back to the laboratory in Carrickfergus, Ryan pulled up on the seafront. He sat for some time, just gazing out to sea. On the horizon, a thin disc of grey cloud hung over the sea. As he watched, the cloud very gradually grew wider and darker as it drifted inland. He knew what that meant. There was rain on the way. That thought suddenly reminded him of his maternal grandfather, a retired seaman, who always said he could tell what the weather was going to do by checking the bunch of seaweed he kept hanging by the back door of their little house in Minorca.

Ryan recalled his grandfather explaining how it was that their tiny area of Carrick had the Spanish-sounding name of Minorca. It had been named in honour of Richard Kane, a Carrick man who, in 1712, was made Governor of Minorca, then a British-administered Spanish island. A man well respected, not least for his road building, he had been honoured by the naming by the islanders of one of his roads as *Camino du Kane*. Thus, the Spanish island and the little Antrim town were forever linked. Ryan had always loved to hear his granda tell him that little snippet of their neighbourhood's history.

He smiled to remember that his maternal grandfather had the implausible name of Albert Ross. Predictably, his fellow seafarers had always called him 'Albatross'. Some said he brought them good fortune; others felt he was a jinx.

171

Albert had survived a major shipwreck, however, when his shipmates did not. What was lucky for the albatross, then, was not so lucky for those who sailed with him.

Ryan had loved his eccentric grandfather, with his quaint ways and old-fashioned sayings. He had been devastated when Albert had passed away. Not so many years later, soon after Ryan had completed his university degree, his parents had both perished in a car accident. They had not lived to attend his graduation ceremony, but Will had been there for him. Now, he had lost Will, too. Ryan wondered if perhaps he, too, was an albatross. As he sat and gazed at the steadily darkening horizon, his eyes filled with salt water and his heart grew heavy with the extreme burden of his loss.

Chapter 40

Out at Donaghadee, Dave Lloyd, too, sat gazing at the horizon. Carole was seated on a garden chair next to his on the lawn in front of Aunt Ellen's house. The day was delightfully warm. Equally delightful was the sea view before them, despite the advancing cloud.

'It's going to rain, soon,' Dave warned. 'Look at that cloud.'

Dave reflected how, on their last visit to Donaghadee a year and a half earlier, he had found himself agreeing with Carole's suggestion that this would be a wonderful spot for them to retire to, when eventually they both decided to quit the Security Service. Now, however, glancing at the grey, stone steps where Carole's uncle had met his untimely and brutal death, he was not so sure. As charming as the Down coast was, and as reasonable as local property prices were, the suggestion had now lost a little of its appeal for Dave.

Ellen now joined them. She carried a tea tray. Dave rose to take it from her and placed it on the garden table. He was pleased to see that, in addition to the tea things, there were slices of buttered soda farl neatly arranged on a pretty china plate. He had never eaten soda bread before coming to Northern Ireland but he had developed quite a taste for it. The faded hand-painted shamrocks on the vintage Belleek china tea set were similar in design to the silk-embroidered shamrocks on the bedspread and curtains in the guest room he and Carole occupied. He guessed both items had been inherited and he could understand why they were cherished.

The house was indeed charming, and not just because of the beauty of its coastal setting and the fresh saltiness of the sea air. There was also an indefinable atmosphere about the place. It was light, airy and timeless. There was an old,

173

weathered sledge in the porch on which the milkman left their daily bottles of the full cream milk which came no further than a couple of miles from the local dairy. Carole had recounted Christmas holiday adventures when the sledge had been used for its intended purpose, whenever snow had come to the Mournes.

The fishing tackle and keepnets on the hallstand, the tennis racquets in the understairs cloaks and boot cupboard, and the stack of children's annuals stashed in the kitchen dresser, along with the boxes of draughts, dominoes and monopoly, all spoke of happy times. These were the tangible symbols of Carole's golden childhood. He could see why Carole loved the place, and why she would love to live here. He knew her roots were here, and so were Ellen's. He knew that he, too, could put down roots here, if it were not for the underlying danger he felt was still present.

However, uprooting Ellen and bringing her to live in their comfortable but small London flat did not seem like a viable alternative. Yet, given her fading memory and the fear that, soon, she might be too forgetful to look after herself, something would have to be done. Arrangements for her care would have to be made. But how unkind it would be to remove her from all this – from the familiarity of her home and neighbours, from this pretty house which held such happy memories for her, albeit that those memories were slowly deserting her. Whatever, they decided to do, Dave knew it was going to be a tough decision.

Carole poured their tea and was offering Dave the soda bread when her mobile phone rang. She saw the call was from Mike Malone's mobile, so she stepped away down the path towards the front gate to take the call. It was just possible that what she and Mike would discuss was something she might not want her aunt to overhear. As she reached the gate, she spotted the blue Mazda again, parked up on the coast road.

She took in the information Malone had to impart and thanked him for it. It crossed her mind to ask Malone to check out the registration number of the Mazda, but, on quick reflection, she decided not to.

Once she had ended the call, she noticed the Mazda had gone. She returned to the table to drink her tea.

'That was Mike,' she told Dave.

'Any news?' Dave asked.

'Those images I sent him – you know, Caffrey's list of names from the admissions register at the Shearwater Point home.'

'Yes?'

'He's traced the birth identities of a significant number of babies born to women whose details appeared in the home's register and he's cross checked them on a variety of databases. Seems a few British passports were issued in those identities. Yet the babies were all sent to the States for adoption soon after birth.'

'Wouldn't they have issued passports to the babies so they could get US visas and travel to join their adoptive families?'

'They did, but these are subsequent issues to adult males. The applications were made some thirty to forty years later. And those applications weren't from people living in the US. They were from applicants living here in Northern Ireland. An application for a British passport was made in the Killian Devereux identity just a few days ago, but that one was made by the real Devereux – by Dominic Caffrey.'

'Didn't anyone at the Identity and Passport Agency think it unsatisfactory to have such a gap between all these passport applications?'

'Well, perhaps not. After all, the birth certificates presented in support of the latest passport applications were original birth certificates, the ones issued soon after birth. They'd been stolen from the adoption authorities' files, but the thefts were not noticed at the time. The IPS staff only really get suspicious about an application when the birth certificate is one which has been issued very recently.'

'Sounds like you were right, then. It's a major identity theft racket. What's Mike doing about it?'

'He's got the police looking at electoral registers, driving license applications, bank accounts. Dan McKittrick's red-flagged the identities in case they come to light. If one of them so much as jumps a red light, he'll get to hear about it.'

'Does Mike think one of them might be your uncle's killer?'

'He says he'd give it fair odds.'

Dave gave Carole's hand a gentle squeeze and nodded in the direction of her aunt. Ellen hadn't been listening. Mercifully, she was gazing out to sea and she was smiling contentedly.

Chapter 41

The spring rain beat against the glass of the sash window and ran down in stuttering rivulets. The skies over Belfast were grey and unseasonably cold. Hughie grabbed the bottle of Bushmills from his bedside table and reached across Eileen to pour some more into her glass.

'Oh, no more for me,' she protested. 'I'll have to be getting home soon.'

'Ah, go on. Sure, it's cosy in here. You don't wanna be going out in that rain.'

'Have to. The boys'll be back soaked and starving from football practice soon, and I'll need to get something out of the freezer for Doug's supper.'

'You sure you don't want another wee one for the road?'

Eileen was naked. She swung her slim legs over the side of the bed and felt around on the bedside rug for her bra. She put it on and gathered up the rest of her underwear and her uniform shirt and trousers.

'Will the boss man not miss his best whiskey, then?' she asked as she quickly dressed.

'Ach, he has plenty more. Sure, he orders it by the case. He's not gonna miss the odd bottle.'

'How the wealthy live, eh? You've never said how he makes his money?'

Hughie shrugged.

'Well,' she pushed, 'I don't suppose he'd tell you, would he? You're just his driver and errand boy.'

'That's what you think.'

'By the look of this place, he doesn't pay you much. And you with all your army skills. You'd have earned more if you'd joined the police. And you'd be guaranteed a pension.'

'Like I say, that's what you think. He pays me well enough for what I do.'

'I very much doubt that, Hughie. He's clearly worth a lot, and he doesn't even trust you to know what his business is.'

'I know all I need to know. He's an importer of certain commodities, and a very successful one. And I help him with distribution. That's all *you* need to know.'

Hughie poured a generous amount of whiskey into his own glass. Eileen sat on the edge of the bed to put on her shoes. He leaned over towards her and ran his fingers down the centre of her back. She tensed and turned to look at him.

'Has anything been mentioned about Alistair?' he asked.

She turned away and finished buttoning up her shirt.

'They haven't identified him yet. His fingers were badly burned when he tried to beat out the flames, so there wasn't much left to fingerprint. While he was alive, they were busy trying to treat his burns. Now that he's dead, though, they'll probably concentrate on trying to ID him. You'll need to be careful they don't connect him with you.'

'I'm sure I can rely on you for an alibi, can't I?'

Eileen rounded on him.

'No, you damn well can't! Doug has a terrible temper on him. If he knew about us ...'

'Chill out, Eileen. He won't find out from me. Don't you worry. Are you sure you have to go so soon? The sight of a woman in uniform really gets my motor going.'

He took another mouthful of the whiskey and, sliding back down under the bed clothes, he stretched out lazily and ran a hand over his close-cropped hair.

Eileen didn't answer. She stood up and stepped across to check her appearance in the mirror on the dresser. Tidying her hair with her fingers, she glanced at the framed photograph on the dresser. The photo was of Hughie in his former para's uniform.

'You didn't keep *your* old uniform then?' she asked.

178

'If I did have it, would that entice you back to bed?' he grinned.

She paused for a moment, then she glanced at the watch on her wrist and picked up her jacket and handbag. Taking out her car keys, she shook her head.

'No, I really have to get going.'

She crossed to the bedroom door, opened it and paused to look back at him.

'Bye, lover.'

'Bye, Mrs O'Neill,' he winked mischievously.

Chapter 42

Coffee in hand, Ryan followed Harpreet into the Specialist Fingerprint Unit.

'What's that you're working on?' he asked, as she brought up on screen the enlarged fingerprint image.

'It's a couple of partials.'

'Which case?' he asked.

'Suspicious death up at the Royal.'

'Oh, yeah?' he said, casually, trying not to sound unduly interested.

He shuffled a few papers in his own file and sipped at his coffee whilst his colleague gazed at the twin screens of the fingerprint comparator. After what seemed like an age, he finally heard the printer whirr into life. The sound told him Harpreet had identified the owner of the fingerprints. She took the print-outs and left the room.

Ryan remained, sipping his coffee and waiting around until a decent amount of time had passed before he followed her back to the main lab. He would wait. It didn't matter how long he had to wait. She would need to visit the ladies' room sooner or later. He would wait for her to leave, then he would find the print-outs in her file and quickly photocopy them before she returned.

Half an hour passed, but Harpreet seemed too engrossed in her work to even contemplate her own immediate physical needs. Eventually, however, she stood up.

'I'm gonna make some tea, Ryan. Can I get you one?'

'Yes, please,' he smiled and handed her his mug. 'Can I be a nuisance and ask you to give it a quick rinse? I had coffee in it and I've let it go cold.'

'Sure,' she smiled.

To his great relief, she set off for the kitchen with his mug and hers.

An hour later, his tea long consumed, Ryan had put together a full profile of the young arsonist who had been suffocated at the Burns Unit, and whom Harpreet had identified from the partial fingerprints. There was a list of his priors from his CRO, his mugshot, his last known home address and as much information as Ryan had been able to glean from the young man's social media accounts. Ryan now knew where Alistair Henry had liked to eat out, which football team he had supported and, more importantly, perhaps, who his friends and associates on social media were.

Chapter 43

It was raining in London, too. However, at Number Ten Downing Street, it wasn't the weather which had upset the prime minister.

'Fucking bloody hell!' Ivan Thompson cursed as he slammed his copy of *The Times* down onto his press secretary's desk. 'How the hell did they get hold of this?'

Joy Cooper grabbed the paper and quickly scanned the front-page story, whilst the Prime Minister continued to splutter and rage.

'They've managed to link that half-baked MOD treaty I wouldn't sign with the security for Joe Biden's visit. And they didn't even clear the story with us before they went and got a response from the European Defence Agency.'

'Well, surely that's helpful, isn't it?' Joy said. 'I mean, the EDA say we can't do it. They won't allow Ireland to sign a bi-lateral agreement with us. And you didn't want them to, did you?'

'No, of course I didn't. But tomorrow we'll have all the tabloids screaming *'how dare the EU tell the British PM what he can and can't do'*. I'll be expected to stand up to them over the issue. It's bad enough that the Americans are in favour of the treaty. They're using it as a bargaining chip in our trade talks with them.'

'But do the Irish want it?'

'Of course they do. Under that treaty, they'd get the use of our intelligence, our planes, our ships, and all for free. And joint policing has been dragged into the equation as well.'

'But, Prime Minister, what about your defence spending plan? You can ask for even more money if you have to help defend Ireland as well. And you'd already said you were going to recruit twenty thousand more police officers.'

'I know what I *said*, Joy. But the plan was to recruit to fill *existing* vacancies in the police, not to increase their numbers. It was only supposed to *look* like an increase. And the defence spending was going to be on nuclear stuff, not boots on the ground or ships in the Irish sea. But who the hell could have leaked this?'

Joy thought for a few moments before suggesting a possible culprit.

'Well, presumably it would have been someone inside government. Or, maybe it was leaked by someone who used to be here in Number Ten and who had knowledge of the proposal, but who isn't here any longer. Someone who's disgruntled, disaffected. Someone who might have an axe to grind or a score to settle?'

'What? Well, who?'

'Well,' she ventured cautiously, 'there's Malcolm Donald.'

Thompson immediately drew breath to dismiss her suggestion, knowing there had been no love lost between Joy, his press secretary, and Malcolm, his former special advisor. Why would she think it was Malcolm Donald? After all, Malcolm had been dead set against the defence treaty with Ireland. He'd cautioned against confronting the Russians and had persuaded Thompson that the Chinese were the ones to watch, not the Russians. But it suddenly occurred to him that she might just be right, and so he didn't rush to refute the accusation.

It now occurred to him also that Malcolm hadn't been happy to have lost his position of power within Number Ten. He was a devious bastard and he might just have it in for Thompson. Malcolm had publicly accused the PM's fiancée, Sally Austin, of influencing his fall from grace. He had also blamed Sally's friends and allies within Number Ten, and chief amongst those allies was Joy Cooper. Thompson recalled how Malcolm had habitually sought to denigrate his press sec by referring to her as 'Mini Cooper'. However, whilst Joy would have strong personal reasons to attribute blame to Thompson's former special advisor, that didn't mean she was wrong.

In fact, the more he thought about it, the more he thought she probably was right. It now occurred to him that any act of revenge on Malcolm Donald's part, some of which would be aimed at his press secretary, was bound to involve leaking something to the press, and what better issue to leak than something on which he and Malcolm had been in agreement? That way, Malcolm could disclaim responsibility for the leak. Thompson could already hear Malcolm bleating *'why would I risk upsetting the Russians by disclosing that we even considered engaging in joint patrols with the Irish? I was the one who told you it would be a bad idea.'*

Yes, it made sense that Malcolm would be the source of the leak. Malcolm was a tricky character and he would never have gone down without a fight, without seeking revenge. Thompson nodded to himself. Joy was indeed right. And to think that he had even made Malcolm head of MI5, and in the face of fierce opposition from the Cabinet Secretary, Sir Henry Mortimer. Henry had been right, too, of course. That appointment had been a grave mistake. Thompson had once thought Malcolm his most loyal supporter. It had taken a long time for him to realise it, but he now knew that Malcolm Donald had only ever been on Malcolm Donald's side.

Just then, the phone on Joy's desk rang. She answered it, then covered the mouthpiece with her hand and glanced towards the Prime Minister.

'It's the White House press office,' she announced. 'They want to know our response to *The Times*' article, and they ask if we are reconsidering our position on the joint defence treaty? The President would like to know.'

'Fucking bloody hell!' Thompson exploded again.

Chapter 44

The rain had cleared up overnight and the morning sun shone down again on Belfast's busy streets as Dom Caffrey emerged from St George's Market clutching the large paper cup of coffee and plate of buttered toast from one of the market's café stalls. Sitting at one of the pavement tables, he ate his breakfast whilst perusing the newspaper he had also just purchased. He had picked it up with a view to seeing what films might be on television later that evening. He didn't want to eat dinner out every night and so he thought he might buy a few items in the market for a little TV supper back at the apartment.

He began reading *The Times*' main story. He didn't really have any great interest in the Brits' opposition to a joint defence treaty with the Irish, but one part of the article caught his eye. It was the mention of a Russian submarine having sunk a fishing trawler near Ardglass. He recalled having seen Ardglass on his map. He realised that wasn't too many miles from the pretty spot on the County Down coast that had been his own birthplace.

Caffrey began wondering what Russian subs would even be doing in the Irish Sea. It made little sense to him. Then again, why would that Russian who was staying at the Europa Hotel have gone to stay at Shearwater Point? He was suddenly put in mind of an old film, *Ryan's Daughter*. He had watched it as a young man interested in the Irish struggle for independence from the British. What now came to his mind, however, wasn't the politics behind it all, but the bit in the film where guns and ammunition had been landed on Irish shores, apparently from a German U-boat.

He began to wonder if that's how the arms he had chanced across at Shearwater Point had got there.

Of course, he reasoned that it wouldn't be the Germans providing arms to the Irish subversives. Perhaps those Russian subs sneaking up and down the Irish Sea, weren't simply spying on the British and testing their response capabilities, as the press suggested. Maybe they were landing munitions, just as the Germans did a century earlier? His thoughts turned to Carole Murray, the lady whose uncle had been murdered. She had been interested in that Russian. What was his name? Kirov? No, Kirasov. Might Kirasov have had something to do with the weapons in that basement at the old mother and baby home? Caffrey didn't really have a clue what was going on, yet he sensed there was something more to all of this.

As tragic and shocking as the discovery of the infants' remains at Shearwater Point had been, the publicity which had arisen out of that grisly find had helped him get the issue of cruelty and human exploitation at the maternity homes tabled for discussion by the US President. The uncovering of those remains could not have been better timed, as far as Caffrey's quest was concerned. But could there be something even more sinister going on out at Shearwater Point, something involving guns and Russians? Although deep in thought, he suddenly became aware that someone was waving to him from across the street. One of the taxi drivers parked up outside the Hilton Hotel was waving to him from his open car window. It was Joe Doyle.

Leaving his newspaper on the table, Caffrey stepped across to speak to Joe.

'Morning, Dom. How's things?' Joe greeted him warmly.

'Grand, Joe. How are you, and how's business?'

'Aye, things are picking up now the tourist season's in full swing. Are you still at the Europa?'

'No. I decided to stay on in Belfast for a few more weeks, so I've rented an apartment down by the river. Say, Joe, I don't suppose you could find out something for me, could you?'

'Depends what it is.'

'Last week, a Russian businessman named Kirasov took a taxi from the Europa out to Shearwater Point. I'd like to know what address he went to. Would it be too much trouble for you to ask around in case one of the other drivers recalls taking him there?'

'Kirasov? No problem, Dom.'

'That'd be great, Joe. Here, let me give you my business card, it includes my cell phone number.'

'Do you still have my number, Dom? Only I'll be happy to take you anywhere you need to go.'

'I do, indeed, Joe.'

Meanwhile, twenty miles away, the man who, for the past eleven years, had been living as Killian Devereux, was also contemplating having breakfast. He had just made his first cup of coffee and had taken it out onto the terrace when the doorbell rang. Fastening the belt on his dressing gown, he went to the front door and glanced through the spyhole. A slim, fair-haired young man was standing there. Opening the door, he saw the caller held, between his white cotton gloved hands, what appeared to be a bottle wrapped in tissue paper.

'Mr Devereux?' Ryan asked.

'Yes.'

'I'm from Cleery's, the spirit dealers. There may have been a wee problem with your last delivery.'

'Oh, yes?'

'Seems we've been having a bit of pilfering at our warehouse and some of our customers have found their boxes were a bottle short.'

'Oh?'

'Yes. We've no way of knowing whose orders were short, as not everyone has opened their boxes just yet, so, just in case yours was one of the orders pilfered, we'd like you to accept this with our deepest apologies.'

Devereux unwrapped the bottle proffered and saw it was a bottle of his usual Bushmills sixteen-year-old single malt.

'Oh, well, since you mention it, I believe I was a bottle short in the last box. I thought mebbe the cleaner had whipped it. Well, thank you very much, son.'

'And Cleery's thanks you for your continued custom, sir,' Ryan smiled and held Devereux's gaze just long enough to take in the sleep-filled eyes – one being blue and the other green.

As Devereux closed the door and returned to his coffee, Ryan stood on the doorstep for a moment, glancing around at the property and grounds. There appeared to be no security cameras, not even a doorbell-activated one, just a peephole in the wooden front door. He supposed the remoteness of the location and the lack of any neighbouring properties was security in itself. This, he told himself, was no fortress. It was the home of someone who never expected to be targeted. It was the home of a Cleery's customer who went by the name of Devereux. It was the home of Samuel John McClure, the man whose CRO mentioned his unusual eyes.

As Ryan walked back to his car, he saw there were two other vehicles parked in the drive. One was a Mercedes saloon. The other was a white transit van. As he climbed into his car, he saw another vehicle arrive at the property and pull up in the driveway. Ryan took his time starting up his engine and fastening his seat belt as he watched, via his rear mirror. He observed the well-built, crop-haired man in his late thirties, step out of the car and let himself into the house with his own key.

Ryan picked up his notebook and pen from the front passenger seat. Crossing through the list of Cleery's remaining customers, for he now knew he'd found the owner of the thumb-print found on the petrol bomb, he wrote down the index number of the crop-haired man's metallic blue Mazda. He also recorded the index numbers of the Mercedes and the transit van. Glancing at his watch, he rolled down the driveway, turned out onto the coast road and headed off back towards Carrickfergus, stopping only to buy petrol on the way.

Chapter 45

Tomasz Bartosz was weary as he got off the train at Belfast's Sydenham station. He actually hated working the nightshift, but the money was good and it fitted in well with his wife Anna's nursing shifts at the hospital. He would be glad to get home, take off his security guard's uniform and climb into bed. He glanced at his watch. It was twenty to nine. Normally, he'd be getting home shortly after eight in time to see Anna and have a coffee with her before she set off walking their girls to the local Catholic primary school. This week however, he had to travel by train, and his journey home took him longer than usual. He hoped the car would be back in action next week. He also hoped that, once it was repaired, it wouldn't suffer any further damage by vandals.

As he passed along the row of red-brick terraced houses, each one very much like his own, he thought how lucky he was to live in such a nice neighbourhood. The houses in this part of east Belfast were small and modest, but his street was tree-lined and it was conveniently located for the station, the park and the local shops. The neighbours were lovely, too. The mortgage re-payments had been a little more than they had hoped to pay, but he decided it was worth it to be able to bring up his daughters in a safe place. He didn't have to worry about Anna coming home alone after a late shift, either. At least, he hadn't needed to worry until quite recently.

As he turned into Invercastle Avenue, a car came racing past him. He thought the driver was being a bit reckless to be tearing through the residential estate at such a speed when there were children walking to school. He looked at his watch again. It was ten to nine. He supposed the two men in the car must be really late for work. The metallic blue Mazda disappeared off in the direction of the by-pass. As Bartosz approached the far end of his avenue, he suddenly saw smoke coming from one of the houses. His heart sank as he realised it was from his own end of the block.

His first thought was for his next-door neighbour. Seventy-four-year-old Jimmy Clancy was a very heavy smoker. 'Smokin'll be the death of me, Tommy,' Jimmy often joked to his Polish neighbour. Bartosz feared he might be right one day, for the old chap was careless in his habits and a little forgetful, too, these days. As he drew nearer, however, he saw it wasn't Jimmy's house which was on fire, but his own. He ran even faster and, as he reached his two bedroomed end-of-terrace, he saw the fierce, black smoke pouring out of the broken front window.

In his panic, he struggled to get his key to turn in the front door lock. As he managed to push the door open, he was met by a thick pall of acrid fumes. Holding his handkerchief over his nose and mouth, he raced in, calling out Anna's name. He searched from room to room, but was relieved to realise she and the girls were not there. Mercifully, they had already left for school. The fire had already taken a firm hold though, and he realised there was nothing he could do. He made his way outside again and took out his mobile phone to call the fire brigade.

He met Jimmy out on the pavement.

'Tommy,' the elderly man shouted, 'Anna and the weans, are they in there?'

'No, Jimmy, they're not. They're at the school.'

'Oh, thank God. I've already called nine-nine-nine. They're on their way.'

The fire engine was there within ten minutes, though it seemed a whole lot longer to Bartosz. Jimmy did his best to console him whilst the firemen got to work and the blaze

191

was soon extinguished, but they could see the extent of the damage the fire had caused. Soon Anna appeared running back down the street. She ran into her husband's arms. She didn't ask what had happened. She didn't need to. They both knew. A couple of weeks earlier, a brick had been thrown through their kitchen window in the middle of the night whilst they were sleeping. Then, a few days later, the car had been vandalised overnight, its windscreen and headlights smashed and some sort of corrosive liquid poured over the paintwork. And now this.

Bartosz remembered the graffiti someone had scrawled on the plywood he had used to board up the broken kitchen window temporarily. 'For locals only', it had read. The message had been clear. Not all the locals were as lovely as the neighbours on his own block. There were some people who wanted them out. It didn't matter to them how many people Anna had nursed back to health, and at great risk to herself during the Coronavirus pandemic. Nor did anyone care that Tomasz Bartosz worked long hours as a security guard at the same hospital. They were Polish, and, just because they were Polish, somebody wanted them out.

Looking in at the charred furniture, most of which was not yet paid for, Anna began to sob. Her husband held her tightly.

'Come youse into my house,' Jimmy urged them gently, 'and I'll make us a nice pot of tea.'

Chapter 46

At Thames House, MI5 Director General Helena Fairbrother appeared in the Counter-espionage section and made a beeline for Adrian Curtis's office. He was glad he had just put away his newspaper and had files spread out on his desk instead. Usually, he received the royal summons to see Helena upstairs in her office. It was less usual for her to come down to see him. He decided it must be something important which had brought her downstairs.

'Good morning, Helena,' he smiled. 'How are you, this morning?'

Helena's smile was even broader than his and her eyes flashed with delight. It suddenly put him in mind of a time, a very long time ago, when she had always looked at him with excitement in her eyes. Of course, things were different now. Their relationship could never have survived her rapid promotion. He wondered if, these days, someone else was putting the fire into those brown eyes of hers, or was this momentary delight simply the result of a work triumph?

'I'm very well indeed, thanks, Adrian. Not sure the same could be said for our illustrious leader, though.'

'Oh dear. Has something upset the PM?'

Adrian's tone was one of mock concern. He knew very well what would have upset the Prime Minister, and he knew that Helena knew it had been Adrian's doing.

'You could say, that. Apoplectic would be the word to describe his mood.'

'Oh dear.'

'It was most unfortunate that *The Times* got wind of that Anglo-Irish defence treaty.'

'Mmh,' he nodded.

'And even more unfortunate that they tied it in with security concerns over Joe Biden's visit to Northern Ireland.'

'Mmh.'

'And now it looks like the treaty's back on the table again. Thompson's arranged another meeting between our Defence Minister and his Irish counterpart.'

'Sir John will be pleased, then.'

'I'm quite pleased myself, Adrian. The Home Secretary's been asked to send police officers from three UK mainland forces over to Northern Ireland on temporary detached duty. It's to cover the President's visit. And that's not all. He wants additional Security Service staff sent over as well. They're to go immediately to augment the intelligence effort at our regional office at Holywood.'

'Brilliant!'

'Mike Alford's agreed to send a couple of his Counter-terrorism people. Can you spare anyone?'

'Well, as it happens, Helena, I've got two of my staff over there at the moment.'

'Have you? Who?'

'Carole Murray and Dave Lloyd are taking leave over in County Down. Carole went to arrange an uncle's funeral and Dave is on annual leave. In fact, they're staying less than half an hour's drive from our Holywood office.'

'Excellent. Well, if they're happy to stay on, tell them they're no longer using up their leave allowance. They're on detached duty and on full subsistence rates. Now, is there anything else happening in the province that I should be aware of?'

'Well, yes, as a matter of fact there is. I'm sorry to say that Carole's uncle didn't die of natural causes. He was gunned down on his own doorstep.'

'Oh my God! That's awful. Do they know who did it, and why?'

'Not yet. Seems he was a retired member of the judiciary and he'd put away a lot of bad boys during the troubles. Could be any number of suspects. Local MIT are all over it, according to Carole. Also, Harry Edwards is liaising with our Holywood office, because a Russian who's flagged up by us as a person of interest has recently pitched up in Belfast.'

'Who's that?'

'Ilya Kirasov. A major operator in Russky Obraz, one of the worst of the neo-Nazi outfits. Remember the lawyer's head in the Moscow trash can affair?'

'Good God! Why the hell are Russky Obraz interested in Belfast?'

'Probably extending Putin's ultra-right network. Mike Malone over at our Belfast office is looking into it and Harry Edwards is liaising with him.'

'Is there any connection between Kirasov and the murder of Carole's uncle?'

'I shouldn't have thought so. If there is, though, Mike and Harry will find it.'

'Okay. Keep me in the picture, won't you? I'll be down at The Fort for the next few days but I'll be contactable there if you need to call me.'

'At The Fort?' Adrian queried.

He was familiar with MI6's training facility down on the south coast and indeed, had been there several times himself for conferences and high-level meetings, but he wondered what it was that would take his own DG there for a stayover.

'Yes, Bob Vanbrugge and I are giving a joint talk to some Allied Services personnel. You know the kind of thing, inter-agency co-operation, resource-sharing, threat analysis.'

'Well, you'll have nice weather for it.'

Helena mentioning her MI6 counterpart, Sir Robert Vanbrugge, caused Adrian to wonder if there might be

195

something going on between them. After all, Vanbrugge was a good-looking chap in his mid-fifties, always immaculately groomed and expensively dressed. Adrian didn't know whether there was a Lady Vanbrugge. He didn't know very much at all about the head of the Secret Intelligence Service, other than the fact that he and Helena seemed to get on very well, especially when it came to presenting a united front to stand up to Downing Street. He felt a sudden twinge of something akin to jealousy. He also felt, as he often did, a measure of regret over what might have been.

He couldn't believe, though, that he had just blurted out a comment about the weather. How pathetic that must have sounded. He supposed he'd intended it to cover his real reaction. Perhaps, though, he was reading too much into Helena's visit to Monckton Fort. It wasn't as though she and the sartorially elegant MI6 head were spending a weekend in Paris in a luxury hotel. This was an MOD establishment with pleasant and perfectly adequate residential accommodation, but it wasn't, so far as he could recall, the sort of place one would choose for a romantic getaway.

Of course, there was a bar, and some very acceptable wines were available, and he knew that Helena, once the love of his life, who was so upright and professional in the workplace, could nevertheless throw off her inhibitions under certain circumstances. Adrian reminded himself, however, that he was happily married, and Helena was happily single. He had no right to wonder what romantic attachments she might have. He hadn't had that right in a long time, not since the days when he and Helena had been at the same point on the pay scale.

'You've been to The Fort, haven't you?' she asked.

'Oh yes, several times over the years. Nice golf course down there at Stokes Bay.'

He winced. Now he had added a comment about sport to his observation about the weather. How feeble was that? He bit his lip. *'Shut up, Adrian!'* he thought, *'before you make a complete arse of yourself.'*

In the outer office, the phone rang suddenly and Harry Edwards answered it.

'Carole, how are you? And how's your aunt?' Harry smiled, pleased to hear from his colleague. He hadn't forgotten how kind Carole had been when his fiancée Lorna had been killed. But for Carole's kindly ministrations, he would have fallen apart. Now, it was Carole who had suffered a sudden and tragic bereavement.

'I'm fine,' Carole assured him, 'and Aunt Ellen's as well as can be expected, under these awful circumstances. But could I ask you to do me a favour, Harry?'

'Of course. Anything at all. You know you only have to ask.'

'I'd like a DVLA check on a car index number. I may be imagining things, but I've seen this blue Mazda a few times over the past couple of days and I think it might be following me. I'd ask the local police here to check it out, but it might just turn out to belong to one of their guys. You know, they might be watching to make sure no harm comes to us, and I wouldn't want to embarrass them by letting them know I've spotted it.'

'No problem. Do you want to hold or shall I call you back?'

'No urgency, Harry. Here's the number…'

Harry noted down the number and hung up. It was around ten minutes later when he called Carole back.

'Hi Carole. Yeah, that car, the blue Mazda. It's registered to a Hugh McCalmont at fourteen Lissadell Street, Belfast. Before that, it was owned by the Ministry of Defence. MOD often give their own staff the first option to buy their redundant vehicles, so I checked with MOD and they confirmed McCalmont is ex-army, a former para and a trained sniper, in fact. He served in Kosovo. His unit also did a couple of tours in Northern Ireland. He was based at Palace Barracks in Holywood. Isn't that where our Northern Ireland branch is?'

'Yes, it is.'

'So, he'll be familiar with that location. However, nothing adverse is known about him. No CRO or anything.'

'Okay. Thanks, Harry. That sounds reassuring … I think.'

Chapter 47

Caffrey was pleased at the response to the articles he had placed in the Irish and Northern Irish press. Having learned that infants born at the Shearwater Point home had also been sent to England for adoption, he had copied his article to the *Liverpool Echo*, the *Birmingham Post*, Glasgow's *The Herald*, and the *Manchester Evening News.* These, he had been advised, were widely read in UK cities with the largest concentration of Irish readers. He had sent it also to *The Guardian*, which he understood was a major national newspaper with a social liberalism ethic. From *The Guardian*, his piece seemed to have been even more widely syndicated.

He had written his emotive feature from the perspective of the adoptee who, no matter how improved his lot may have been by overseas adoption, had been denied the fundamental right to know his biological parents and to discover his true ethnicity and heritage. His piece had been all the more emotive for his unashamed use of terminology such as 'modern day slavery' in terms of the mothers' incarceration and unpaid employment, and 'child trafficking' in relation to their sold babies. Though he had feared that some of the mothers who had passed through Northern Ireland's homes might not wish to come forward or be identified, he was pleased nevertheless to see mail rolling in to the designated post box number included with the article.

Perhaps the most moving of the letters which had arrived in response to the article was one from a sixty-two-year-old woman, a Mrs Marie McDaid. Though apparently not a particularly well-educated woman, Mrs McDaid had written a heartfelt account of her time at *La Mère du Bon Pasteur* home at Shearwater Point. As she lived in Belfast, Caffrey had invited her to come to the apartment and tell him her story in person. He had the tea things all laid out in anticipation of her visit. She arrived promptly at eleven that morning, as arranged.

Over tea and cake, Mrs McDaid told Caffrey she had grown up in the town of Ballynahinch in County Down and, having found herself pregnant to her teenage boyfriend, had given birth at *La Mère du Bon Pasteur* home in nineteen seventy-six. She explained that her father, a Protestant, had died when she was very young and, with a further four children younger than Marie, her Catholic mother had found it hard to make ends meet. There had been no question of Marie keeping her baby or returning to her family. Following the birth and subsequent adoption of her son, she had been sent to Belfast to find work, she explained.

Caffrey reasoned that Marie McDaid's time in the home might have crossed with that of his own mother who had also given birth to him there in nineteen seventy-six.

'Do you remember meeting one of the other young mothers there? Her name was Alice Devereux, or Devricks?' he asked, hopefully.

'Alice Devricks? Well, of course I remember her. She was from Wexford. She and I became friends. She was fifteen and I was just turned sixteen. We were probably the youngest girls there at the time and there was just a few months between us in age. We looked out for each other, so we did. I was sent away first, to Belfast. I wrote to her at the home as soon as I was settled, but I imagine she'd gone by then, too. I'd love to know what happened to her.'

'She went back to Wexford to her father's place,' Caffrey said.

Mrs McDaid's face fell on hearing this piece of news. Something in her expression suggested to Caffrey that

Alice had confided in her friend Marie and that maybe, just maybe, his suspicions about his paternity were true. The thought suddenly cut into him like a knife. He had found it disappointing that his birth mother was an ill-educated and simple Wexford woman, but the notion that his father was the kind of man who had forced himself upon his own daughter really turned Caffrey's stomach. He tried to dismiss the thought, however, and concentrate on the reason he had invited Mrs McDaid to visit.

'I understand they sent your babies away for adoption?' he asked.

'Yes, they did. Her wee boy Killian and my wee Jimmy. Mine went to America, so he did.'

'So did Alice's boy. In fact, Mrs McDaid, it's me. I'm Alice's boy. I was Killian Devereux, but my adoptive parents called me Dominic Caffrey.'

Suddenly, Marie's face was filled with joy.

'Well, God love you! Would you ever … but, does that mean you came here to find your mother?'

'I did.'

'And did you find her? Is she alive and well?'

'Yes. I met her for the first time less than two weeks ago. She's still living down in Wexford on the family's smallholding. Would you like her contact details?'

'Oh, I would. I'd love to get in touch with her again. I'm so happy to know she's all right.'

As he wrote down his mother's address and telephone number, Caffrey was puzzled about one thing. He had been over and over the names on the list of admissions in the register, but he couldn't recall seeing the surname McDaid.

'Was your name McDaid back then?' he asked.

'No. I married a McDaid. I have two grown up daughters now, and three grandchildren. But your mother would have known me as Marie Maharg.'

'Maharg?' Caffrey started. 'So, your son Jimmy's birth was registered as James Maharg?'

201

'Yes.'

'And you say he went to America? Did you ever meet him again?'

'No. It wasn't for want of trying, though. When my husband died five years ago, I thought mebbe the time was right to try and find my firstborn. I told my eldest daughter all about it and she helped me track him down. She's great with that there interweb stuff.'

'And did she find him?'

'Well, she got details out of an adoption agency in New York. They'd changed his name, of course. She found out he'd had a troubled life over there. Seems he ended up in some sort of boys' home. I think they called it a 'joovie'. Anyway, my daughter found a death record for him. He'd died of a drugs overdose when he was just twenty-two. I'll always be wondering if things would have been different if he'd been able to stay with me, his mammy.'

Following Mrs McDaid's departure, Caffrey felt quite drained. He realised that many of the accounts from those who had responded to his article would be harrowing to hear. He wouldn't be able to help Marie McDaid to see her son again, but he would damn well get some sort of acknowledgement from the authorities and possibly some compensation, too.

Of course, he realised that no amount of compensation could ever make up for the kind of suffering Marie and Alice had endured. They might have been able to put behind them the pain of unassisted childbirth and the mistreatment they had endured at the hands of the nuns, but, surely, the pain of losing their babies must have stayed with them always. Surely, every year when their stolen babies' birthdays came around …

The ringing of his mobile phone disturbed his sad thoughts. He picked up the call. It was from Joe Doyle.

'Joe. Thanks for calling back. …You did? Okay, let me write that address down … So, how would that be spelled?

... Ardmore. Yes, I've got that. ... Okay. That's great. Thank you so much.'

Next, Caffrey called the number he had for Carole Murray.

'Miss Murray? Dom Caffrey here. Are you still interested in that Russian, Kirasov? Well, I found out where he went when he checked out of the Europa. He went to stay at a private address, Ardmore House, out at Shearwater Point. My contact says it's right up on the top, higher up than the abandoned maternity home. Ah, but he's not there now. The same taxi driver was called to take him to Belfast International Airport three days later. Seems he's left Belfast, but the taxi driver didn't know where he was flying to.'

Caffrey was pleased to know that his information was welcome. Then, it occurred to him that there was something equally interesting that Carole Murray might want to hear.

'Oh, and, you remember the guy named Maharg who paid his hotel bill? ... well, it may just be a coincidence, but there was a James Maharg who was born at the Shearwater Point home the same time I was. He was adopted by a New York family at the same time I went to Boston. But it can't be the same Maharg ... Why? Well, because that James Maharg died in New York around nineteen ninety-eight.'

Chapter 48

Dr Mairead Mulroney found her two ASOs busy down in the laboratory.

'Ah, Harpreet,' she smiled. 'Just had a message for you from the Major Incident Team at Musgrave Street. They send their thanks for your quick ID on the young man in the morgue. Well done.'

Harpreet Gill beamed with modest pride.

'And Ryan,' Dr Mulroney continued, 'any joy on the evidence from the fire at the Indian diner?'

'No, I'm afraid not, doctor.' Ryan shook his head. 'I'd hoped to get a print off the remains of the bottle that was used as a Molotov, but turns out it was too badly charred.'

'Well, never mind, Ryan. I know it wasn't for lack of effort on your part. In fact, you've been working long hours on that. I think we should've eased you back into work more gradually. You're looking pale and tired. Look, why don't you take the rest of today off. Go home and get some rest.'

'Well, if you're sure you don't need me. I must admit, I am very tired. My hands are still very sore, too. I have some emollient stuff I'm supposed to rub in several times a day but I left it at home.'

'Well, that settles it. You go home right now. Put your feet up and treat your hands with the ointment. Oh, and when you get a chance, please call your surgery again. Tell them we still didn't receive your return-to-work certificate.'

That evening, Ryan parked up outside the leisure centre and waited. Soon, various young men began arriving. He would give them a chance to get inside and change before he wandered in himself. He knew exactly where they would be, for, according to Alistair Henry's page on social media, he and his mates had a regular booking at the centre for the same evening each week. This week, of course, Alistair wouldn't be joining them. Ryan couldn't be sure which, if any of his friends might be party to Alistair's arson activities, but, so far, the dead man's connection to these young men was all he had to go on.

Once inside, he headed upstairs to the viewing balcony from where he could look down on several of the sports halls. The five-a-side kickabout was already under way. Clearly, they had quickly found another chum to replace their deceased player. He watched them for half an hour or so, trying to get some clue from how they looked, how they interacted, as to whether any of them might be so psychotic, so lacking in morality that they could cause innocent human beings to burn and suffocate to death.

Disappointingly, he could see nothing to suggest this. They were just a mixed bunch of young working-class men. They were, according to their profiles he had found on social media, a couple of mechanics, a shoe shop assistant, a shipping clerk, and one who worked for the city's sanitation department on the refuse collection. Their posts suggested they mainly knew each other since school.

Ryan now realised he was wasting his time. Observing these young men wouldn't get him any closer to finding out who had wanted Will and the others at The Rainbow Room killed. This and the other fire-bombing incidents might not even be linked. It might just be by chance that this group had an arsonist amongst their members. Maybe Alistair Henry was just someone who'd had a bad curry once at Firoze's Fusion Diner. Disappointed, he went outside and sat in his car, wondering what to do next. Perhaps he should just go home and let the healing process take its course. Well, his hands might heal, but he wasn't too sure his heart ever would. Besides, home didn't feel like home any longer, not without Will.

He now saw the young men emerge from the leisure centre, laughing, invigorated after their knock-about. He saw them head for their cars. He started his own engine. Then he suddenly noticed the metallic blue Mazda parked opposite him. He recognised the index number immediately. He saw a crop-haired man step out of the car. It was the same man he had seen at Ardmore, the house at Shearwater Point – the house occupied by the man who ordered his whiskey in the name of Devereux but had a CRO in the name of McClure.

He heard the crop-haired man call out a name – 'Billy'. One of the football group reacted to the shout and the older man beckoned him away from his friends. Ryan watched as the two engaged in furtive conversation. He would have given anything to be able to hear what they were saying, but even with the car window wound down he couldn't hear. Soon, their conversation ceased and the crop-haired man walked back to the Mazda.

Ryan waited until the Mazda had exited the car park and was a little way up the road before he began to follow at a discreet distance. Eventually, the Mazda pulled into Lissadell Street, one of North Belfast's older streets of terraced houses, and the driver parked up. Ryan parked up too, a little way down the street. Looking back, he watched the man let himself into one of the houses. Ryan got out of his car and walked down the street past the house. He made a mental note of the house number and walked on around the block. He took the precaution of approaching his car from the other end of the street, so he wouldn't pass the house a second time – just in case the man should be looking out of his window.

Now, he would go home and put his feet up for a while. Now he could relax. Now, at last, he felt he had something to go on. Tomorrow, he would check out the address. He would find out who the man was and what connection he might have with Samuel John McClure and the house out at Shearwater Point.

Ryan climbed back into his car and scribbled the address into his notebook. He was just about to start his engine and head off when another car, a grey mini, entered the street. Cars were parked along both sides, leaving no room in the road for two cars to pass, so he waited for the mini to reverse into a space before switching on his ignition. A red-haired woman in police uniform got out of the car. Removing her dark green uniform jacket, she threw it onto the rear passenger seat, took out a plain blue cardigan and slipped it on over her uniform shirt. Taking her handbag from the front passenger seat, she locked the car. As Ryan drove slowly past, to his surprise, he saw the woman entering the very same house the crop-haired man had entered.

His first thought was that the police must be acting on Harpreet's identification of Alistair Henry's fingerprints and that they were following the same line of enquiries as himself. But why would they send a lone female officer to speak to a man who might be a vicious killer? And why did she make a half-hearted attempt to cover up her uniform? Perhaps she lived at the house. Might she be the crop-haired man's wife? He circled the block again and made a mental note of the index number of the grey mini. Then he pulled in on Lissadell Street again and sat watching the house.

The light was now fading and, since no-one seemed to be leaving the house, he began to think he should go home. Suddenly, however, he saw the light come on in the front bedroom of the terraced house and, as he watched, he saw the bedroom curtains being closed. It was a little early for the occupants to be retiring for the night. He was confused by what he had just seen. He felt he had gathered some more pieces of the puzzle, but could he make them fit? He was persuaded of one thing, however. Whatever he decided to do next, it might be better not to involve the police, not just yet, anyway.

Chapter 49

DS Dan McKittrick had just left Musgrave Street police station after a particularly long day. He was weary and bleary-eyed from all the case notes he had been reading on the various criminals whom the late Judge Murray had put away. He had also been perusing the various allegations and snippets of information gathered so far on Alternative Ulster. Mrs McKittrick had had an equally long day and had phoned to ask him to call in at their favourite local Indian on his way home and pick up a takeaway. He was just a couple of streets away from collecting their supper when his mobile rang. Thinking his wife might have had a change of heart over her choice of *murgh makhani* and *tarka dal*, he pulled over to take the call.

However, the call was from one of the detective constables back at the station. Knowing his interest in the recent discoveries out at Shearwater Point, the constable wondered if he'd also be interested in knowing that a fire had just been reported at a large house out there. The fire brigade was already in attendance and had just reported that it seemed to be another case of arson. Activating his blue emergency light, McKittrick headed out for the coast.

The fire had been extinguished by the time he arrived at Ardmore House, and his arrival coincided with that of the SOCOs. The fire officer in charge of the shout approached and advised him of his findings.

'The fire was started at both front and back doors simultaneously,' he advised. 'There's melted plastic on the step at each site, probably from plastic petrol containers ignited right by the doors. Whoever started this didn't intend for anyone to get out.'

'Casualties?' McKittrick asked.

The fire officer pointed across to the two ambulances parked, one behind the other, further down the driveway.

'The householder was holding a business meeting inside. He and four other men are being treated for smoke inhalation. No serious injuries, though. There was no-one else on the premises. Says his wife lives over in England. He rented the house only recently and the wife was due to join him soon. Since he hasn't been living here too long, it may be the arsonist was after a previous occupant of the premises. Still, that's your area of enquiry.'

'Cheers. Do you have the names of the casualties?'

'No, the ambulance crew will, though.'

'Is it safe to go inside, yet?'

'Should be all right if you go in the back way. Just watch yourself in the front and back hallways. The floorboards are gone.'

McKittrick spoke to the ambulance crew. They had recorded the names of the rescued men on their clip board. He copied them into his notebook. The names of Messrs, Kennedy, McClusky and McKenna meant nothing to him, but he was surprised to see the names Killian Devereux and James Maharg on the list. He would certainly like to speak to them at some point. First, however, he decided to take advantage of the fact that the men were in the ambulances to have a look inside the house.

Apart from the house's wooden front and back doors having been completely destroyed, as was the flooring just beyond them and the ceilings above them, most of the interior damage, extensive thought it was, seemed to be from smoke and soot. Clutching his handkerchief to his mouth and nose to avoid inhaling the fumes which still hung heavy in the air, he wandered around the ground-floor rooms.

In the dining room, he espied a number of whiskey glasses set around a dining table. There were several bottles of Bushmills single malt on a sideboard, one of them three-quarters empty. He drew the attention of the SOCOs to these items and asked that they be bagged and tagged and sent for fingerprint checking. He noticed there was some singed paperwork spread over the table and he asked that this, too, be bagged.

A brief wander around the upstairs and into the kitchen threw up nothing further of interest to the detective, apart from a safe, which unfortunately was locked, so he headed back towards the front door. Stopping only to scoop up some heavily heat-charred paper from the hall table and leave it on the dining table in place of the documents SOCO had taken, he went outside.

Looking into each of the two ambulances in turn, he confirmed with the ambulance crew that the men were unlikely to feel like talking right now, since each was hooked up to a breathing mask. He was advised that they would be taken to the Royal Victoria to be checked over and would almost certainly be kept in overnight.

Content that there was nothing more he could do here for the present, McKittrick stood outside and looked back at the house. Given the size of the house and its excellent location, he guessed it must be quite an expensive place to rent. Suddenly, he remembered the errand he was supposed to be on. He had forgotten all about his supper. He checked his watch and realised he had just half an hour to get to the takeaway before it closed. If he didn't, he knew that, like Ardmore's floorboards, he would be in for a roasting.

Chapter 50

Two days later, DI Sarah Lawrence and DS Dan McKittrick attended a meeting at MI5's Palace Barracks office at Holywood. Malone had received more intelligence which needed greater evaluation, and McKittrick had further developments on which to report.

'So, you know Carole Murray,' Malone said as he welcomed the DS into the briefing room, 'but have you met her husband, Dave Lloyd?'

'Yes,' McKittrick said, 'Dave and I met at the funeral. How is Mrs Murray?'

'She's not doing too well,' Carole said, 'but at least we'll be here a while longer to keep an eye on her.'

'Carole and Dave have now been attached to us on temporary duty,' Malone explained, 'mainly to assist us in risk assessing the President's visit. We needed extra resources as there's any number of groups and individuals whose interests might be served by disrupting that visit.'

'Might one of those groups be Alternative Ulster?' Dave asked.

'Indeed, it might,' Malone agreed.

'Actually, I'd say they're the front runners,' McKittrick added, 'and we believe we've now identified some of their members.'

McKittrick looked to his DI before expanding on the findings of his investigation so far. Sarah Lawrence nodded her assent. He produced some images of driving licence records

'There was another arson attack a couple of nights ago out at Shearwater Point.'

'At the mother and baby home?' Malone asked.

'No, it was at a private house, a large rented property called Ardmore House. The man who's renting the house was holding a business meeting with four other men. Whilst they were sitting around the table, drinking whiskey, someone set burning petrol cans at both the front and back doors to the property. Whoever did that intended to kill them.'

'Ardmore?' Carole asked. 'Dominic Caffrey found out that's the house the Russian, Kirasov, went to after he left the Europa. But he's left Northern Ireland now. Was anyone killed in the fire?'

'No, there were no fatalities. We can deduce that the arsonist wasn't very familiar with the property. He, or she, didn't realise there was another way out via the French windows onto a raised terrace and from there down into the garden.'

'So, who were these businessmen?' Malone asked.

'Well, the property is rented to a man calling himself Killian Devereux.'

'That's the fake Devereux, presumably,' Carole asked, 'not the American, Dominic Caffrey?'

'That's right. The other men gave the names you see on these copies of driving licences, James Maharg, Eamon Kennedy, Dermot McCluskey and Donal McKenna. The cars that were parked on the driveway at Ardmore House are registered in those names, too.'

'Wait a minute,' Carole interrupted excitedly. 'James Maharg, that's one of the names Caffrey found in the birth records. There was a James Maharg born at *La Mère du Bon Pasteur*. Presumably, the Maharg who obtained that licence is the same Maharg who paid Kirasov's hotel bill. But the real James Maharg was another adopted baby who died in the US almost twenty-five years ago.'

'Yes,' McKittrick agreed, 'and, in fact, all those names, including Kennedy, McCluskey and McKenna, they all appear as infants born to women listed in the admissions register which Caffrey photographed and which Mike kindly sent me. All the men who met at Ardmore the other night are using identities of infants who were born at the home and were adopted not long after birth.'

'I wonder why our enquiries didn't come up with Devereux's driving licence until now?' Malone puzzled.

'His was issued only recently by the DVLA,' McKittrick explained. 'I can only assume he's been using a driving licence in a different identity until he moved here. He may also have other documents in different identities that we don't know about.'

'Dan found business papers on the dining table where they were holding their meeting,' DI Lawrence added. 'They included some sort of accounts book. It was heavily singed and we're still trying to make sense of the entries in that book. There was also a map of Ireland with what appears to be the proposed route of the President's journey from Belfast to County Louth marked on it. Looks like they were planning some sort of disruption of Biden's trip.'

'When they realise you have those, aren't they likely to change their plans, and maybe even go to ground?' Dave asked.

'I'm hoping not,' McKittrick said. 'You see I had the SOCOs remove them, then I substituted a load of burnt paper which I found in the front hall. There was a telephone table right near the front door and the phone directories and other bits of paperwork on that table had been burned to a crisp. I put those burnt papers on the dining table in the hope they'll think they were their accounts ledger that caught alight with the heat.'

'That was quick thinking, Dan,' Malone said. 'But we still don't know who Devereux and co really are.'

'Well, actually, we do, now,' McKittrick assured him. 'I also had the whiskey glasses taken away for our FPOs to check out. They found the men's prints on AFIS. It seems Devereux was first fingerprinted back in the early 'nineties

214

under the name Samuel John McClure. Sammy McClure was a regular villain and he did a twelve stretch for murder back then. He was sent down by your uncle, Carole. The others all have CROs from that era as well.'

'So, they've all been living under assumed identities,' Malone surmised. 'And, for an organisation which seeks to promote a Protestant state, I see some of them have taken on names which are plainly Catholic.'

'That may have been deliberate,' Sarah Lawrence added. 'No-one would suspect Catholics of involvement with a group promoting a Protestant state. Or it may simply be that they'd targeted births of adoptees from a Catholic home, all of whom would have been Catholics. Anyway, now that we know who they really are and where they live, it'll be easier to keep an eye on them. We also have an idea what they have planned. This is it, guys. This fire was our lucky break.'

'It was indeed,' Carole agreed. 'I'll work with MIT's analysts and we'll capture the phone traffic between the men who were at Ardmore House. We'll draw up telephone link charts to link them with each other and association charts to see who else they've been in contact with. Using their phone data, we should be able to pinpoint who was where during each of the incidents we believe are connected, in particular my uncle's murder. We'll also check out who countersigned their passport applications. If it's the same person, that points to conspiracy. We should be able to put together an intelligence package for prosecution purposes.'

'And I'll work with your team to go over all the witness statements and CCTV again in each incident, now that we know the addresses of more individuals linked to Alternative Ulster,' Dave added. 'But, Dan, who do you think was responsible for the fire at Ardmore?'

'Not sure,' McKittrick said. 'Could have been a rival criminal gang, I suppose. But whoever it was, he did us a favour, as it flushed out five members of Alternative Ulster. I do have one potential suspect for the arson attack, and I intend to visit him this afternoon.'

That afternoon, McKittrick called at Alfred House again to speak to Aminullah Miah, but the lawyer wasn't at work. Maeve McCutcheon, an experienced lawyer herself, was a new addition to the staff. She introduced herself as 'the new girl'.

'So, Mr Miah is getting his additional resources, then?' McKittrick observed.

'Yes. There's been a sudden increase in casework so I've been taken on and we've another new member of staff joining us next week. I'm afraid Mr Miah isn't in today, though. You may be aware they released the body of his brother yesterday, so he's busy organising the funeral. Is there anything I can help you with?'

'No, thank you. I was just passing and I thought I'd enquire as to how he and the family are.'

'Well, I'll tell him you called ... er ... DS ...?'

'McKittrick. Dan McKittrick. Oh, but before I go, actually there is a legal query I have which you might be able to help me with.'

'Sure, if I can.'

'Would you know what the penalties are for using a fake identity?'

'Well, that depends. It's not an offence to change your name, and you don't have to change it by deed poll. So long as you're not doing it to commit an offence, such as fraud, you can use whatever name you like.'

'But if a person uses someone else's birth record to obtain a passport? For example, if the real holder of that ID is now using a different identity, say, because they were adopted.'

'Well, that would depend *why* they did it. Under the Identity Documents Act, possession of false identity documents without a reasonable excuse could result in a custodial sentence of two years, and also a fine. However, if you can prove they made false statements to procure a passport *and* that they did so with improper intent, then they could get ten years' imprisonment. But it's not always easy proving improper intent.'

'So, if someone said they'd only assumed that identity and obtained the passport to cover up for old and spent convictions, would they only get two years?'

'To be honest, if that were the only reason, then yes.'

'Okay. Thank you for that advice. That's very helpful.'

As McKittrick left the HRC office and walked back to Musgrave Street, he was deep in thought. He determined not to bother the Miah family at this difficult time for them. His gut instinct told him Aminullah was an unlikely suspect for the fire at Shearwater Point, but he had been obliged to at least make an attempt to speak to him about it in order to rule him out. He couldn't see how Miah would even have known that the suspect in the abduction and murder of his brother was living at Ardmore House – unless, of course, the source of the leaks from their Major Investigation Team had told him.

It irked McKittrick that he still hadn't managed to identify who, on his team, was releasing small details of their investigations. He had his suspicions, but he couldn't be sure. Several of his constables had been sent to take turns at keeping eyes on that Russian at the Europa, but it wasn't clear which one of them had, either negligently or deliberately, missed him checking out.

Even if Aminullah Miah had found out about Sammy McClure and his connection with Alternative Ulster, Miah was a human rights lawyer. Surely, McKittrick thought, a man dedicated to preserving human rights wouldn't turn arsonist himself. Fire was as indiscriminate a weapon as were bombs. Anyone raised in Belfast knew that. No, he dismissed any notion of Miah being involved. The possibility of it being down to a rival drugs gang seemed more feasible.

He felt bad that he had let the Miah family down in the past. He wondered if perhaps a greater effort could have been put into the investigation when Mohinullah Miah had gone missing. Yet he recalled the witnesses' descriptions of the young man's possible abductors had been so sketchy and contradictory. Two young men and one slightly older man, were the only descriptions upon which the witnesses had agreed.

Some had thought the four young men they had seen were just larking around, play fighting. Another felt the older man, a man in his thirties with his hair cropped quite short, had gripped Mohinullah in a Jackie Chan style hold, suggesting he had some knowledge of restraint techniques. And that was all they'd had to go on. No-one recalled seeing a car involved. There had been no CCTV evidence. Mohinullah Miah had simply been spirited away. Now, however, his body had been found out at the mother and baby home. At least Mr and Mrs Miah now knew for certain that their elder son was dead and they could lay him to rest.

McKittrick had no doubt the Alternative Ulster thugs were responsible for Mohinullah Miah's murder, yet he had no way of proving this. It seemed highly likely they were also responsible for the threats made against Aminullah Miah's legal colleagues which had persuaded them to resign. Still, at least he now knew who the major players were in the organisation. That was a start.

As he walked back across town, McKittrick reflected on how little evidence they had regarding the bodies found out at Shearwater Point. He'd considered the possibility that the European women might have been trafficked here for the sex trade, though he had no proof of this. Identification was usually the starting point but, so far, no-one had come forward with suggestions as to who the other bodies might be. The bullets taken from the bodies were all he had to go on. He just needed to find the gun that had fired them.

As for the mass grave of the innocent babies also found at *La Mère du Bon Pasteur*, his enquiries into that horrific discovery had also come to a temporary halt. The religious order had been disbanded in the 'nineties and the church authorities were dragging their feet in tracing the nuns who would have been based there. They argued that most would probably have passed away by now.

In his frustration, McKittrick kicked a discarded drinks can from the pavement into the gutter. There was only one slight ray of hope in that aspect of the investigation. Maybe a bit of pressure from Dominic Caffrey and the Human Rights Commission, not to mention from the President of the United States of America, might force that issue into the open.

Then, there was the murder of the judge. McKittrick had no doubt that was the work of the Alternative Ulster organisation, too, but, once again, proof was lacking. He had briefly interviewed Devereux, whom he now knew to be Samuel John McClure, and his business associates. It had been convenient that they were all in one place, at the hospital on the morning after the fire. Their varying accounts of what business they had with each other had left him in no doubt that they were lying. He could arrest them all right now for having obtained British passports on the basis of false information, but unless he could prove they had obtained those identity documents to facilitate the commission of a crime, they might only face two years in prison.

No, it might be highly frustrating not being able just yet to take any action against Sammy McClure and his cohorts, but McKittrick determined that, when he did get them, he would get them good.

Chapter 51

At the forensic science laboratory in Carrickfergus, Harpreet Gill was engrossed in her examination of a large notebook.

'Ryan, you speak Irish, don't you?' Harpreet asked. 'Would you have a look at this for me and see if you can make out what language it is?'

'Sure,' Ryan smiled. 'What is it?'

'It's some kind of business record or accounts ledger, I think. MIT brought it over. The amounts given are in sterling. See the pound signs? But the comments next to them aren't in English.'

Ryan perused the pages of the ledger. It wasn't written in Irish. At first, he thought it might be written in German, but some words looked more like a misspelling of English words. After a few moments, he realised exactly what it was that he was looking at. In his head, he could hear Will reciting some of the words. In his heart, he felt a sudden stab of pain.

'I think I do recognise this,' he said, at last. 'A close friend of mine was learning Ullans. He used to leave his notebooks and dictionary lying around the flat. I used to take the mickey out of him and say it wasn't a proper language, not like English or Irish.'

'But what is Ullans? I never heard of it?'

'It's a variant of Lallans. Lallans is a Germanic language spoken in the Scottish Lowlands. It came to Northern Ireland with the Scots settlers during the Plantation era. Over time, it evolved into a slightly separate dialect that they called Ullans. Sort of Ulster Lallans. Like the English language, its roots lie in German.'

'So, can you understand it?'

'No. I mean, I recognise the odd word here and there, but that's all. See, the word *kist* appears a lot. That means box or chest, or, maybe a crate. *Echt* I know, means eight; *twunty* is twenty, of course, and *tha nicht* means tonight. It looks like this is some sort of sales or delivery record.

'So, are there people in Northern Ireland who only speak Ullans?'

'No. Everyone here speaks English, and many can also speak Irish. No, I imagine whoever decided to write this in Ullans did so as they didn't want everyone to know what they were writing about. And, whilst the Irish-speaking population are mainly Catholics, Ullans would be understood mainly by some Protestants of Scottish descent. Where did the ledger come from?'

'From that fire at Ardmore, the house out at Shearwater Point.'

Once again, Ryan tried not to show too much interest in the incident.

'Uh huh? Well, if I were you, I'd contact the university and see if they have an Ullans speaker who could translate it for you. Alternatively, there's an Ulster-Scots society which promotes the language. My friend used to receive their newsletters. I think they're called something like *Tha Boord O' Ulster Scotch*.'

'Thanks, Ryan. I'll look them up. The police officer who brought it over is waiting outside. I won't remember what you said about all that Lallans and Ullans stuff. Would you be able to explain it better than me?'

'Sure, I'll have a word and tell him what we're intending to do to get it translated.'

Ryan went to the reception area to find the police officer. To his surprise, it wasn't a policeman who awaited him there, but a policewoman. In fact, it was the same red-haired policewoman he had seen entering the house of the crop-haired man in north Belfast. He was taken aback for a moment. So, she was working on the investigation into the Ardmore House fire and, at the same time, she was visiting an associate of an arsonist, and she was spending time in his bedroom with the curtains drawn. That struck him as highly dubious.

'Hello,' he greeted her civilly. 'Just to let you know we've no idea yet what that paperwork is. We'll hang on to it for the time being, though, and continue to try to work it out, that's if you're happy for us to do so?'

'Great. Thanks.'

'So, if you could let me have your name and extension number, I'll call you the minute that's done.'

'Yes, of course,' she smiled. 'I'm Constable Eileen O'Neill and this is my number.'

Ryan spotted the wedding ring as she handed him the paper on which she had scribbled her number. So, she was married. But was she married to the crop-haired man? He watched her leave, and he wondered just what the hell was going on. Maybe it was time he did reveal what he knew to the police. But could he trust the police?

Chapter 52

At Holywood's Palace Barracks, a major conference was under way. Mike Malone's boss, Gerald Gilmour, kicked off the introductions by explaining the roles of his local Security Service team, and by introducing the Thames House contingent, Carole and Dave, and their colleagues from MI5's Counter-terrorism section. Also around the table there were two officers from Irish military intelligence and four from the *Garda Síochána*'s Special Detective Unit in Dublin. The leader of the SDU team explained that their most pertinent remit was presidential, ministerial and diplomatic protection. There were also two Americans present, FBI officers sent by the US embassy in Dublin.

Each person present had been given a map which Mike Malone had produced, showing the proposed route of the presidential motorcade. Wisely, the map was not annotated to show what the marked route was for, nor who would be taking that route nor when. This was a precaution in case someone should lose their copy. Gilmour outlined the situation regarding the President's visit.

'From Hillsborough Castle where the President will stay, the motorcade will head south. There will be no stops made within Northern Ireland. The first stop will be a photo opportunity outside historic King John's Castle in County Louth, followed by a lunch stop just a little further on at the town of Carlingford. After lunch with local dignitaries, the motorcade will head on down to the Cooley Peninsula where the President will visit some family graves at Kilwirra cemetery and chat to locals. After that, they will continue on down to Dublin. Later in the week, he will fly from Dublin to West of Ireland airport for a one-day family visit in County Mayo. Then he'll return to Dublin by air, and from there, it's back to Washington the following day. The UK's responsibility ends at the border, however, and it is that very handover, at the border between Counties Down and Louth that we feel is the weak spot in terms of security protection.'

It was one of the US delegates who raised the first query.

'Are you expecting there to be trouble?'

'Well, yes, we are,' Gilmour said, 'though not from the same source as the threats to President Obama emanated. If you recall, Barack Obama's visit to Ireland came just weeks after the assassination of Osama Bin Laden, and a number of plots by radical Muslim groups were foiled just prior to his visit. Mike here will explain our current fears with relation to Mr Biden's visit.'

'There never is an ideal time for a state visit,' Malone explained, 'the state of the world being what it is, but this year brings its own particular challenges. Twenty twenty-two marks the centenary of Irish independence and of the partition of Ireland, an event which was welcomed by many but which, equally, was resented by many.'

'Why would that be a threat to the US President, though?' one of the FBI men asked.

'There's ill-feeling in some quarters in Northern Ireland, that it was partly the influence of Irish-Americans which led to partition. Even a century later, some people still resent the ceding of three of the nine northern counties to the Irish Republic. An attack on the US President would not only reflect that resentment, it would also embarrass the British government, the British having been the main architect in carving up the island.'

'So, we're not talking the IRA, here?' the American asked.

'No,' Malone agreed. 'We're looking at one organisation in particular. Alternative Ulster is a group committed to re-partitioning Northern Ireland. They want to amalgamate all the nine counties of Ulster into a single province, and an entirely white Protestant one.'

'And how big a deal is this organisation?' the FBI man's colleague asked.

'It's not huge, but it has branches across Northern Ireland and its membership is growing. Its thugs have been conducting a campaign of violent attacks, abductions, murders and arson against ethnic minorities. It's believed they've also killed a retired judge.'

Malone gave Carole an apologetic glance before continuing.

'This ethnic cleansing has attracted the attention of the Kremlin. You may know that Putin encourages his home-grown neo-Nazis to form alliances with similar groups in other western countries. The latest Russian organisation to express an interest in Alternative Ulster is Russky Obraz.'

'And how does this Alternative Ulster get its funding?' the first FBI man asked.

'Very recently, one of their accounts ledgers came into our possession. It strongly suggests that, whilst they gather subscriptions from their membership around Northern Ireland, they also seem to be on top of the drugs trade. They run the import and distribution of class A and class B drugs all over the province. We believe they've also been importing weapons and explosives. We recently found one cache of weapons but it's likely they have more. Intelligence suggests the Russians have been supplying them with arms.'

'But, given your assessment of the threat, why does British involvement cease at the border?' the first American asked. 'Can't we have the Irish and the British security accompany the president the whole way?'

'That would be eminently sensible,' one of the Irish intelligence officers agreed, 'but European Union regulations won't allow it. Whilst our British counterparts are agreeable to our men accompanying the president on the

British side of the border, I'm afraid Brussels won't agree to police, military or intelligence staff from a so-called 'third country' operating on our side of the border, since it's within the EU.'

'That's crazy,' the American protested. 'That should be an issue for the Irish government to decide. But I guess that sort of bureaucracy is why you Brits left the EU.'

Having strong feelings on that score as well as some inside knowledge on recent developments, Carole decided to add her opinion to the debate.

'Well, the bureaucracy has got a whole lot worse since we left. You could say we brought it upon ourselves. But, it's just possible that the situation could change between now and the state visit. The British Ministry of Defence has drafted a treaty which seeks greater co-operation between our police, military and security agencies and that of our Irish neighbours. The prime minister has now signed the treaty, as has his Irish counterpart. It just needs the objections from Brussels to be overruled.'

'Do you think that will be implemented in time for the visit, though?' the American asked.

'I'm not sure anything Brussels does is done in a timely fashion,' Gilmour interjected, 'but there are precedents which could persuade them to agree eventually. A similar treaty exists between the Nordic countries, only two of which are full EU members. Iceland and Finland are non-EU states but they conduct joint sea and air patrols with Sweden, Denmark and the EEA state of Norway.'

'The thing is,' the FBI man said, 'does this Alternative Ulster organisation know that the Brits can't cross the border with the president?'

'Oh, I'm sure they do,' Malone answered. 'There was a bit about it in the press recently. And that's why I think any attack may happen either close to the border or just over the border, down on the Irish side. Our thinking is that it's most likely to be close to the border, as that would embarrass both British and Irish governments.'

'Couldn't the route simply be changed?' Dave asked.

'It could be changed, and indeed, in view of what you've told us, I guess it should be changed,' the FBI man agreed, 'but the president won't agree. He's decided who and what he wants to see, and when. He wouldn't want to disappoint those who are expecting to see him. Anyhow, even if it was changed at the last possible moment, the people he's due to meet along the way would need to be told of the changes, and word would quickly get around.'

'So, gentlemen, and lady,' Gilmour concluded, 'we'll just have to check out the route in advance and try to identify areas where the motorcade might be most vulnerable to attack. Then we need to saturate those areas with our people.'

Chapter 53

Dan McKittrick was trying to make sense of all the loose ends in the case files on his desk when his thoughts were disrupted by a call from reception, announcing he had a visitor on his way upstairs. His visitor was from the forensic laboratory at Carrickfergus.

'Mr Donovan. Take a seat. What can I do for you? Have you deciphered the ledger we sent you?'

'Yes, we've sent it back to your Constable O'Neill already with a transcript. But actually, I didn't come about that. I was at The Rainbow Room when it was fire-bombed. I was injured and my partner, Will Gibson, was one of those who died in the fire. I suppose I've come here looking for answers. Do you know who did it and why?'

McKittrick looked at the young man. His initial irritation at being put on the spot by a victim's relative quickly abated when he saw the deep sadness in the young man's eyes and felt the pain of his bereavement.

'I'm so sorry for your loss, Mr Donovan, and I can tell you that, yes, I'm satisfied I know who did it. I believe it was the same arsonist responsible for a couple of other incidents in the city. But I'm also satisfied that he is dead.'

'So, you believe Alistair Henry, the burns victim suffocated up at the hospital, was responsible for the pub fire as well as the attack on the Indian diner?'

'How did you know who he was?'

'My lab processed the fingerprint evidence. But why? Why did Alistair Henry set out to kill so many innocent people?'

'Well, I believe I may know the answer to that, and we're investigating others who were associated with him.

We've got to proceed with caution, though, and spread our net wide in order to catch others who may be involved. You do deserve answers, Mr Donovan, but I'm sure you'll understand why I can't share anything with you just yet.'

'I understand. And thank you for seeing me. But, before I go, there's something I feel I should share with you ,,.'

Across town, another meeting was about to take place. Caffrey was both excited and puzzled as he made his way to Stranmillis to the office of the US Consul General. He felt a slight trepidation as he entered historic Danesfort house. The high Victorian mansion with its mix of mansard roof and conical towers, put him in mind of a French château, not that he had ever visited a French château. Of course, there was every possibility that he might do so one day, especially as, thanks to his newly issued Irish passport, he was now officially a European. This ornately elegant building was equally grandly appointed on the inside, he noticed as he waited. Eventually, he was escorted into the Consul General's office.

'Good morning,' the diplomat smiled as she extended her hand to shake his, then indicated he should sit opposite her. 'I'm Viveca Holmberg. Thank you for coming over.'

'Thank you for inviting me, Ms Holmberg,' he said.

He took in the splendid marble fireplace and the artwork on the walls of this very bright room.

'I'll get straight to the point, Mr Caffrey. I've been contacted by White House staff who are making arrangements for the president's visit to Ireland next week. The president thanks you for drawing his attention to the issue of the historic abuses at the province's mother and baby homes and the lack of action on that issue. You may have read in the press that he intends to raise the issue at Stormont.'

'Yes, and I am very grateful to the president for his interest.'

'A contact of yours in the office of the US Ambassador to the United Nations, a Mr Spence, has told the president that you, yourself, were born at *La Mère du Bon Pasteur* home in County Down. I hope he wasn't breaking any confidences when he revealed that information?'

'Oh, not at all. I've been publicising the fact myself in order to encourage contact from women and adoptees who passed through that home.'

'Well, I have to tell you something which I need you to keep confidential.'

'Oh, absolutely.'

'The president has been advised by his own researcher that someone with whom he has a tenuous family connection was a young woman who also gave birth at that home.'

'May I know the name of the young lady? You see, I have copies of the admissions register and I could get more information …'

'No, I'm not at liberty to disclose the lady's name, nor that of her child, and it's not a close family connection, in any case. His own researcher has come up with all Mr Biden needs to know. But this discovery has given, shall we say, added impetus to the president's desire to push this issue to a firm conclusion.'

'I can understand that.'

'So, he now thinks he would like to visit the home at Shearwater Point. He hopes it might give him a feel for the place, and an idea of what life was like for his relative – his *distant* relative. Being seen to visit the home in person would show that his interest in the issue is genuine. It would be a good photo opportunity, too, and a way of getting the press onside.'

'Well, it sure would do that.'

'He would also like to meet you, Mr Caffrey.'

'Me? Our president wants to meet me?'

'Yes, if you wouldn't mind. Perhaps you could arrange to be at the home when he arrives, and maybe you wouldn't mind being photographed shaking his hand. This would be a stop off on his way from Belfast down to County Louth in the Republic. Just in case his discussions on the issue are not well received during his talks at Stormont, a little press call at Shearwater Point would add weight to the issue. What do you think?'

Caffrey thought it would indeed add weight to the issue and it would help his crusade. On a more selfish basis, it would also be great publicity for his own law firm. He was thrilled.

'I think that would be wonderful, and I'd be very happy to be involved. Very happy indeed.'

Chapter 54

Eileen O'Neill parked her mini up Lissadell street away from Hughie's house. Walking back down the street, she glanced around to make sure no-one was watching before she let herself in. He was drinking beer and watching football on television. He barely looked up when she entered the living room. Instead, he pointed to the kitchen.

'Wanna drink, Eileen? There's some wine in the 'fridge.'

She put down her canvas shopping bag and went into the kitchen. Taking a wine glass from the cupboard, she held it up to the light and grimaced at the greasy film on it. Having washed the glass and dried it, she took a bottle of white wine from the refrigerator, unscrewed the cap and filled her glass. Returning to the living room, she sat down next to Hughie and wearily took a long draught of the wine.

'Did you bring any food?' he asked.

'No, I can't stay for supper. I brought you something better than food, though.'

'Oh yeah?'

'Yeah. Something belonging to your Mister D.'

Hughie glanced around at her quizzically. He picked up the remote and switched off the television.

'What is it?'

She got up, walked over to where she had left her shopping bag and drew something from it. She handed him the large ledger and sat back down on the sofa to drink her wine.

'What's this?' he asked.

'It's his accounts book.'

'Where did you get it?' Hughie looked shocked.

'Forensics lifted it from his house during the fire. I lifted it from their lab.'

Hughie skimmed through the pages of the ledger.

'What's all this mean?'

'They said they couldn't make head nor tail of it at the lab, so they released it. I collected it from the lab. I was supposed to take it back to Musgrave Street, but I thought your boss would want it back.'

'I'm sure he will, whatever it is. You say they couldn't understand it?'

'No. A chap who works there said they thought it was high German or something. But they didn't think it was of any importance. Of course, you and I know better, don't we? We recognise the lingo, don't we? We know exactly what it is.'

'Do we?' Hughie said, cagily.

Eileen took another large draught of the wine.

'Come off it, Hughie. It's a list of imports and deliveries, isn't it? Your boss is importing and distributing drugs, and maybe other things besides.'

'But you're not going to be telling anyone, are you?'

'Why would I? I wouldn't have brought it to you if I was going to tell anyone, would I?'

'True,' he smiled, and he reached out and kissed her on the cheek. 'You're a good girl, so you are. Are you sure you won't stay and eat? I could get us a takeaway.'

She took another large sip of the wine, stretched out her legs and kicked her shoes off.

'No. I must get home before seven. Got things to do. Gotta get the boys' school clothes sorted for the week. I'm going to be pulling a couple of all-nighters next week. We've got to mount an OP for the president's visit.'

'An OP?'

'An observation point. The president's using *the beast*, you know, his armour-plated official vehicle. So, nothing's going to happen along the road. The places where he'll be stopping off are already saturated with security. There's FBI, MI5, our lot and the Irish diplomatic protection guys, not to mention half the Irish army. It's believed the most likely spot for a possible attack would be down at the border. But the White House have just announced he's made a slight change to the route, so we in MIT have been drafted in to help check out the additional location he's planning to visit.'

Hughie looked up suddenly.

'He's changed his route? So, … where's he going now?' he asked, trying to sound only mildly interested.

Eileen drained the contents of her glass and thrust it at Hughie.

'I suppose I could manage another of these before I go,' she said.

Outside, at the top of Lissadell Street, Dan McKittrick sat in his car and waited until, eventually, he saw the grey mini pull away. The young scientist's suspicions had been confirmed.

Disappointment clouded the detective's face as he watched his constable leave. In the fading light of early evening, Eileen O'Neill hadn't seen him, but he had seen her. He sat for a while and considered what action he ought to take. Soon, however, he saw the crop-haired man emerge and jump into his own car. McKittrick watched the blue Mazda drive past before he started up his own engine and slowly rolled out of the street, heading south in discreet pursuit.

It was dusk by the time Hughie pulled up outside a large modern bungalow, in the city's southern suburb of Newtownbreda. From the far end of the road, McKittrick saw him ring the doorbell and be admitted. Cruising past slowly, the detective spotted a large Mercedes saloon parked in the driveway of the bungalow. He pulled in across the street and quickly jotted down in his notebook the address of the bungalow and the index numbers of both the

Mercedes and the metallic blue Mazda, then he headed further down the road and found another spot to park up, out of view of the bungalow. Flipping back through the pages, he spotted the number of the Mercedes already written in his notebook. It was one of those numbers he had recorded on the night of the fire at Shearwater Point. It was the car he had already established was registered to one Killian Devereux of Ardmore House. So, now he knew where Sammy McClure, the fake Killian Devereux, was hiding out.

He thought for a few moments and decided against involving his own back office in checking out the address and the other car numbers. He thought about calling Sean Rafferty, an old friend of his in Belfast's CID, and asking him to carry out some urgent checks for him. He began to dial the CID number, but something caused him to stop. It now occurred to him that, whilst Eileen might be the source of the recent leak of information from MIT, she might not be the only source. There might be other bad apples within the local police. He had no doubts about his friend, but Rafferty's return call might be overheard by others in CID. Heaven alone knew who else might be in league with Alternative Ulster. Of course, they might even have someone within DVLA itself, but he had to risk that as he needed the information. On impulse, he called Carol Murray's mobile.

'Hi, Carole? It's Dan McKittrick, here. I need to ask you a favour.'

'Of course, Dan. Ask away,' Carole said.

'Listen, I'm down in south Belfast at the moment and I need some DLVA and voters' list checks done, but there's no-one in back in my office at Musgrave Street at this time of the evening and, well, for reasons I'd rather not go into just now, I'd prefer it if neither my warrant number or the PSNI were shown on the computer as having requested the checks. I don't want to call the local DVLA office at

Coleraine. I understand you're authorised to undertake such checks and that you could do them via the DVLA in England?'

'Yes. In Wales, actually. Give me the details and I'll contact DVLA Swansea.'

McKittrick read over the car numbers for Carole to run past the Driver and Vehicle Licensing Authority, and he also gave her the addresses of the Bungalow in Newtownbreda and the Lissadell Street house for voters' list checks to be conducted.

'Well,' Carole said, 'I can tell you right now who lives at that Lissadell Street address. It's the same person who's the registered keeper of the blue Mazda you just mentioned. His name is Hugh McCalmont, and he's a former soldier in the British army. He's an ex-para, a sniper who saw action in Kosovo.'

'Bloody hell! How did you get that info so quick?' a surprised McKittrick asked.

'Because I've already had cause to check him out. He and his blue Mazda have been following me around over the past few days.'

'Well, it looks like he's an associate of the man I believe is running Alternative Ulster, in which case, Carole, you'd better take care. You may well be in grave danger.'

McKittrick decided not to wait where he was for Carole's call back with details of the other car numbers and the Newtownbreda address. He didn't want to risk being seen by the occupants of the bungalow. He started up the engine and headed for home.

Inside the bungalow, meanwhile, Sammy McClure was pleased to be back in possession of his ledger, and even more pleased to hear about the change of route.

'Well, would you credit it?' he mused. 'McCalmont won't have to go to the Cooley Mountains after all. The man from the mountains is coming to McCalmont. That couldn't have worked out better.'

236

'And you were right about that woman,' McCalmont told him.

'What woman?'

'The one Billy and I saw meeting up with the Yank. The one we followed to the judge's house. Seems she's Murray's niece. She's been asking a lot of questions.'

'What sort of questions?' his host frowned.

'Questions about Killian Devereux,' McCalmont said. 'And the Yank's still here. He's been out to the Shearwater Point home again. If it hadn't been for him poking his nose in, they'd never have found the bodies out there.'

He produced the Glock from within his jacket and ran his fingers along the barrel.

'Mebbe Billy and me should pay them both a wee visit.'

'No,' McClure said. 'What can the niece know? And anyway, it's too near to the big event, now. We don't want to be drawing attention to ourselves, do we?'

'Whatever you say, Mister D.'

Chapter 55

The following morning, an urgent summons upstairs saw McKittrick standing in the office of his DCI. O'Keeffe had some news for him.

'We've been advised that there's been a bit of a change to the route the president will be taking when he leaves Hillsborough.' O'Keeffe told him.

'A change?'

'Yes, his motorcade will now be diverting north towards the coast before they head south to County Louth.'

'What for? Just to look at the sea views?'

'No, he intends to stop off at Shearwater Point.'

'Why, in God's name, would he want to go there? Not to look at the birds, surely?'

'He now wants that American lawyer, Caffrey, to meet him at the old mother and baby home. They'll be arranging for a small clutch of pressmen and a few other interested parties to be there. We've insisted the reporters should only be told of the location a little beforehand, with just enough time for them to get there.'

'But why does Biden want to see the home?'

'It seems the President's taking a keen interest in the maternity homes abuse scandal. He'll have raised it at Stormont, the day before, and he wants to see the Shearwater Point home for himself before he leaves. He intends to have a few publicity photos taken there. They have cleared up the disinterment site, haven't they?'

'Yes. All the bodies have been removed and the excavation is all filled in now. But he's going to be much more vulnerable out there. And the Alternative Ulster thugs know that area well. He'd be a lot safer if he stuck to a fast dash down the A1 route. Could we not talk them out of it?'

'Well, we don't want to do that. You see, we've just had some fresh intelligence which suggests there *will* be an attack on the president but it won't be down at the border, as MI5 thought. Alternative Ulster have already found out about the change of plans and we've been tipped the wink that they're going to make their move out at Shearwater Point.'

'Wait a minute, gov. How did Alternative Ulster find out about the change of route before I did?' McKittrick asked, though he feared he already knew the answer.

'Well, who knows? But it'll work to our advantage, Dan. Now that we know exactly where they'll strike, we'll have the place staked out well in advance and we'll catch them. You were hoping to have something much better to charge them with than identity theft. Attempted assassination of a head of state should do quite nicely. It'll be quite a coup.'

O'Keeffe glanced across at the photograph of himself receiving his QPM from the Queen.

'In fact, there could be a gong or two in this for some of us,' he added.

'Yes, but, gov, that won't be an easy area to stake out.'

'Oh, we'll manage it. Now, I've asked Sarah Lawrence to arrange an OP there. She'll be there to supervise from the night before. She'll take Eileen O'Neill with her and an armed response unit. You can take the rest of the team and join them on the morning of the visit. We'll have the whole area checked out for explosives the day before and we'll keep it staked out until the president departs.'

McKittrick sat down heavily.

'Eileen O'Neill? You've got Eileen O'Neill in on this?'

'Yes. She used to be with the drugs squad, you know. She's used to stakeouts and OPs.'

'But, gov ...' McKittrick paused.

The implications of his constable's involvement hit him like a side-swipe from a truck.

'But what?'

'Gov, you need to know about Eileen. Look, I'm sorry to say it, but I believe she's the one who's been leaking information. She's been observed several times visiting the home of a character named Hugh McCalmont. He's an ex-para, a trained sniper, in fact. He's also an associate of Sammy McClure and some of the other Alternative Ulster members. If Eileen tells him we're putting all our resources up at Shearwater Point, then they'll change their plans again, move the attack elsewhere and we won't know where.'

Thomas O'Keeffe sat back in his chair and smiled. He didn't seem at all shocked by McKittrick's disclosure. McKittrick was both disappointed and annoyed at his DCI's lack of reaction. However, O'Keeffe had a little disclosure of his own.

'You're right, Eileen is the source of the leaks.'

'You mean, you knew about her and yet you've kept her on the case.'

'Dan, Eileen's working to me. She's been acting on my instructions. She got close to McCalmont with my knowledge and blessing. Whatever snippets she's leaked to him have been cleared with me first. She had to get his trust, you see. He thinks she's a tame police officer, an informant, but she's not. She's an experienced under-cover officer.'

'Why didn't you tell me?' McKittrick protested.

'I couldn't. She's been engaged in this sort of under-cover role ever since she was with the drugs squad. You see, Hugh McCalmont was a principal target in their investigation into a major drugs and organised crime group. When it was realised that particular OCG was also a political organisation and that they were behind these abductions and arson attacks, they ceded the case to us. Since she was already under cover and well in with

McCalmont, we inherited Eileen along with the case. Strictly speaking, she's still the drugs squad's officer, not ours. I couldn't disclose her role to anyone.'

McKittrick's mind was reeling. He could scarcely take it in.

'Does Sarah know?' he asked.

'No. It's not that I didn't trust you both, but you know how these things work. Only her handler should know what she does. And I'm her handler. She reports directly to me, and only to me.'

It suddenly occurred to McKittrick that it was a good job he hadn't told O'Keeffe *all* he knew about Eileen. If what young Ryan Donovan had told him was true, it looked as though Eileen was sleeping with the man she was reporting on. It was absolutely forbidden for under-cover operatives to cultivate a sexual relationship with the enemy. He knew Eileen would be sacked if her alleged intimacy with McCalmont were known, and the whole under-cover operation would be blown.

He wondered what the hell she was playing at. She was certainly playing a dangerous game. She was risking her career by sleeping with one of the principles in the investigation. He wondered why on earth she would take that risk. He also knew that one of the dangers of forming too close a relationship with a target was that the under-cover officer could be turned and could switch their loyalties.

'But, that ledger. It was good evidence of their drugs trade. We could have used it. She didn't bring it back from the forensics lab. She must have given it to Hugh McCalmont.'

'Yes. She did. That was my idea. She felt she was losing his trust a little, and she wanted to get him to open up a bit more about the group's activities and about their plans. It seems to have worked. Don't worry about the ledger.

241

We've got a translation of it and we'll retrieve the original again when we round them all up.'

As McKittrick headed back downstairs to his office, he was still reeling from the shock of the DCI's disclosure. Having someone virtually inside the organisation was useful, and, indeed, it would be a coup if they could catch the gang poised to assassinate the president. But supposing O'Keeffe was wrong. Supposing Eileen O'Neill had turned. What if she were to tell McCalmont about the stakeout and he decided to strike at different location. It could all go wrong. In fact, it had the potential to go most horribly wrong.

Chapter 56

Over the next few days, every available PSNI police constable was deployed to scour the countryside and farm buildings along the route the presidential motorcade would take between Belfast and the province's southernmost border. Barns and outhouses were checked, as were vacant properties and holiday homes. Woods were searched and so were some of the caves along the coast. Two constables were tasked with checking properties in the immediate vicinity of the abandoned mother and baby home at Shearwater Point in particular.

Hughie McCalmont, accompanied by Billy Boyd, drove the white transit van into the driveway at Ardmore House and parked up in front of the property. Hughie first checked that the *'B&J Property Repairers, Bangor'* decals were still firmly adhered to the van's sides, before he and the youth set about unloading the vehicle. Half a dozen floorboards were taken out of the van and propped against the front wall of the property, then tins of paint, bags of plaster and a few joinery tools were piled up near the front door.

When he was satisfied that everything looked right, Hughie produced the fisherman's canvas rod bag from the back of the van and handed it to the youth, with instructions to hang it in plain sight on one of the hooks inside the garage. Propping one of the floorboards against the back doorway of the van as a ramp, Hughie carefully wheeled the motorcycle out of the van and pushed it into the garage. He rubbed his hand in the dust on the garage floor and smeared it over the rod bag which contained the rifle. Hopefully, the bag would look as though it had been there a long time and would not attract attention during any search.

'What do we do now, Hughie?' the youth asked.

'Now, we have a cup of tea and we wait,' he said. 'Fetch the flask and the biscuits from the van, will you.'

Hughie and his accomplice sat on the steps, enjoying the sunshine and drinking their tea. The tranquillity of the place was disturbed from time to time by the police helicopter which circled overhead. As they expected, it wasn't too long before a police car appeared up the driveway. The two constables got out of the vehicle and looked around them. One glanced in through the open front door of the house at the badly damaged floor, walls and ceiling of the hallway. The other went to search the garage.

'Looks like you've got your work cut out there, lads,' the first constable said.

'Aye, we have indeed,' Hughie agreed.

'Are you gonna be working up here tomorrow?'

'I should think we'll be here all week, officer. After all, we need to pace ourselves,' Hughie smiled, genially and raised his plastic tea mug by way of emphasising his lack of urgency to complete the job. 'Would you fellas like a cuppa tea?'

'No thanks. We need to have a look around the house and garage, though, if you've no objection.'

'It's not my house,' McCalmont grinned. 'Knock yourselves out.'

The search was a thorough one, and, as Hughie took his flask and cups back to the van, he saw one of the constables was up in the loft, ensuring that the line of sight from the loft window presented no threat. The constables searched the garage and the transit van, too, and, once they were satisfied that the house was empty, largely because much of the downstairs was uninhabitable, and since there seemed to be no signs of guns or gunmen, they headed back to their car and took off. To McCalmont's relief, if they had noticed the canvas fishing bag hanging in the garage, they hadn't bothered to look inside it.

'Do you think they'll be back?' the youth asked.

'Aye. I expect they'll come back again in the morning, so we'd better pull up a few of those floorboards and clean a bit of the soot off the walls. We'll make it look like we've at least done a bit of work.'

'What about eating, tonight?'

'No problem. Mister D said to help ourselves to any of the food in the kitchen fridge and freezer. I'm guessing that includes his best whiskey.'

As McCalmont and his cohort began their desultory attempt to tidy up some of the fire damage, forty miles further north, at the port of Larne, a more assiduous effort was being applied by Border Force officers who were observing the disembarkation of the ferry from Cairnryan in Scotland. One freight lorry in particular was the focus of their attention this morning, but their instructions were to observe and not intercept the vehicle. One of the observers was MI5's Mike Malone.

As the lorry passed through the checkpoint, Malone took out his mobile phone and dialled Harry Edwards' number.

'Harry, it looks like your intel from the phone intercept was spot on. Yes, it's just gone through now. According to the paperwork, it's delivering office furniture to an office in south Belfast. ... Yes, we already have eyes on the address. We'll let them make the drop and we'll keep them under obs. We won't move in until they look like they're going to move the stuff on. Many thanks again, mate.'

Chapter 57

McKittrick was relieved that, so far, the president's visit had gone smoothly. Of course, Biden's diatribe about the final shocking total of seventy-two babies found buried in a septic tank at the Shearwater Point home, and his assertion that this was probably just the tip of a very chilling iceberg of Titanic proportions, had ruffled a lot of feathers at Stormont. He had caused upset in the previous days at Westminster, too, by reminding the British parliament exactly whose fault he felt it was that his ancestors had been forced to migrate from Ireland to America in the famine era.

To add further injury to insult, Biden had also reiterated his displeasure at the UK having quit the European Union. He hadn't appreciated it when one bold MP had suggested Britain's withdrawal from Europe had been less injurious than America's withdrawal from Afghanistan. All in all, it was with some relief that the dignitaries, both in London and Belfast, had waved Joe Biden farewell as he had set off on his journey towards the Irish border.

However, for McKittrick and his colleagues, and all the other agencies involved in security for the final leg of the visit, their challenges were only just beginning. McKittrick arrived at Shearwater Point at six-thirty on the morning of the visit and checked in with his DI who had been there all night. Sarah Lawrence certainly looked as though she had been up all night, and she and Eileen were pleased to accept the large box of doughnuts and flask of coffee McKittrick had brought for their breakfast.

'Well, Dan, there's absolutely nothing to report,' Sarah yawned. 'The detector dogs didn't find anything explosive, and firearms officers conducted patrols at intervals right through the night, but nothing stirred, not even a mouse. Any action your end?'

'No. I had the Newtownbreda address under obs all night, too, but Sammy McClure didn't stir either. And there's nothing to report from the MIT over in Londonderry either, but they've got their targets under surveillance. They'll await a signal from us before they make any arrests. More worryingly, perhaps, there was no sign of Hughie McCalmont. His lights were on all night but no-one's seen him leave his house. We can't be sure whether he's in there or not, but we didn't want to check in case we spooked him.'

'Yes, all we can do now is sit and wait.' Sarah said, as Eileen climbed out of the car to join McKittrick. 'Don't slam the car door, Eileen. I'm going to try and grab forty winks. Wake me up when the motorcade's in sight.'

A couple of hours later, more people and vehicles started to arrive at Shearwater Point. First amongst them was Joe Doyle's taxi. Once the vehicle and its occupants had been checked over by police officers and McKittrick had given them the nod, the taxi was allowed to ascend the driveway and park up in front of the home. Joe had been promised he'd get a glimpse of the President so he parked the taxi in a prime spot, facing the front of the building. Dom Caffrey and Aminullah Miah climbed out of the taxi. The sun was up already and the morning was quite warm, despite which, the two lawyers both wore smart suits and ties for their meeting with the forty-sixth president of the United States of America.

'It was good of you to invite me along,' Miah said, as he and Caffrey found a spot with the best backdrop for the photographers.

'Not at all,' Caffrey insisted. 'The Consul agreed with me that you've done so much work on this project you should take your share of the plaudits.'

247

McKittrick looked around him continuously. He knew there were police and army secreted all over the area, even if he couldn't see them all. All the nearby cottages and holiday homes had been searched, including the fire-damaged Ardmore House, which had been so recently deserted by Sammy McClure. But that didn't make him feel any less worried. He told himself he would stop worrying when someone called to say they definitely had eyeball on former sniper McCalmont and that he was still over in north Belfast.

An old, battered orange Volkswagen was the next vehicle to roll up the driveway and park up. Carole and Dave stepped out.

'I wonder where Mike Malone is,' Dave asked. 'Is he going to be here for the jamboree?'

'No, he's taken another armed response team down to the border, just in case,' Carole informed him. 'And it's not going to be a jamboree. I know you hate fussy occasions, love, but, really, this will all be over in ten or fifteen minutes. The President will hop out of *the beast*, exchange a few words with Caffrey and the chap from the HRC, a few photos will be taken and then the motorcade will take off again.'

'I do hope you're right. This isn't the easiest place in the world to carry out surveillance. What's that out there?' Dave pointed out to sea.

'The Copeland Islands,' Carole told him.

'Who lives over there, then?'

'Just the shearwaters and their chicks.'

Eventually, the signal came that the president with his entourage and security escort had been sighted a short way off on the coast road. Suddenly, everyone was on high alert. Minutes later, the various vehicles, including the American's bullet-proofed *beast* of a limousine, turned up the driveway and coasted to a halt in front of the abandoned maternity home. Immediately behind them were several cars full of newspaper reporters and photographers.

A dozen secret service men in suits leapt out of the leading vehicles and began pacing around the area immediately in front of the home. The US Consul General, Viveca Holmberg, stepped out of her official vehicle and went to stand alongside Caffrey and Miah. Having been given the nod by his security staff that the coast was clear, the president emerged from the back seat of his armour-plated presidential vehicle and walked across to be greeted by the Consul General. Ms Holmberg shook his hand and began to make the introductions.

A burly, square-jawed bodyguard with a reassuring bulge visible under the left side of his jacket, stood very close to the president, continually pressing the earpiece he wore further into to his right ear. Meanwhile, the various press men began milling around, photographing the president from all angles as he shook hands and chatted with the two lawyers.

An amused Dave pointed out to Carol the secret service men's lapel badges which bore the words 'Secret Service'.

'Some secret,' he whispered.

'I know,' Carole smiled. 'They're not what we understand to be secret service. I believe they're US Treasury officials, really.'

Unlike those of the onlookers, the eyes of the secret service men were not focused on the president. Instead, they continually scanned the surrounding hillsides. Some gazed over the cliff edge to check for any unwanted interlopers from that direction. McKittrick, too, kept looking nervously around. The feeling of unease he had begun to feel on awaking that morning was growing more intense with every moment the president spent here at Shearwater Point. Luckily, he thought, the visit shouldn't last much longer now.

Looking out to sea, all McKittrick could see was a couple of fishing vessels in the distance, doubtless returning to shore after a night out at sea. They chugged past harmlessly enough, on their way, he supposed, to Donaghadee or Ardglass. He hoped there wouldn't be any Russian submarines in the Irish Sea on this of all days. Reassuringly, though, there were police launches out there, too.

As he turned his gaze inland again towards the headland to the north of them, something glinted momentarily. It was little more than an instantaneous flash, but he had seen it. He waved to catch the attention of one of the armed response unit officers nearest to him and pointed up towards the hillside where the sudden burst of light had been. He could see nothing amiss for a second or two, but then it came again. The ARU man now spotted it, too.

McKittrick was unsure what it could be. The risen sun was shining from the south east and was reflecting off something very small but very shiny up amongst the trees on top of the headland to the north of them. In any other situation but this, he might suppose it to be a discarded glass bottle or a shiny bird scarer in someone's garden, but it suddenly occurred to him that it could equally be the sights of a sniper's rifle. The same thought had clearly occurred to the armed response officer who was now looking intently through binoculars.

'Look out!' the officer yelled suddenly. 'Sniper! Sniper!'

All the armed personnel spun around rapidly and immediately raised their weapons in the direction in which McKittrick and the ARU man now pointed. Caffrey acted quickest of all, however. He immediately shouldered his president sharply sideways, just as three shots rang out in quick succession. The noise reverberated all around the hillside, and Joe Biden overbalanced and toppled over onto the cinder surface of the car park, whilst everyone else ducked. Several members of the armed response unit immediately returned fire towards the dense foliage of the headland. Secret service personnel and police rushed forward to shield the president. Dave, however, had pulled Carole to the ground and was shielding her with his body.

'Bloody hell!' he gasped.

'Is anyone hit?' Carole asked.

Dave quickly looked around. The president was on his feet, now, being dusted off by a number of concerned people as they rushed him back into the safety of his bulletproof vehicle. Just yards away from him, however, two figures lay motionless on the ground. McKittrick rushed forward, his heart in his mouth. He saw the square-jawed bodyguard lying flat on his back, his arms outstretched and his drawn weapon clutched, unfired in his hand. He was bleeding from one shoulder, but at least, he seemed to be alive. Next to him, another man in a smart suit lay, unconscious.

'Get the ambulance up here,' McKittrick yelled. 'Caffrey's been shot.'

From the direction of the road, the sound of a racing motorbike engine could be heard roaring away into the distance. A cacophony of excited yells and sirens ensued as various armed and uniformed officers dashed to their vehicles and started up their own engines. The first car to leave the site, however, its wheels squealing on the tarmac of the access road, was a grey mini.

As a number of police vehicles pulled out onto the main road in pursuit of the gunman, an ambulance, its blue lights flashing, suddenly appeared from the other direction and turned in up the driveway. It came to a halt in front of where the casualties lay. McKittrick was pleased he'd had the presence of mind to arrange for the private ambulance to be parked a little way up the main road, just as a precaution. He bent down and checked Caffrey's pulse. He was

251

relieved to find there was one. Then he stepped aside to make way for the paramedics.

The two casualties were soon stretchered into the ambulance, and Aminullah Miah, insistent on accompanying Caffrey to the hospital, climbed in, too. Moments later, the ambulance took off for the city. As everyone gradually recovered from the shock and began to take stock of the situation, officers were despatched up the hillside to search for physical evidence of the shooter's presence. McKittrick headed over to the DI's car where Sarah Lawrence sat, still sleeping soundly, blissfully unaware of what had just happened.

Chapter 58

Eileen arrived at Lissadell Street before McCalmont did. Parking her car around the corner in the next street, she walked back and let herself into his house. Heading straight upstairs to the front bedroom, she pulled the bedside cabinet forward and reached for the handgun McCalmont kept taped to the back of it. Checking it was loaded, she released the safety catch and made her way down the landing to the tiny back bedroom, where she sat down on the bed to wait.

Hughie McCalmont cautiously cruised up and down past his house several times. He had taken the bike through woodland and across farmland but it had taken him some time to evade the helicopter surveillance. Satisfied that the police were not in the area around Lissadell Street, he now parked the bike and let himself into the house. He had avoided CCTV cameras by taking back roads. Once he had hit the city, where there were numerous cameras, he had driven relatively slowly, in case those monitoring the security cameras might already be looking out for an assassin fleeing at speed.

Time was of the essence now, however, and so, taking the stairs two at a time, he went first to the airing cupboard on the landing. He pulled out all the towels until he found the one inside which the sizeable bundle of banknotes was wrapped. Dividing the bundle in two, he stashed a half in each of his jacket pockets. Heading into the bedroom, he yanked open the wardrobe and grabbed his holdall from the top shelf. Then he snatched several pairs of jeans and some tee shirts from the hangers and stuffed them into the holdall. He placed the holdall down on the bed and stepped across to the dresser.

Lifting the framed photo of himself in uniform, he turned it over. His passport was sellotaped to the back of the frame. He tore off the passport and stuffed it into his pocket, then turned to drop the framed photo into the bag. It was only then that he caught sight of Eileen standing in the doorway. He saw the Glock in her hand.

'I wasn't going to leave without you, lover,' he stammered, 'at least, I was, but I would have sent for you.'

'I wouldn't have come ... lover. But that doesn't matter, for you won't be going anywhere.'

He froze, his face a mixture of, firstly, confusion and then fear. There was a distant squeal of tyres from up the road and the chilling wail of police sirens. He picked up the holdall and made to leave, but Eileen blocked his way. He moved to grab the gun from her but he wasn't quick enough and she immediately pulled the trigger. The impact knocked him backwards onto the floor. Clutching at the spreading red stain on his chest, he looked at her, his eyes wide with shock and pain.

'Why?' he gasped.

'You killed the father of my boys,' she said, coldly.

'I never met Doug, let alone ...' he broke off as blood began to fill his lungs and he started to cough.

'Not Doug O'Neill. Andy Robinson was my first husband. He was the father of my children. He was also an undercover drugs squad officer. And you killed him.'

'Don't remem ...' he began, but he began to choke on the blood that was now in his throat.

Hughie now writhed around, gurgling, coughing and struggling to breathe. A fine blood mist sprayed into the air from his nose and mouth as he tried unsuccessfully to turn onto his side. He raised a hand out to her for help. She did not move. Calmly, she watched him. Her face reflected nothing, no pity, no anger, nothing. His expression was one of incredulity. She derived some satisfaction from seeing his shocked disbelief at the realisation that she had betrayed him. She knew he'd believed her to be in thrall to him. She congratulated herself that she'd done her job well. She'd gone far beyond what she had been expected to do, but it had all been necessary, and it had been worth it, for Andy – the love of her life. Suddenly, McCalmont fell back. He had lost his fight to breathe and he lay still now, his eyes staring lifelessly at the ceiling.

Now, there were heavy footsteps on the stairs. Quickly, Eileen bent over Hugh McCalmont's body. Placing the gun into his hand, she pressed her own hand onto the back of his to transfer the gunshot residue. She stepped back and raised her hands, just as the armed response officers burst into the bedroom.

They trained their weapons on the man on the floor and on her, until they realised that he was dead and she was unarmed. Eileen shook her head.

'Constable Eileen O'Neill. MIT,' she said. 'I was too late. Looks like he shot himself.'

Once the ARU men had satisfied themselves as to her identity and had begun radioing in, Eileen headed downstairs to the kitchen. She picked up the bottle of Bushmills sixteen-year-old single malt from the work top, unscrewed the cap and took a swig straight from the bottle. She needed to get rid of the bad taste in her mouth, and she had some sorrows to drown.

Chapter 59

The following day saw a few fluffy clouds hanging over a calm sea out at Donaghadee. There was just enough of a sea breeze to warrant the pink pashmina Carole Murray draped around her shoulders as she took a seat at the little garden table out in front of the house. Dave was tucking his mobile phone into his shirt pocket as he came out of the house to join her.

'Ellen's making poached eggs on toast for lunch,' he said. 'They're from her own chickens. It'll taste all the better for that lovely Irish butter she gets. Much nicer than that olive oil spread we have at home,' he said, pointedly.

'Was that Adrian who called?' Carole asked. 'Is he mad at us?'

'Not at all. He says it was unfortunate that two Americans were shot but it was fortunate that neither was the president. Actually, he sounded quite pleased.'

'Really? What did he say?'

'He said the fact that it happened on UK soil, yet we had Irish police and army co-operating with our own forces here, has gone down well at home. I told him that both PSNI and the Irish military had returned the gunman's fire. He sees it as an example of effective cross-border co-operation. Oh, and the White House has issued its thanks.'

'Sounds to me like some of the negatives have been turned into positives.'

'Yes, and he said the fact that the attack happened at the coast has highlighted the importance of some MOD treaty on joint sea patrols. Adrian seemed particularly pleased about that, for some reason. Who was your call from?'

'Oh, that was Mike Malone. He told me the police moved in last night and arrested dozens of Alternative Ulster members. They've taken out people across five counties, from Belfast to Donegal, and in Derry, Cavan and Monaghan. They also nabbed a big haul of Russian-made weapons and explosives. They were intercepted whilst being moved from an address in south Belfast. The occupants of that address, including one Samuel McClure – the man who's been calling himself Killian Devereux – they've all been arrested.'

'Result!'

'They've found a lot of damning paperwork and, together with my analysis reports, Mike says the police will have enough to charge them with conspiracy over uncle George's murder, as well as with the attempted assassination of the US President.'

'They'll never see the light of day again,' Dave said, gleefully.

'Oh, and forensics did a rush job on a hand gun found in the possession of Hugh McCalmont, a former para, and they've confirmed it was the same gun that killed Uncle George. It was also the same gun that killed those adults found buried at the mother and baby home. They found a Russian-made *Chukavin* sniper's rifle dumped out in the woods at Shearwater Point. Forensics are still looking it over, but it's almost certainly the one used in the attempt on the president's life. And More *Chukavins* were seized in the South Belfast haul.'

'Are they able to connect Hugh McCalmont with this fake Killian Devereux?'

'Oh, yes. You remember in my reports there was an unregistered mobile phone which had been calling McClure's phone numerous times, but the digital forensics people hadn't managed to identify the user? Well, that mobile was found on Hugh McCalmont.'

'Brilliant!'

'And McKittrick had seen them together at the bungalow they just raided in south Belfast. Also, McCalmont had on him a set of keys to Ardmore House out at Shearwater Point – the house Samuel McClure was renting. It seems McClure has been making regular payments into McCalmont's bank account. McClure should get a life sentence this time around. Sadly, though, McCalmont won't stand trial.'

'Won't he?'

'No. He's dead. Looks like suicide.'

'Did they find out who it was who set fire to Ardmore House?'

'No. It seems likely it was a rival drug gang. I don't suppose they'll ever know.'

'Still, that's a great outcome. Seems our work here is done. Adrian says he'd like us back in the office on Monday, but we still need to decide what to do about Ellen.'

'Oh, I forgot to mention it to you in all yesterday's excitement, but I think I might have found a temporary solution.'

'Oh, yes?'

'Ellen's next-door neighbour over there, Elizabeth Begley, she's a good friend of Ellen's. She's a widow in her early fifties and is as fit as a flea, but she's just lost her part-time job at the local independent supermarket. It was another casualty of the covid lockdown. Everyone's been getting groceries delivered by one of the bigger supermarket chains, so the little supermarket's gone out of business. I asked if she'd be interested in popping in for a few hours each day to look after Aunt Ellen and maybe do a few household tasks for her and a bit of shopping. I said I'd pay her, naturally. She said she'd have done it for nothing, but I insisted.'

'Well, that's a relief. It's better than having a stranger looking after her.'

'It isn't a permanent solution, but it'll be a stop-gap until we decide what to do for Ellen's long-term care.'

'I suppose the best solution in the long-term would be for us to move here and look after her,' Dave said.

Surprised, Carole turned and looked at him.

'I thought you'd gone off the idea of retiring here. Surely, yesterday's events must have put you off even more?'

Dave glanced out at the horizon, where a handful of sailing boats scudded past on the azure waters, and he sighed. His gaze shifted along towards Donaghadee harbour, where several sturdy fishing boats, each with an accompanying halo of screeching gulls, were returning home with their catches.

'Well, love, I suppose nowhere is completely safe, these days, not here, and certainly not London. There's a nest of serpents in every paradise, isn't there. But, you know, when you look out at all of this, who would want to be anywhere else?'

Chapter 60

Dom Caffrey winced as the taxi hit a slight bump in the road. It had been eight weeks since the shooting and, although his ribs were still tender where the sniper's bullet had smashed its way through them, he knew he was on the mend. He would certainly have something to tell his colleagues and friends back in Boston. To have been shot defending his president was a rare privilege. The scar tissue adorning his chest was, perhaps, as prestigious as any congressional medal of honour.

He looked out at the gentle Wexford landscape and, somehow, it didn't look as lush and green as it had on his last visit. The summer was coming to an end and crops had been harvested, leaving sun-baked stubble in the fields. He hadn't thought he would come here again, but circumstances had changed his mind. He now wanted to present the cheque to Alice in person.

If he were honest with himself, he really wanted her to be proud of what her son had achieved. He wanted to see her face when he told her he had gained both recognition of, and an official apology for what she and other women and girls had suffered. He had scored many a legal triumph over the years, but, somehow, this one felt more satisfying than most. This would seem more tangible and worthwhile to her than his college degree. She had suffered to bring him into the world. By comparison, his efforts to secure her compensation had been easy and painless, unless he counted the bullet wound in his chest. That had hurt like hell.

He knew she hadn't really understood what an attorney did, and he wanted to see her reaction when he told her that he, personally, had won compensation for her and for many more like her – with a little help from the US president, of course. He didn't know if the sum would be life-changing. He hoped, though, that it would go some way to brightening her existence, to adding some light and comfort into her small, modest world. It would at least pay for her to have a washing machine installed in that tiny scullery.

It was true that he hadn't really felt any kinship to her, and yet he was quite looking forward to seeing her again. This time, he'd remembered to bring a gift. He didn't think flowers would stay fresh and beautiful during the long journey down here, so he had brought a large box of chocolates – the largest box Lily O'Brien's Belfast chocolate shop could offer. He would give her the chocolates first, he decided, and then the cheque.

As the taxi pulled up outside the little farmstead, he asked the driver to return in an hour. He didn't think it would take long to explain to Alice the reason for the windfall and to take his leave of her. They hadn't had a lot to say to each other at their first meeting, so he couldn't imagine they would have much more conversation now at their last. Clutching the chocolates under his arm, he knocked at the door. He knocked several times but there was no reply, so he walked around to the back. He knew country folks often left their back doors open.

There were no chickens scratching around in the dirt at the back of the house, and the back door was locked, too, so he wandered across to the field. He expected to find Alice there, clad in her apron and tending to her calves. However, there were no cattle in the field, and the meadow grass was grown long and was beginning to turn brown. He wondered if this might be the time of year when the cattle went off to auction. He had no knowledge of such things. He had no idea when cattle were born and weaned and when Alice would take delivery of a new herd of weaners to graze in her little field. This world, which was entirely driven by the seasons, wasn't his world. He was simply a visitor here, a hapless onlooker.

Further along the lane, he saw a neighbouring white-washed farm and he recalled Alice had said it belonged to a family named Kinsella. He thought Alice might be visiting the Kinsellas, so he wandered up the lane to enquire. Mr Kinsella was sitting outside his front door enjoying the sunshine whilst sharpening some knives against the stone-edged doorway. Judging by the many grooves worn into the stone, he supposed generations of Kinsellas must have sharpened their knives in this way. This was a place where very little changed over the years, the decades, the generations.

'Mr Kinsella?' he called out. 'Would Alice Devricks be here, by any chance?'

Kinsella arose and ambled down to the gate to meet him.

'Alice?' he said, surprised. 'Well, no, she isn't. I'm afraid Alice passed away around six weeks ago. Are you a relative?'

'Oh, well, yes. Passed away, you say? How?'

'They say 'twas her heart gev out. Sitting by her fire she was, with a cup of tea turned cold at her elbow. A peaceful death, it seemed. She'd just slipped away. My wife heard the cattle creating when they'd no water to drink and she went into the house and found her. Stone, cold dead, she was, and been there several days, by the look of her.'

Caffrey was taken aback. So, his mother was dead, and at the age of just, what, sixty-one, maybe sixty-two now? The quiet little life she had led was now ended. He didn't know how to feel over the death of this stranger. She was the woman who had given birth to him, yet she had never been a mother to him. It seemed grossly unfair, though, that death had cheated her out of her compensation. He, too, had been cheated out of the satisfaction of seeing her reaction to receiving the cheque.

He'd hoped to see how surprised she would be, how pleased, and maybe even proud of the son whom she'd borne but not been allowed to raise. He felt he'd done something good for her – a small reward for the pain she had gone through to give him life. Now, though, she would never know what he had achieved. For the second time since he had arrived in Northern Ireland, Caffrey felt hot tears welling up inside him. Kinsella interrupted his thoughts.

'So, would you be a blood relative, then? I guess you'll be inheriting the farm, so. Only, if you are, I'd be interested in buying the land. It wouldn't be too expensive, I would imagine?'

Kinsella looked hopeful. Caffrey shook off his sadness for a moment. He was indeed Alice's next of kin in biological terms, but, with his understanding of legal matters, he knew that, in law, he was not.

'No, I mean, yes, I am a blood relative, but I was adopted out of the family years ago, so I wouldn't inherit anything. It'll all go to the Irish state, I expect.'

Caffrey couldn't quite believe Alice was dead. He now felt guilty that he hadn't spent more time than he had in conversation with her. They hadn't had much to say to each other, however, and yet, now, when he had something really important to tell her, now it was too late. Somewhat irritatingly, Kinsella persisted with his enquiry about the land.

'So, how would I be going about buying the land, then? Would you know?'

'Uh, … I guess you could get in touch with a local land agent. They'd enquire on your behalf. Was there a funeral, by the way? Do you know where Alice is buried?'

'There was. A small little funeral there was. Me and the missus went, and a few others from around here. She's buried in the churchyard down the road there along with her mother and father. There's no headstone. She had no close family to pay for one. And, sure, what would be the point, for who would ever come and look at it? Did you come all the way from America to see her? I expect it'll be a shock for you to hear she died. Will I make you a cup of tea?'

Caffrey thanked him but declined. He noticed Kinsella's curious glances at the huge box of chocolates. On impulse, he handed the box to the neighbour.

'I'm grateful to you for your kindness to my ... relative,' he said. 'Please accept these with my thanks.'

The man readily accepted the chocolates, and Caffrey took his leave of him. He walked back up the lane to await the return of his taxi. He wouldn't go to the churchyard just to look at a freshly dug mound of earth. He could see no point in that. He would return to Belfast. There was nothing for him here now. In truth, there never had been.

The late summer weather was wonderful. Caffrey had Joe Doyle drive him out for one last look at Shearwater Point. He stood for quite a while and stared out at the sea. There was a great deal of avian activity between the coast and the Copeland Islands. It truly was one of the most beautiful places he had ever been. His heart should have soared with the gulls over the darkening waters and on up into that periwinkle blue, cloudless sky, but it was too heavy to do so. This was a place of great beauty, but also a place of deep sadness.

As he gazed around, he wondered what it was that he had hoped to find here. He told himself he should have realised there couldn't be any kind of fairy tale ending. Alice Devereux wasn't the elegant lady in taffeta whom he'd expected to find. They'd had some similarities in looks, but that was all. They'd had nothing else in common. He was never going to inherit an Irish estate, and nor was he ever going whisk his birth mother off to live in Boston to be introduced to all his friends and to Boston's own brand of Irish-American culture.

It now occurred to him that the Ireland that Bostonians sang about only really existed in song and inherited memories. The mawkish sentimentality of Saint Patrick's night celebrations in Boston bore no relation to the reality of life on an impoverished little farm down there in quiet County Wexford, or to the murderous activities of a bigoted set of gangsters here in County Down. If he'd lived out his life in Wexford, by now, he'd have been another Mr Kinsella. He'd have spent his time sharpening his knives on the door frame, not sharpening his legal wit in a courtroom.

He wondered if his Irish odyssey had changed him in any way. He decided it hadn't. He had always known *what* he was, and he had come to a different continent hoping to discover *who* he was. Now, however, he arrived at the disappointing conclusion that *who* he was wasn't really any different from *what* he was.

In his search for his Irishness, his expectations had not been met. Sure, he now had an Irish passport, and a British one, too, but, in essence, he was still an American. Notwithstanding those passports and the birth certificate and student ID, he wasn't Killian Devereux and he never would be. He was Dom Caffrey. His rightful place was back in Boston, not here. Now that he had achieved an apology and financial settlements for many of the women who had suffered as Alice had, he had abandoned all thoughts of expanding his legal empire to Ireland. What would be the point?

'They're all getting ready to leave, Dom,' Joe interrupted his thoughts.

'Who?'

'The Manx shearwaters. They'll be feeding in a frenzy each night, now, fattening themselves up for the thousands of miles they'll soon be migrating. Ah, but it's an amazing sight when they go, Dom. They'll be taking off for South America any day now.'

'It's time I was taking off, too, Joe. I'll be flying off to north America in a coupla days' time myself.'

'Do you think you'll ever come back?'

Caffrey shook his head.

'Are you kidding me? Having wrestled with a maggot-ridden corpse, been arrested twice and then shot in the chest? No, Shearwater Point is an extraordinarily beautiful place, perhaps one of the most beautiful places on earth. But, you know, it's not my place. I may have been born here, but I don't belong here. I never did. In fact, Joe, as lovely as it is, if I never see Shearwater Point ever again, it'll be too damned soon.'

ABOUT THE AUTHOR

Retired civil servant, Denise Beddows has a background in research, investigation and intelligence analysis. Her career has taken her to work in a number of different countries across several continents. She writes – as Denise Beddows – true crime and thrillers, and – as DJ Kelly – local history and biographical fiction. This is her fourth standalone story in the series featuring MI5's Counter-espionage team. A member of the Society of Authors and the Crime Writers' Association, she regularly contributes articles to local, national and international press and journals. She reviews books and films for publishers and journals, and is a volunteer researcher for her local history and heritage group. A trained and experienced public speaker, she regularly gives talks on different topics to a variety of community groups and at literary festivals. She is married, with a grown-up daughter. She and her husband and their pet whippet live in Buckinghamshire.

Also by this author:

ESPIONAGE FICTION:

The Hunt for WOTAK
By Denise Beddows

The Cold War has never been colder than in 2020's Brexit-era Britain. In the midst of the mounting chaos of cyber-attacks and a global pandemic, a sinister entity calling himself WOTAK claims responsibility for much of this 'hybrid warfare' and seeks to hold the nation to ransom. A series of brutal murders, including that of the Foreign Secretary, raises the pressure on the Joint Intelligence Committee to establish who or what is WOTAK. With a little help from his friends, the Security Service's Harry Edwards seeks to track down and neutralise WOTAK. However, he has no idea of the enormous personal cost this complicated operation will involve.

Amazon #3 best seller in Espionage thrillers

'Full of intrigue, beautifully written and meticulously researched ... a really impressive read' – Robert Howe, author of 'A Short Life on the Ocean Wave'

'Fast-paced with a good story line and feels as if it has been meticulously researched' – Geoffrey Gudgion, Author of 'Saxon's Bane' and 'Draca'.

'An original and tense spy thriller, set in a wholly believable, locked-down, apocalyptical Brexit-era Britain. A salutary warning of what might be and, at the same time, a gripping read.' – Joe Silmon-Monerri, author of 'A Secret Son'.

*****

When the Grey Wolf Sings
by Denise Beddows

When an elderly Russian is burned to death in his car in north London, his 72-year-old friend, former KGB man Nikolai Volkov, determines to avenge his death. Meanwhile, the 'cyber-war' waged on the west by Russia, and a global viral pandemic, both threaten the health, the economy and the security of the nation. When former policeman turned MI5 agent-handler, Dave Lloyd and his colleagues are tasked with identifying the mysterious 'Ringmaster', help comes from an unexpected source.

Amazon #5 best seller in Espionage thrillers

'I thoroughly enjoyed the concept of the tale. In fact, it is all too believable... Shades of John Le Carré are all through the book, but, I think, with a lot more humour.' – ***** Librarything Reviewer.

'A resourceful and likeable central character with an exciting plot.' – *****   Amazon reviewer

'Superb spy novel! Have friends retired from US intelligence agencies and this rings true. Most spy literature puts me to sleep, but this book is a refreshing exception to the norm' ***** Amazon reviewer, retired US homicide sergeant

A Long Road to Revenge
by Denise Beddows

A decades-old Russian bio-terror weapon is being deployed on the streets of London. People with no apparent connection are dying, horribly, and there is no clear motive. MI5's Harry Edwards and Counter Terrorism Command's Detective Inspector Kit McGlone identify potential suspects – only to see them assassinated too. What deadly secret did the murder victims share, and who is killing the killers?

269

Rated amongst Amazon reader's Top Ten spy/political thrillers

'A complex but intriguing web that spans cultures, political machinations and devious trade craft. This has a 'Line of Duty' feel about it and would make a cracking TV drama.' – ***** Amazon reviewer

'A well-written tale of intrigue with a glimpse of intelligence operations in the modern world ... shows us the human side of this shadowy struggle between nations. There are twists and turns enough to keep the reader fully engaged.' –
**** Goodreads reviewer

'I love the topicality of the story which is set in our present COVID ridden, Brexit ridden, political 'circus' of 2020 and 2021. Moves at a fast pace and is difficult to put down.' –
***** Amazon reviewer

TRUE CRIME:

Odd Man Out – A Motiveless Murder?
by Denise Beddows

WINNER OF THE GEORGINA HAWTREY-WOORE AWARD

The true and tragic story of transgendered bus conductress Margaret 'Bill' Allen who, despite desperate campaigning by loving friend Annie, was hanged for the 1948 murder in Rawtenstall, Lancashire, of Nancy Chadwick, an eccentric old woman whom Bill barely knew. Did she do it? If so, why did she do it? If not, who did it?

The author uncovers evidence which was suppressed at the time, questions the death sentence and asks whether society's treatment of Bill would be very much different today.

'... a vivid picture of post-war Rawtenstall and of the difficult lives of three women – a murder victim, her killer and the killer's lover ... an exceptionally well researched account of a true crime and a sensitive exploration of the difficult life and brutal death of this transgendered woman whom history has forgotten.' – Murder Monthly

*****

The Cheetham Hill Murder – A Convenient Killing?
By Denise Beddows

One hot July afternoon in 1933 saw Frances Levin brutally and fatally attacked in her own home in one of Manchester's affluent districts. A recent BBC TV programme revealed that the man hanged for the killing could not have done it. The Author uncovers police corruption, malpractice and suppression of crucial evidence, and reveals a more likely motive and an obvious suspect who was never investigated.

'An old murder case is re-visited in this highly readable book ... a shameful miscarriage of justice is explored and fresh research brings up fresh motives and fresh suspects. The author's conclusions are indeed persuasive' – Bloggs on True Crime

All are available from Amazon or from all good book shops

Printed in Great Britain
by Amazon